THE
EXILE
WAITING

THE EXILE WAITING

by Vonda N. McIntyre

NELSON DOUBLEDAY, Inc.
Garden City, New York

Printed in the United States of America.

*For Ursula and Charles
with fond memories of their
Charitable Home for Writers*

Unlock, set open,
set free, the exile
waiting in long anger
outside my home.

—*Ursula K. Le Guin*

THE
EXILE
WAITING

1

Contacts in a spaceport bazaar are tenuous and quickly broken. Most of the people are transients—I'd leave too, if I could. I never had to think about money before, and the sudden realization that it's necessary is disconcerting. But I won't ask my father for support, nor have I petitioned my mother's estate. I've been thinking more about myself and my numerous faults than about money. I've been lonely. Yet, somehow, I'm more content than I was as a respectable reader at university, learning everything and knowing nothing. I've just begun to realize how much time I've wasted.

Ichiri has not quite disowned me. He simply did not answer my letter. I won't write him again—I'm not even sure why I feel I owe him any explanations. All I want is an attempt at understanding. He may be hoping I'll give up and come home, so he can pretend he never knew about my brief bout with rebellion and—to him—insanity. Then neither of us would lose face. I don't know yet, but I think I'm stronger than that.

If I never went home, he would be able to forget that his only offspring has blond hair, and he would be able to immerse himself completely in his fantasies. I can't bend myself to them anymore—they have become stronger, more pervasive, and, worse, more intrusive on other people's lives. Yet I can't forget him. I still love the old man, on a level much deeper than that of my resentment.

I sat in a bar all evening, keeping myself mildly intoxicated. That helps very little. I become introspective. If I got more intox-

1

icated, maybe I could begin to believe my father's fantasies. I could proclaim myself legitimate son of the bastard son of the emperor of ancient Japan, then they could ship me home and I would live happily ever after in a world of stories and words that no longer have any meaning. I see by those lines that I am still a little drunk.

I met a retired navigator while I was drinking. She is almost deaf and almost blind—she's outlived many of the ships she served on. Her hair has aged from ebony to white, her eyes from black to luminous gray. Too many flights have battered her, and stray radiation has turned her corneas to ground glass. They could be restored, but not the optic nerves. Yet she has a dignity about her that her tremors and deafened near-oblivion cannot strip away. She is ubiquitous, yet unique. A hundred castoff, worn-out relics wander in this bazaar alone, but she is the first with whom I've talked at length. She could go to one of the homes established for her kind, but she would have to leave space to do that, and she says it would kill her. She says she was born on old earth: she says it defiantly, with her clouded eyes glaring from her dark face, and she dares anyone to say she lies, or to be repelled by her. She was born there—it's true in spirit. And perhaps even in fact, though I've always been taught that earth was dead and abandoned.

The old navigator and those like her rely on the aid of the younger members of their society, who know they in turn will be cared for. Tonight she and I talked so long that everyone else went off to sleep through daybreak, so she came with me to my cheap little room. Now, while I write, she is dozing on the cot, lying close to the wall, because, I think, she does not wish to displace me from my bed. She has given, now she will accept—but she does not take.

The scarlet darkness cooled gradually to maroon as Mischa followed the rising caves toward Center. She was tired, thirsty, hungry. She had been in the deep underground for several days, wandering and exploring, guided by intuition and the experience of other, similar escapes. But now it was time to return to the city.

She wished she could stay away longer and extend the limits of her range. The strangest sights were deepest in the earth, delicately sculpted by eons, or, rarely, rarely, built by people who had abandoned their immense constructs when they had no more need for weapons of war.

Mischa heard a noise and stopped. The sound came again, a faint scratching of metal against rock. A few shards of stone clattered down the wall and fell at her feet. She looked closely, at shoulder height, and laughed. A tiny machine quivered at the edge of a small new hole, seeming to sniff the air. As Mischa watched, the antenna mouse extruded a shiny metal lead and backed away into the darkness, leaving behind a new connection to the communications network. This far from Center there was no one to use the leads, but the mice worked on, directed in a random and useless pattern by some lost and forgotten program.

Mischa continued upward; the cave was no longer completely natural, but had been smoothed and straightened into a long, regular passage.

A faraway glow appeared and increased as Mischa walked toward it: light-tubes, marking Center's outskirts. Few other people ventured beyond the illumination, for they were afraid. Some of the fear Mischa understood. An hour before, she had caught a glimpse of a cave panther: amber eyes, smooth, black pelt, wide strokes of whiskers, when it started at her silent approach and sprang away. But the outcast people of the deep underground were more feared. People who half-believed in them used their presence to frighten disobedient children. Mischa *knew* the underground people existed, though she had never met them. She had seen their painted symbols on the tunnel walls, and learned to heed the caution, but she found no reason for fear. The outcasts were shyer than the panthers.

Mischa reached the light spilling from the small round room ahead: a wellcell, the only source of good water for this section of the city's fringes. Cut rock gleamed softly with condensation, and the air was sharp with the cool damp tang of limestone. In the middle of the circular chamber, the rim of the well projected a few handsbreadths from the floor. A tall figure in purple and black lay on its wide edge. His near-white hair spread across the worked stone. Mischa hesitated, then went toward the young man. She sat on the wall and reached out to shake him, but stopped with her hand almost on his shoulder when she saw the green flash of his eyes. Her brother stared straight up at the light above him.

"Hey, Chris." She did not understand why he was not in Center. He never went home; he had not needed to for two years.

"Go away." His voice held a thin note, a whine that had never been there before. His hand hung in the water, and his shirt, wet to the shoulder, clung to him as though his arm were only bones. He was much thinner than the last time Mischa had seen him.

"What's wrong?"

"No dreams," he said, sounding close to tears.

"Come on."

"Go away." He flung his arm over his face, covering his eyes, flinging sparkling drops of water across the bright sand and dark water. His hand was pale blue and parchment white, seeming translucent. Veins and bones protruded beneath the skin. Above the shush of water, Mischa could barely hear his slow and shallow breaths. For a moment, with a heavy fist of apprehension in her stomach, she wondered if he had stopped breathing altogether. He had not, yet her apprehension coalesced: she knew why she felt afraid.

She slid off the edge of the well and touched him. "Chris—"

He struck out as though he had forgotten who she was or that she was ever there. Because he had not planned it, because she had not expected it, he hit her, hard enough to knock her back. She lunged and reached for him, but he lost his balance and rolled. The water closed over him and sloshed against the well's side, reflecting in irregular waves.

Mischa straddled the wall. Her face might be bruised, but Chris was not strong enough to hurt her. He floated motionless, face down. She reached out and down and caught the tail of his shirt. As she pulled him toward the rim, he revived, flailing and choking, trying to fight her. When he almost pulled her in, she let him go and waited.

His struggles slowly ceased. He hung in the water; ripples surrounded him. He looked up at her, and intelligence leaked back into his eyes.

"Give me a hand." Still whining, self-pitying, yet trying to demand.

"I tried," she said. She brought her bare feet up on the wall and crossed her arms on her knees.

Chris paddled slowly toward the edge, reached for the stone, caught it and held on. "Bastard," he said.

"And you too."

He pulled himself half onto the wall, stopped, and swung his leg up

4

to hook his heel over the corner. Water splashed out of his boot and dripped from his shiny black pants and bloused sleeves. He held himself there, trembling, unable to pull himself any farther.

"Misch . . ." His voice was very weak.

She dragged him out of the water, over the wall, into the sand. He fell against her; she supported him. He tried to lie down, but she would not let him. "Home, Chris, huh?"

"I want to go to sleep."

She did not answer, but pulled his hand across her shoulders and put her arm around his waist, turned him and took him away, down a radius and toward Center. He stumbled, and leaned on her heavily, but he came.

Chris was twenty, half again as old as she. He looked taller than he was, as Mischa would when she finished growing. Chris's hair was pale, almost colorless, fine-textured, tending to fall across his eyes. Mischa's was darker, a shade between dark blond and brown, untidily cut, but it had the same texture and the same tendency. Her forehead was wide, her jaw strong and rather square. Chris's face was more delicately built, and the fine bones were accentuated by his painful thinness.

What marked them truly close was their eyes. The startling green was an unlikely shade, but no one had ever asked either of them if they heightened the color.

"Why'd you come down here?"

He took some time to answer. "Where?"

"So near his niche." For Mischa and Chris, their uncle had no name.

"I didn't know I was . . ." His voice trailed off, and Mischa kept him walking until he began to make weak and ineffective movements of escape. "Why don't you let me sleep?"

She stopped, let him go, and looked up at him. "Could you? Even if I let you try, right now?"

He met her gaze, for just a moment. It was like looking deep into a person she could too easily be, if she ever let herself become as frightened as Chris was now. He looked down. "I can't dream, Misch. I forget . . ." His voice rose, and he grabbed her shoulders as though to shake her in anger, but he had to use her as a support. "I never dream anymore." Terror and despair were the only emotions he had left.

There was nothing Mischa could say, nothing she could do but put her arm around him again and lead him through the tunnels, back to Center, back to his niche. He came obediently, silent now. Glowing

5

light-tubes began to outnumber dead ones. As they passed beneath the lights, their shadows lengthened and shortened like turning spokes.

Nearer Center were more people, but they took no notice of Chris and Mischa: a couple of kids, one sick, no account.

Mischa's clothes were wet down the side where Chris leaned, clammy and warm against her in the heavy air. But she felt him begin to shiver; she moved her hand against his side and found that all the warmth came from her own body. Chris was cold, all the way through, his energy depleted by exhaustion because he could not sleep and by oblivion because he could not dream.

His boot slid across the stone; he stumbled and fell, pulling Mischa with him. She knelt beside him, holding him up on his knees, engulfed in his limp arms. "Get up, Chris, come on."

"Leave me alone."

She could not carry him and he could not stand.

"Get out' the way!"

Mischa looked up, startled. A miner swayed above them. Mischa could smell the alcoholic taint of his breath, but she had not felt his approach. The sight of helplessness excited him. He struck out at her; he wore heavy rings on every finger of his soft white hands. Mischa threw herself backward into the sand. The miner turned from her to Chris and kicked out viciously. The heavy boot caught Chris in the lower ribs, lifted him, and threw him against the wall. He slid down next to a little pile of trash.

The miner chuckled low in his throat and went toward him, clenching and unclenching his fingers, head low, shoulders hunched. Mischa darted in front of him. She tossed her head and her hair flipped back; he was confronted with anger on the edge of irrationality. "Don't," Mischa said. A touch flicked the crystal blade of her knife straight out. The point just grazed the miner's stomach. As he jumped back, a spot of blood spread on his shirt. Mischa followed him, one step. He backed away. His gaze jerked down to the well-blooded knife. He backed another step, and when she did not follow, he turned and ran.

Mischa wiped the blade. It remained bright, clear ruby from other encounters in which it had tasted blood more deeply. The miner, Mischa reflected, should never have left his Family's safe rich dome and the machines that did all their work.

Chris was curled around himself, unconscious or simply unaware. He did not move when she shook him, though his eyes were open.

6

She supported his head and slapped him gently until he closed his eyes and opened them again. False euphoria, backed, then overwhelmed, by depression, crept up in Chris and leaked to Mischa. She resonated to the pitch of his exhaustion.

"Let's go, Chris," she said, very softly, and he did the best he could.

They walked. Their surroundings grew brighter, warmer, more crowded, noisier. Mischa kept Chris near the wall so she would be between him and other people. She ignored the few who noticed them. None offered help. She did not want it.

"Why were you there?"

"You know why." She could not quite keep the bitterness from her voice. "I always go to the underground after I have to go home." She needed the solitude and silence and petrified fragile beauty of the lower caverns, as well as their danger, perhaps, to renew her faith in herself. The echoing paths that humans had never despoiled restored her.

Chris was silent for so long that Mischa thought he had forgotten they were talking; when he finally spoke he might as well have said nothing. "They can still call you, huh?"

Her temper flared, but she damped it and did not answer.

Chris closed his eyes and let her lead him. "I didn't think Gemmi'd live this long. I really didn't."

And again, Mischa had no answer. The sick, stupid feel of their sister remained in her mind. Gemmi's aura had to fade slowly, like a foul odor. She lived only through others, in the consciousnesses where inhibitions held, and in the soft underparts of the mind where animals still lurked. It was best that she had so little intelligence; she would have been driven insane otherwise. Had her body been so deformed, she would have been exposed to the deep underground as soon as she was born.

"She hasn't tried to call me," Chris said, "not for, oh, a long time."

"Shut *up*, Chris." Mischa had kept her own invisible differences almost secret for so long that the defense was automatic. It worried her that Chris was no longer so cautious. The wrong word at the wrong time, and he—or both of them—might be banished from Center.

When Mischa left the city, as she was determined somehow to do, it would be of her own will, her own plan. She had no intention of being driven out because of an ability for which she did not even have a word. Mischa imagined being chased into the deep underground: as a prison, it would lose its beauty and its fascination. And she would be doubly trapped. If she were seen near the city again, she could be killed; if she stayed in the underground and tried to defy Gemmi's inevitable call to return, she would go mad.

Involuntarily, Mischa shuddered. Gemmi had called her, toward insanity, many times. Chris felt her tremble and pressed his hand against her shoulder. "Hey . . ."

She could not become angry over his undependable concern; she was too used to his unconscious selfishness and his occasional abrupt generosity. "Gemmi sucks out my brain and licks at my eyes," she whispered. "He's making her call me more often now—"

"It won't be long," Chris said. "We're leaving earth. We're going to the Sphere."

Mischa was caught with surprise and hope. She could hardly believe that he had found a position, after so long. If this were true, everything they had been through was worth it. For two years Mischa had stolen for both of them, to placate their uncle and support their younger siblings and to free Chris for his own work. She had begun to despair, and the changes in her brother had seemed to confirm her fears.

Chris's eyelids flickered and he smiled his small diffident smile of keeping a secret until the right moment. "I'm leaving Center. Like we talked about. We'll be so far away Gemmi will never be able to call us. . . . You do want to come?"

Mischa protected herself with distrust. "When?"

"One of the shipowners saw my stuff . . . my new stuff . . . Hers is the last ship out . . ."

"That's great, Chris." Mischa clenched her teeth and kept back tears. "Sure." The last ship had taken off long before, barely avoiding the first sandstorm of the winter. Chris felt as though he believed what he said, but Mischa could not tell if that truth were reality or the remnants of their dreams. Now it hardly mattered.

She shifted her supporting grip on his waist to ease her shoulder muscles, but stopped abruptly when Chris gasped at the pain of his cracked bones. The same pain flared in tandem in Mischa's side, beating at her reserves of strength and endurance. Chris stood hunched over, swaying. Mischa touched his ribs more gently and found the place that made him wince.

"Don't—"

"It's all right," she said. "Just a little farther. I won't do it again."
He let her start him walking. His emaciated muscles had no tone.

A long time passed before they reached Chris's niche. It was almost
in Center itself, on the first circumference out from the main cave.
In a crowded and competitive place, Chris had kept his home because
fighting with a knife or barehanded, he was good. But soon some
chuckie would realize that he no longer had the desire or the ability to fight for anything.

The door was open. Mischa led Chris inside, locked the door behind
them, pushed aside the hall curtain, and stopped abruptly, staring. The
niche was a five-meter cube cut in stone, rough-polished. The wall facing the entrance had been a quiet, bright scene of a world where things
grew, a vision of what she and Chris had imagined of other places.
Now the wall screamed with color. "You changed it—"

Chris's hand slid limply off her shoulder, as though he were giving
up the little strength left him, as though he did not need it in this familiar place. He seemed to feel safe. Mischa felt threatened. The left wall
had been painted over and experimented on a hundred times since
Chris had come here; Mischa had seldom visited without finding a new
picture, or design, or invention.

This time, what was left of the top layer of paint was smeared, and
the wall had been smashed with a stone. Flakes of paint lay scattered
in the sand, and the wall was a mosaic of old work in bits, almost recognizable. Mischa looked at it for a long time, until finally, with a deep
breath, she was able to pull her gaze away. She tried not to look at it
again, but the brilliant disaster kept catching on the edge of her vision.

She moved between heaps of Chris's flamboyant clothes to
straighten his bed. She threw the filthy tangled blankets on the floor
and rummaged for cleaner ones. When she turned back, Chris was
curled in fetal position. She sighed, at the point of frustration. "If you
want to lie there soaking wet—" She stopped. There was no way to
make him feel guilty about himself.

He had wrapped his arms around his head and buried his face between his knees; she could not reach the fastenings of his shirt. She
pulled one arm away but it crept back like a sick snake to shield his
eyes. The slow-motion wrestling match made her fruitlessly angry.
Eventually she got the front of the shirt pulled apart. Once she had
dragged the bright frayed material off one arm, the other was not so
difficult.

9

Over sharp bones, under fine gold hairs, a black bruise marred Chris's blue-white skin. Old scars stood out in darker ridges on his chest and forearms. His boots came off with a faint squelch. When Mischa had finally made him straighten out his legs, his pants were too loose to be much trouble. Naked, he looked very frail. He went limp when she tried to get him to his bed. She shook him and cursed, and very nearly kicked him in the side herself.

Whatever his reasons, he must have been wandering awake near the deep underground for days, because he had passed through hyperactivity and euphoria and false clarity of mind, hallucination and paranoia, and reached the last stage of exhaustion before coma.

"Chris?"

"Uh?" His translucent eyelids flickered.

"Is there any sleep here?"

"I don't want it." His voice was just a whisper, but the whine had returned.

"You started," she said. "You can't stop now."

"It helps," he said. "It used to . . ." He lifted his hand to gesture at the one new wall, but his arm trembled and fell back across his chest. "That's what I did when I started. It was so good—"

"You were good before."

"Not that good. Not good enough . . ."

"And this?" She gestured toward the ruined wall, without looking at it. Chris did not answer, but turned his head away. Mischa shrugged. The changed room reached out with tendrils of color, mindlessly, probing at her. It was full of a nervous and dissipated kind of energy. The controlled power of Chris's earlier work was unleashed here raw.

"You lose a lot when you sleep," he said. "You have visions that would be the best things you could ever do, but you can't remember them when you wake up. Your whole brain gets used, but you forget. That doesn't happen anymore."

"Now you don't dream at all." She said it, and instantly regretted the needless cruelty.

His voice turned ugly and defiant. "Maybe it was worth it."

Mischa looked around, at the walls of the room where she had been able to sit and imagine what it would be like to leave Center and be free, where now she could only withdraw into herself and hope to escape quickly. She wished she did not care. If she had not cared, she could get up and walk away from him and never come back.

With no emotion, Chris said, "It's in the carryall."

She went through the pack and found a vial of round transparent capsules. Fine white filaments writhed slowly inside them. "How many?"

"Just one."

She could feel the lie. She shook two into the palm of her hand and took them to him. "I can tell, Chris. You're not clear like Gemmi, but I can tell." She wanted to grab him and shake him, or scream, or cry: Two! You need two! And you never looked for me, you never let me help.

He closed his hand around the capsules. There was hate in his skeleton-face because she would not let him kill himself now, because next time, alone, he might not have the nerve.

He swallowed the capsules and lay back, changed, gradually relaxing. He reached out blindly for Mischa. His hand was skin and bone, starved muscles and sharp, dirty fingernails. She held his hand until his grip slackened and he slept, a dreamless, necessary, torturing sleep, the only kind he had anymore. She felt it come upon him. For the thousandth time she wished her mind were closed to others. In the spectrum of her strangeness, Mischa could feel Gemmi the most strongly; her sister was not only detectable, but could force herself clearly into Mischa's thoughts from a great distance. At the farthest end of the spectrum, a few people were so calm, so self-contained, that Mischa could hardly sense them at all. She could feel Chris a little more than she did most people: never whole thoughts or words, only vague currents of emotion.

She stayed beside him for a few minutes. Her concern for him was useless. She wanted to cry, but no tears would come, nor could she trace the tangled strings of her sorrow. She had to be selfish to survive, but if her feelings had been due to selfishness she could only have been angry. She could not cry, but she could not hate him either.

She left the cluttered niche and the new painting and the shattered works of genius without looking back. Behind her, Chris was as deep and empty of dreams as the well. The momentary hope he had given her was broken and bitter, and the destruction went deeper because he had left her so alone with their mad childhood visions. She felt much older now, and Chris . . . she could see herself just like him, starting the day she was not strong enough to defy their uncle.

The radius through which she walked ended on the beta-helix that crawled up the inside wall of the underground city. Below, above, and to either side stretched the immense cavern of Center.

Light-tubes spread across the ceiling like the gills of a mushroom. The instantaneous impression was one of chaos, of tiny gray projections climbing each other to reach the ceiling, spotted here and there with color or movement. Mischa knew the city well enough to see the underlying order: five parallel spiral ramps leading up the walls at a low pitch, giving access to the vertically stacked dwellings. The helices were almost obliterated by years of building over, use, and neglect. The walls of the cavern, crowded with single-unit box-houses piled against the stone, looked like shattered honeycombs. To Mischa's left, and below her, Stone Palace was an empty blotch of bare gray rock on the mural of disorder. Its two entrances were closed to the rest of the city; before it, the Circle, the wide sandy way that led around the perimeter of the cave, was almost deserted.

In front of her, stretching to the right, the Three Hills rose up, as crowded with dwellings as Center's walls. Their interiors were mazes and warrens, labyrinthine beyond mythology. Far to her right, at the other end of Center, the gleaming gray hemispheres of the Family domes were just visible, clustered in their own uncrowded section. Below her, in the Circle and in the valleys between the hills, a few people, usually alone, moved on their trivial businesses, hurrying. The smell of humanity made the air a cloying mass that Mischa was not yet reaccustomed to. The last few days closed in around her, and she felt suddenly exhausted. Instead of staying on the path, she cut across the tacit sanctuaries of tiny unit balconies, drawing a few angry cries and ill-aimed missiles of garbage that she ignored.

The fastest way to Mischa's home was around the Circle, past Stone Palace. Most of the bars facing it were empty and quiet; ship crews were their major patrons, and the ships had all left for the winter. The companions lounged lazily in their decorated nudity, talking and gambling together. They had no audience to which to play, no reason for displaying their physical wares. In an open-fronted bar, curtains of light drifted aimlessly between empty tables, seeming sentient and lonely, searching for companionship.

Even the beggars were lazy, and had, for the moment, forgotten their moans and their feigned, flaunted pain. They ignored Mischa and she ignored them. They revolted her, with their grasping hands and their soft pale bodies and their enhanced deformities. They did not beg for themselves, but for the people who owned them, deigned to feed them, further disfigured them if they grew too healthy, and beat them if they made no profit. Mischa could have pitied them if she had ever seen any one of them defy a master or try to escape, but she could not pity an unthinking acceptance of degradation.

The facade of a lounge brought her up short. She had not seen it before; she did not come this way often. The swirling patterns of sound and color plucked at her, engulfed her, and sawed at her self-control. As they were meant to. A couple of companions, a man and a woman, stopped playing with each other and watched Mischa curiously. She moved toward the facade, drawn unwillingly to it. She brushed her fingers across the tangible boundaries of its masses, and the taste of Chris's wasted energy and talent washed bitter in her throat. If she had seen this work of his before, she would have known about his pain; if she had seen it soon enough, she might have been able to find him before he was lost. She pulled away as though from a part of herself, stood for another moment, suddenly turned and fled. Two-tone high and low laughter drifted behind her.

2

In her niche, Mischa woke abruptly, frozen, sweating, shaken by a nightmare, needing to make any sound or movement to break it, but unable to. Her dream was that Gemmi had crept into her mind again, while she was asleep, insinuating herself so deeply she could never be removed. Now Mischa was awake, and Gemmi was gone, but there was no guarantee that this reality was not another dream out of which Gemmi could pursue her.

Believing that would drive her mad. Released from the nightmare, she turned face down and put her arms over her head. The event would recur, in dream or reality, as long as she stayed in Center, or as long as Gemmi was alive. Perhaps she would die, but Mischa could not count on that. She could only keep fighting. Her thoughts went around in small deformed circles, following the Möbius strip of the phrase, *We've got to get away*.

Chris could help no longer, though escape was more essential now than ever. Mischa knew that no one in Center, even the healers, could help Chris; if he had any chance at all to live, it was in the Sphere, the wider civilization spawned by earth.

Mischa had depended on Chris when she was a child. Now his life depended on her.

Her time was her own, for a little while, until she had to begin thinking again about where she would get the money demanded of her and Chris. Since their parents had died, their uncle had become more and more greedy; Mischa was afraid he would begin to require all her time, and draw on Chris's again as well. With Gemmi, he could do it; and he would, if once he began to disbelieve Mischa's lies about how long her plans required, or if he discovered that she provided Chris's share.

Sitting up, Mischa pulled the cover off the bowl of lightcells. The maroon darkness faded in the blue glow. The cells were dull; often Mischa forgot to feed them, and more often she was not in her niche when they were hungry. She sprinkled powdered food across the convoluted surface. The globe glowed a little brighter. Mischa lay back in the tangle of her bed, looking up at the intricate ceiling. Her small cave was almost completely natural. She slept on a pile of blankets along one side. A large wooden chest, holding her few possessions, stood against the opposite wall. Except for the light, the rest of the chamber was empty. In the back wall, a narrow passage led farther into the rock, to a larger concealed cave with a pool of clear water.

Even her home began to close in, as though the stone were folding. Her dreams of leaving earth were crumbling around her. She pulled them back, clutching at them, but they were mist and dust in her grief and anger. Chris was trapped by his dreamless sleep and Mischa was trapped by her link to Gemmi. Perhaps there really was no way out.

Needing space around herself, Mischa slipped through the narrow fissure that led to the deserted radius outside. Walking down the passage, she passed concentric circumference tunnels until she reached the alpha-helix that spiraled, parallel to beta, up the wall of Center. She sat on the ramp, looking out over the cave. Beyond the Family domes that guarded and controlled essential services, the gate to the outside stood tall and solid, closed for the winter while the black sandstorms raged beyond. Mischa missed the neon-orange sun and the iridescent black sand, the stubby cactus-trees and the changing expanse of rolling empty dunes, the carefree manner of the caravannaires and the occasional sight of a ship landing on the field, and even the gray-brown clouds that seldom let the stars shine through.

"Hi, Misch."

She glanced up. "Oh. You. Hello." Kevin was her age, had bright black hair, eyes the same, and a round, pleasant face. He had caught up to and passed her in height during the last year. A fair thief, he would be better when he finally learned that his impulses were not trustworthy. Even getting caught had not taught him that but he did run with a gang most of the time. He was almost ready to admit to himself that he was a follower.

"How's it going?" He kept his voice deferential, almost unctuous.

Mischa did not want to talk to him or listen to him; he made her think of Dav. "What did Dav tell you to say to me?"

"Misch—" Speaking in two tones slid together, his voice oozed unjust hurt.

"I'm really tired of you trying to get me in again."

"The mess was just bad luck. You only ran with us once."

She did not give him her opinion of bad luck. "That's right. I only ran with you once."

"You could get a lot more with us."

"I could get ruined, too."

"Dav said to tell you you can do whatever you want. Everybody would do just what you told them."

"That's what he said last time. And everybody else said they would too. But they didn't. And I'm the one that got hurt."

"He got you out, didn't he?"

"Uh-huh. Where were the rest of you while he was doing it?"

Kevin shrugged and looked away.

"I work better alone," Mischa said. "Let's leave it at that."

"Okay." But he sounded unwilling, as though he had instructions he was reluctant to disobey.

"Hey," Mischa said.

"What?"

She pointed. At Stone Palace one of the doors swung slowly closed behind a child in a gilded kilt and collar. It minced along in the sand, in unconscious parody of adulthood despite baby fat and long beribboned curls.

"Come on," Mischa said.

15

Kevin followed her down the helix. "What are you going to do?"

"*I* don't know," she said, as though she had definite and malevolent plans.

"You're crazy," Kevin said, making the assumptions Mischa had expected.

"Find other company, then."

He followed her, and they followed the slave child as it followed its memorized route. Mischa was cautious by habit, though the child walked eyes front, incurious, disdainful. It seemed to look down its nose even at things twice its size. It shied away from dirt and disorder, when it should have been making mudpies. It seemed proud of itself, proud of its duties, proud of the collar around its neck.

The slave child walked down the middle of the path, toward the Family domes. Kevin grew increasingly nervous. He and Mischa both were out of place in this part of the city. "But what are you going to do?"

"I told you I don't know yet."

"Why waste time on it?"

"That's just why I won't come back."

Not understanding, Kevin said, "Dav—"

"Dav chews his toenails," Mischa snapped.

Hurt by the insult, Kevin grew silent. He followed her for a few more minutes, then spoke again, hesitantly. "Whatever you're going to do, I don't think it'll work."

"I'll see you around, then."

Having expected her to stop chasing the useless slave, Kevin halted, surprised at the cutoff. Mischa kept going, half-smiling with relief that vanished when he called to her.

"Mischa—"

"What?"

"Dav wanted me to tell you one thing."

"What?"

"He says he misses you."

The tightness in her throat was less, this time, than her anger. "That's too bad," she said. Dav had been a good friend, a pleasurable companion, but he had drawn on their friendship more than once too often. Mischa did not want to see him again. Too many people were

16

trying to control her life. She had missed Dav for a long time, in the day, in the night, but she did not miss him anymore.

She walked away from Kevin and did not look back.

The slave child's presence in Center, unguarded, was a taunt that would never be answered. Its authority emanated from Stone Palace, where Blaisse, its lord, held half the power in Center. Blaisse did not exert his will as much as Mischa had heard his father used to, but the potential existed. Blaisse controlled any ship that landed at Center from the Sphere, and he was said to possess great weapons. At least the Families believed he did, for they never tried to alter the uneasy balance of power. The Families themselves were unquestionably powerful, for they controlled the law, the food and water, access to the outside, raw materials, even the air. And, of course, electricity: the light.

When the slave child reached the Family domes, it was allowed to enter, a courtesy accorded few others. When it had finished giving the bulk orders, it went to franchises to buy prepared goods: cloth or caked and flavored algae or meat made of pressed sheets of cultured cells. Last it visited the little luxury shops for outside imports that could not be made or grown in Center: fruit, animal meat, fur, sun-drugs. The prices had already risen considerably; they would be much higher by spring. The child pilfered choice tidbits with impunity, ignoring guardbirds that would have been loosed to take out anyone else's eyes.

Unmolested and avoided, the child made its loop of Center and returned to Stone Palace, to give up its responsibility and again be a plaything competing with other playthings for the attention of some noble. Mischa let it go. She looked up at the clean gray stone where units had been stripped away and crumbled into rubble to give the Palace and its lord the privacy they required. Mischa felt no animosity toward Blaisse for the destruction; it had been done long before either he or Mischa was born.

Mischa smiled a wry private smile and turned back the way she had come.

Jan Hikaru's Journal:

    My friend the blinded navigator tells stories of greater or lesser credibility, and her words flow like poetry. The blind poet: a character so ancient it has become an archetype: Homer, Miri-

amne . . . and my friend. I listen to her and talk with her for hours every day.

People come to her: children, young navigators, even captains, to tell her of ships about to depart for places I have heard of but never seen. She questions each with equal courtesy, thanks them, and stays. She is waiting for something. Of late she has become restless. I have a feeling that soon she will make her way down to the field, find a ship of whatever destination, and leave.

I'm discovering that I have never been frightened before. I am frightened now, of losing her, of loneliness.

Kirillin was a tall, ugly young woman with knife scars down her cheek and a purple birthmark like a mask across her eyes. She always wore opaque black. She was older than Chris by a few years, and ten years removed from being a sneakthief, but she was a good friend. For many things she had been Mischa's teacher, from tricks of the trade of thievery to biocontrol of fertility. Mischa went to her shop and leaned against the doorframe.

Kiri glanced up. "Hello, Mischa."

"Hi." She gestured toward the back of the room where five kids were playing three-coin. "Need more help?"

Kiri smiled with the half of her face that worked. "What have you got in mind? An honest job?"

"Thought I'd try it."

Kiri raised an eyebrow. "It would be a real shame to distract such a good thief."

"I'm getting old for it."

Kiri's laugh was all she needed to indicate her skepticism. "Just what are you planning?"

Mischa shrugged.

"Let's see," Kirillin said. "My senile old mind seems to recall seeing a Palace footwarmer prancing by a little while ago. I'll be hiring out for delivery soon." She frowned. "Close?"

"But you do need more help."

"That's a hell of a risk."

"I want to talk to Blaisse."

Kiri laughed, quickly, sharply, with surprise and disbelief. "He'd rather have you steal from him."

"Give me a chance, Kiri."

18

"Why?"

Mischa folded her arms and let her hair slide across her eyes. "When did you see Chris last?"

Muscles tensed along the side of Kiri's face. "I don't remember. A long time ago."

"One of the shipowners hired him, but he . . . got sick. I've got to get him out of Center, Kiri, or he's going to die. Maybe away from here they can help him."

"Mischa, but what can you *say* to Blaisse?"

She hunched her shoulders. "I don't know. I don't have a special thing I can do, like Chris does. But I can do anything, if you show me once. I'm pretty smart. I'll just have to convince him to let me on one of his ships."

Kiri levered herself from her chair and stared out the window at the bare gray Palace space, taking time. "I think you'll be hurt," she said.

"Maybe."

"I'm risking something too," Kiri said. "I won't guarantee you. If someone will hire you anyway, all right. That's all I'll do. I'd rather not do that."

"Thanks, Kiri."

She smiled an ironic smile made ugly by scars and paralysis. "Yeah, sure."

Mischa joined the group at the back of the room and gambled with them, allowing herself to win a little, until all the others were hired and she was left alone with Kiri.

"I don't think anyone's going to take you, Mischa."

"They ordered from a lot of places," Mischa said. "I'll wait a while longer." She sat against the back wall with her knees drawn up to her chin. Kiri limped back and forth across the front of her unit, but the movement tired her. Once she bent down to massage her stiff leg just above the knee. Mischa knew better than to suggest that Kiri ask a healer to stop the pain. The response would be a cold glare, and a long, long silence.

Kiri finally sat down by the window, glancing nervously into the Circle now and then through the one-way screen. When her gaze lingered, Mischa stood up, waiting. A merchant entered a moment later. "I need a deliverer."

"It's very late," Kiri said. "I have no one who's guaranteed."

He scowled. "I want some kind of insurance."

"Sorry."

"How long have you had this one?"

"Not very long."

"How does she work?"

"I haven't had any complaints yet," Kiri said.

He grumbled and argued, but finally hired Mischa. Merchants had a tendency to feel demeaned if they had to do their own delivering. Holding her temper, after having been inspected like a cut of meat, Mischa followed him out, and half-grinned thanks to Kiri. Kiri did not smile back.

3

Mischa joined a straggling group of kids in a procession to Stone Palace. As they approached, the supply entrance squealed open against the sand caught in the door's tracks. A slave waved them through. Mischa trudged inside, pulling the heavy cart, jostled by the varied conveyances crowding into the tunnel. She allowed herself to be displaced toward the back of the line, yielding her position to messengers more anxious to finish and get on with other commissions.

The slave led them straight back, through a corridor without side-tunnels. As they continued deeper into the Palace, the air grew warmer and more humid, and a faint cooking smell became stronger.

They stopped at the doorway of the kitchen. Never having been inside Stone Palace before, Mischa glanced around curiously. Most of the huge room was out of use now that it was winter and most of Blaisse's ships and their crews were gone. The kitchen was cluttered with pots and pans, immense vats and grills and griddles, ovens and stoves. Toward the back, five nearly naked slaves stood in a ragged line, heads down, as the steward of Stone Palace chastised them in a low voice. She turned away, and two of them glared at each other while the others moved like wraiths back into the steamy heat.

The tall woman approached the carriers. She wore an unornamented ring on her finger, but she did not stand or walk like a slave. She had a high forehead, a narrow chin: an elegant, guarded face. Her dark eye makeup made her look angry, but she was not, as far as Mischa could tell. The black velvet she wore was embroidered with silver thread. Her long skirt rode low and was slit to her hip on the left; the bodice had a high neck and long sleeves, but barely covered her nipples from above, leaving the lower curve of her breasts bare. A black opal covered her navel, and her black hair was twisted with silver rope. She gestured with a short whip. Silver barbs glinted at the ends of a triple lash, polished, unstained.

"Come along."

They pulled their burdens after the steward, through the kitchen to a storeroom. At the end of the line, Mischa looked for another exit and found it: a tall, wide doorway curtained with brown hangings. As the slave woman gave directions to each of the others in turn, Mischa stood waiting by the storeroom door, watching.

"You, girl."

Mischa started. She did not like this woman; she could not sense her. She was self-contained, guarded, opaque to Mischa's talents. Mischa would have been glad if everyone were so closed, but they were not, so the steward was rare and mysterious, a possible danger. Mischa followed the steward to an open bin.

"Put the fruit in there, and be careful not to bruise it."

Mischa did not answer. The slave woman flicked her whip against her skirt. It made a delicate scraping sound. "Did you hear me, girl?" Her tone was not angry; the discipline seemed the result of duty rather than offense or the wielding of power.

"Yes," Mischa said.

"You should learn manners. Be quick."

But the slave steward did not leave. She stood by the entrance of the pantry, overseeing the work. Mischa felt sure the woman had memorized everyone here and would raise an alarm should she fail to see each one leaving. There were innumerable hiding places in the storeroom, and Mischa had confidence in her ability to sneak past any of the ordinary Palace servants, but the steward appeared a more formidable barrier.

Mischa drew out her job, taking as long as others with larger burdens, arranging the hard-rinded fruit in a regular pattern. The storeroom contained interesting things; it was reasonable for her to stop occasionally and peer around curiously, wearing an innocent expression of wide-eyed wonder, taking a few extra minutes each time. And each time she searched for a way to create a diversion. But all the cabinets and bins were well secured to wall and floor; all were closed and locked except those actually being filled. Mischa's cart was sturdy and stable; she decided that simply overturning it would be a little too blatant.

Only two other kids remained when Mischa finished storing the fruit. The slave steward glanced at her with disapproval despite Mischa's careful look of guilelessness. Mischa began to admit to herself that she had failed, this time; she was annoyed to have taken a job of manual labor with no result. Thieves did not work with their backs, but with their hands and minds.

Mischa brushed fragments of rind into a small neat pile in the corner of the cart. In the next room, a voice yelled angry words; a second voice responded in kind. The steward glanced over her shoulder, frowning; when the argument grew louder, she glanced back into the storeroom. Mischa picked up the handles of the cart and pulled it toward the door. Out of sight, the voices erupted loudly. The steward turned and left the doorway momentarily unattended.

Bonded and obedient, the other two carriers started outside. Mischa let them pass her and followed until they were in the steamy kitchen. She hung back, and when they were a few meters ahead of her and kitchen equipment hid her from the steward, she pushed the cart into shadows and sprinted. Kitchen background noises concealed her soft footfalls and hid any sounds from the corridor, but it felt empty. Mischa ducked through the tapestry.

The curtains along the walls on the other side were clear yellow, geometrically patterned in rust-orange. The thick carpet was like cave moss, soft on her bare feet, deep brown. The lighting cast diffuse multiple shadows. Mischa was alone.

The hallway curved off to the right. Close to one wall, Mischa felt almost secure: despite the narrowness of the space between curtains and stone, the thickness of the fabric seemed almost able to conceal her behind it. She moved away from the kitchen.

The corridor forked three ways. The side branches led sharply left and right at angles of not quite ninety degrees. Mischa followed the central way, which opened into a long dining room. Its curtains and carpets were embroidered with metallic thread; small caged lights on the walls cast striped shadows and caught the myriad prisms of the branching chandeliers. Cushions surrounded a low, gleaming wooden table.

The tapestries soaked up sound, a disorienting effect to someone used to the echoes of caves. Mischa walked cautiously to the opposite end of the long room, up the five stairs to a platform, and through the heavy curtains of another doorway. Beyond it, precious stones joined the metallic thread in the embroidery. Mischa passed thirty meters of opulent mythological scenes worked in silver, gold, and spun jewels. The figures seemed to move at the periphery of her vision, beckoning, teasing, tantalizing. She walked quickly on.

The hallway ended abruptly in an apparent dead end. She looked around, up, into a vertical tunnel. Her feet rose from the floor. She spun, reaching for anything solid, lost her balance, and fell, but never hit the ground. She writhed in the air, searching for a point of stability, but there were no handholds. Steady pressure pushed her upward for what seemed a very long time as she struggled. Light grew brighter and the shaft widened. The pressure lessened and she felt she was going to fall, but she hung in the air. The shaft had brought her through a hole to a small, round room. Gold cords dangled near her, hanging horizontally, wavering like curious snakes. Using one of them, Mischa pulled herself to the floor's edge.

She crouched by the tube, shaken, feeling foolish: she might have been trapped. A few moments of equilibrium calmed her and she proceeded.

The room opened into a larger chamber with a fountain in its center and many corridors leading outward. Behind the brittle play of water, silence lay like a desert at noon. The most ornate hallway was carpeted and curtained in embroidered purple velvet. Mischa followed it uneasily, feeling that the tapestries and jewels and rugs were wasted in disguising a cave revealed by its faint, dank odor.

Shining cords held drapes from the entrances of huge rooms. Furniture hung from the ceiling, projected from the walls, or seemed to grow from the floors. In one room, water poured over the seven tiers of a fountain, changing color like the spectrum, red at the top to violet at the bottom. To Mischa, the effort of building such a construct seemed great compared to the result.

Hearing voices from a room ahead, Mischa stopped. When she was sure no one was approaching, she crept slowly toward the voices, her hand on her knife. Beyond an open set of curtains, violent motion tangled the shiny sheets of a high bed. A fur blanket slid to the floor unnoticed, further revealing the satin-obscured outlines of two people coupling. Mischa watched for a moment; she had never considered that the beings in Stone Palace might engage in such ordinary human pursuits. The clothing strewn around the room should not have seemed so incongruous, yet it jarred against the ornate perfection of everything else Mischa had seen.

She wondered if one of the people might be Blaisse, but the jeweled bits were the clothing of a slave and the rest was a guard's uniform, so she continued. She saw no one else, and felt no one else; the whole immense ostentatious place seemed deserted.

"You!"

Mischa spun, shocked by the lack of warning despite her watchfulness. Behind her, Blaisse's steward glared, but without feeling: the tall slave woman still projected no anger, nothing at all.

Mischa turned and bolted deeper into the Palace, possibly closer to her goal, certainly farther from escape.

She fled around a blind curve. She could see a dead end just ahead. Desperate, she slipped between a last pair of closed curtains, and stopped.

"What the hell—"

The guard facing Mischa put aside her book and stood up. "Now where did you come from?" Mischa half-turned. The slave woman swept the curtains aside, barring her path. Relief softened the steward's haughty face.

"How did she get in?"

The steward stepped into the room. "I do not know."

This room was subdued rather than gaudy, and as Mischa looked for some escape, she realized that the shelves lining it held books, more than she had ever seen or believed existed anywhere in Center.

"This is as far as she gets," the guard said.

The steward reached for Mischa, who ducked the long silver-painted fingernails and lunged into an opening between two cases of books. The guard grabbed at her and tried to hold her, but Mischa hit her wrist with the edge of her hand. The guard grunted with pain and let go. Mischa fled through a corridor and up a flight of stairs.

Sweet steam thickened around her and tile was slippery under her feet. Skidding, she caught herself on the edge of a deep blue pool. She dodged around it just ahead of the guard.

"Stop!"

Mischa ignored the command; the voice was that of the steward, who was not armed. She ran on, and the carpeting resumed, thick and soft.

"What is this?"

The voice held power. Mischa stopped short, looking up at Blaisse. Behind her, the steward and the guard froze.

The Lord wore a long, patterned silk robe. His damp hair fell in tendrils around his face; his gray eyes were hard and as powerful as his voice. They contrasted sharply with his face, which was round and pudgy, pale but pink-cheeked. Behind him stood another slave, a young girl with silver-blue hair and a strange blue cast to her skin, wearing a narrow loincloth and low halter of silver mesh and sapphires.

"Well?"

Startled out of silence, the slave woman spoke quickly. "The girl is a thief—"

"Put that down!" Blaisse cried.

The steward flinched, paled, and stared at the laser lance in her hand as though she had never seen it. The guard took it back and reholstered it, left-handed; she held her right hand pressed against her side.

"I . . . I beg forgiveness, Lord. I did not think . . ." The slave's haughtiness was gone.

"Just explain," Blaisse said, sardonically, calmly, his rage forgotten. The instant mood change had been genuine, and more than upsetting to Mischa.

"I'm not a thief," she said. In spirit, for the moment, it was true: she had not come here to steal. "I want to work on your ships."

The slave woman looked insulted and the guard snickered. Blaisse began to laugh. "Perhaps you'd like me to give you my spare? Do you think you can fly it in the storms?"

"Stupid kid," the guard said with sarcasm. She suddenly turned very pale, and slid her hand under her belt.

"Are you on duty?" Blaisse asked.

"Yes," the guard said sullenly.

"I couldn't have gotten past her and the others if I weren't good enough to join," Mischa said.

The guard frowned slightly. "She can fight," she admitted.

"I never hire Center people," Blaisse said.

"How do you know? Nobody ever asked you before."

"How do you think you know that?"

"They didn't, did they?"

"It doesn't matter. I won't hire anyone from Center."

"That's stupid."

Blaisse glared at her like a resentful child, straightened up, and spoke very softly. "Do you know who you're addressing?"

"Yes."

Blaisse drew his dark eyebrows together and watched Mischa in silence. She could feel the extension of a tentacle of curiosity from him; she allowed herself to hope. Behind her, the young guard felt surprise above her pain and the slave woman revealed nothing.

"What is the meaning of this?"

The curiosity snapped back; the guard's pain dissolved in dislike and contempt.

The Lady Clarissa, standing framed in the doorway as though aware of the frame, using it, glared at them from the opposite end of the room. She had the high forehead and cheekbones, deep widow's peak, and wide, narrow-lipped mouth characteristic of her Family, which controlled the access of Center to the outside, as Blaisse controlled access to the Sphere. Clarissa's hair was bright brick-red and her eyes glittered like jewels, changing color as she moved. "Has it become impossible for one to sleep?" Her tone was petulant. She moved out of the doorway, slowly, carefully, gliding. As she neared them, Mischa caught a scatter of her feelings: not anger, or fear, or even annoyance; simply boredom.

The slave woman inclined her head. "I regret the disturbance, my Lady."

Clarissa's attendant followed her into the room. He was a large man, dark, with dark curly hair and curiously pale eyes. He wore a loincloth of gold and rubies, a wide jeweled collar, heavy bracelets on his upper arms, a ruby in his navel. A chain jingled gently on his ankle.

"It's taken care of, Clarissa," Blaisse said. He addressed the steward. "Madame, throw the girl out of here." He seemed to use the steward's title from habit, not regard or respect.

"It's taken care of for now," Clarissa said. "But what about later, when they find out they can get in here?"

"No one else will come in to disturb your sleep."

"As if you wouldn't rather be in bed," she said. "With that awful alien."

"I won't discuss it!" he cried. Mischa closed her eyes and wished he would not slide off into unpredictable irrationality.

Clarissa sighed and made a gesture of dismissal. "I don't care if everyone thinks you're in love with a slave." She acted bored now, but no longer was; a current of interest and pleasure flowed from her. She leaned against the big slave, tilting her head so her long hair tickled him. Mischa clenched her jaws and by force of will shut them all out: Blaisse and his anger, Clarissa and her taunting enjoyment, the guard and her pain, the attendant and his dull, quivering control, the alien girl and her fear and innocence. And the slave steward, so withdrawn that Mischa could not touch her.

"Madame, do as you were told." He glanced at the guard. "You're on duty until twenty-four hundred?"

"Yes, sir," she said, her tone just short of surly.

"You comb your hair with your feet," Mischa said.

Madame slapped her. Mischa took it without reaction, but glared at Blaisse. "You're actually rather lucky," he finally said. He turned on his heel and left the room. The alien slave slipped out of his way, then followed him.

"I am surprised, Madame," the Lady Clarissa said, smiling cruelly, speaking in a tone one would use with a small errant child.

"It will not happen again, my Lady."

"I should hope not. Have her taken over to my cousins' dome and given twenty lashes as an example."

"The Lord wished—"

"Do as I say or I'll have them take a whip to your pretty skin." She blinked; her eyes flashed scarlet.

"Yes, my Lady."

"That's better." Leading her attendant, she left them, walking carefully in her affected regal manner.

Long nails sank into Mischa's shoulder; Madame propelled her out and past the pool. Mischa remained tractable. The guard followed, more slowly, and in the library sat down and put her head between her knees.

"Someone will relieve you," Madame said.

The guard shook her head without looking up. "Not till Kaz gets here at twenty-four hundred."

"Then I will send the paramedic."

"Thanks . . . and tell Kaz he better not be late today." She sat up, leaned back in the chair, and looked at Mischa. "You know," she said, "I almost thought he was going to let you stay." She shrugged. "You must be pretty crazy to come in here like that."

"He's crazier," Mischa said.

The guard glanced sharply toward the doorway, but then she grinned. "You're right. But he's allowed." She gestured with her uninjured hand toward a recessed speaker grill in the wall. "Make someone from the dome come get her, Madame." She cradled her broken wrist. "You really hit me. I'm sorry we have to do this. But you must have known—"

"I did," Mischa said shortly. The guard gazed at her a moment longer, shrugged, and returned her attention to her injuries. Madame's back was turned as she spoke into the transceiver. Mischa bolted.

The guard cried out; Madame flung herself after Mischa, clawing at her. Mischa thought she might escape, but the slave dug her fingernails into her ankle and hung on. Mischa was hit hard from behind and went down, twisting. Then the guard was above her, raising her hand in a fist.

Jan Hikaru's Journal:

The day came when I felt that my friend would leave; when she awakened, she confirmed my fears. The most recent ship to land was captained by a man she trained twenty years ago. His ship was headed along a chord, almost a diameter, of the Sphere. My poet wants the abandoned center; that ship would take her closer. We sat together until almost midnight, then she stood up and started away, alone. She was slow, and frail, yet sure of her way. Even blind. Then she turned around and seemed to look straight at me, though I know the most she sees is a pearl-white refraction of light and shadow. She smiled, very slightly, and said, "Are you coming?"

I followed her, without needing to say a word. Since then we have embarked on four ships, and stopped at seven planets. I am her eyes. Our journey has been rapid and erratic, but always in one direction, toward a part of this galaxy used up and for-

saken by people, before we learned better: the core of our civilization, now abandoned and decaying.

My poet is ill, though she pretends not to be. I'm concerned about her, but she refuses to stop and rest. She is determined to see earth again before she dies. I am apprehensive about what we may encounter; I'm afraid she will not find comfort, but pain. I could almost betray her and take her somewhere else, to some world of beauty and peace. I could take her to Koen, to the Scarlet Forest where the insects always sing. But she would know. So, for now, we drift through a society of quasi- or extra-legality, as welcomed and as cherished as when we traveled on luxury liners and Sphere ships.

My poet has begun to depend on me more. I used to forget her age, her infirmities, even her blindness. I can't now, and neither can she. Sometimes at night she can't keep from whimpering, though admitting pain seems to shame her. I hold her in the darkness until she can sleep, but in daylight, she tries not to lean on my arm.

Disorientation caught Mischa and shook her. Her eyes were closed and she could not open them. The darkness was the scarlet of her body heat, veined with the images of capillaries in her eyelids, holding nothing but fog beyond. She floated in an environment that lacked gravity, pressure, and light, surrounded by something that soaked up everything she could see or hear or touch or smell. She tried to move, and it seemed she might be able to, in slow, slow motion, through an amorphous, yielding substance, but she strained her arm against it until the muscles ached, and when she finally relaxed she was in the same position from which she had started.

She listened, but heard nothing except the rush of her own blood in her veins. Her brain took the sound and made music of it, searching for any sensation.

Mischa fought a tentacle of panic, but it curled and writhed inside her. She allowed her anger to well up and fight it. That worked, for a little while.

Tentatively, cautiously, she listened with her mind, almost as far as she could reach. She was not yet desperate enough to touch Gemmi. No one was near enough or strong enough to feel. She had not tried to listen to what people were thinking for a very long time. She could detect their presence without needing to go that deep, and their emotional states rammed through unsought and unaided.

She pulled back inside herself so she could not be surprised and hurt while her attention was elsewhere.

For a moment she again fought the restraints, but that was useless, hopeless: she could not even feel what held her. Her fingers would not touch each other; she could not make a fist. Any number of her acquaintances had been caught and flogged for stealing, but none had ever described any experience like this. Mischa thought of drugs that could take away her sight, her hearing, her sense of touch, her balance. She could be staggering about right now, without knowing it, while the people from the Families watched and laughed.

She held herself very still, angry and afraid.

The passage of time was incalculable. Mischa did not try to move again until long after both her fear and her anger had passed. Perhaps she had bored those who might be watching and they had gone away, or perhaps the time was only a few minutes and they were laughing again because she had no more patience than that.

She tried once more to clench her fist, stretching out her fingers, contracting the muscles, digging with her nails like talons, into nothing.

Her fingertip touched a minuscule irregularity in the matrix that bound her. She stopped trying to make a fist and concentrated on that one square millimeter of skin in contact with some kind of reality. She probed the imperfection, wishing she could grasp and tear it. Her nail slipped beneath it and she pulled: an insignificant motion requiring infinite energy. But the bit of material yielded; the flaw grew. She worried it, abraded it, unable to rip it. She felt she should be warm and sweaty, but the matrix around her adjusted to her body temperature and absorbed her perspiration without allowing her even that sensation.

She felt the spark of someone's approach. In anger and frustration, she struggled with the single tiny opening. Her hand broke through into a textureless foam or gel.

Bright light cut off her struggles.

Mischa blinked into the spotlight, dazzled, dizzy. Beyond the glare stood two great dark figures who reached down and dragged her from the close restraints. The artificial skin pulled away from her like a glove, and the gel sucked it back.

The two shadows were very strong. They lifted her easily. Even their harsh touch and the painful brilliance of the light were welcome, after so long. She braced herself against the high side of the horizontal cabinet that had imprisoned her. Her eyes adjusted slowly.

She recognized the two people who had come to get her. Their Family dispensed a form of justice, ordered what existed of Center's law, and guarded the property of those who could afford their services.

The administrator glanced inside the cabinet. One side of the suit shriveled as the gel expanded against it, but the other swelled as gel protruded into the tear Mischa had made. The administrator probed and found the hole.

"Industrious little brat," she said. She had a beautiful voice, and eyes like blue diamonds. "Who checked this out?"

"I don't know," said the young, blue-eyed man, who looked enough like her to be her twin, but who was probably no more closely related than first cousin.

"You should," she said. "Call some practice sessions." There was a sneer in her tone, uglier because her voice was still so lovely. She looked down from her great height as Mischa straightened slowly. "Don't you like the way we treat dangerous criminals?" She gestured toward the door.

Mischa came forward slowly, watching her. She watched Mischa as carefully.

"We don't need to tie you, do we?" The young man's voice was falsely hearty. Mischa shook her head. The administrator said nothing, but the corner of her mouth twitched up: she knew a lie.

They walked for a long time down a straight and unbranched corridor, entered an elevator and rose some distance, stopped, and went into another hallway. Mischa had never been in a Family dome before, but there was nothing to see except closed doors every few meters. Mischa walked slowly past them, hunched against the fear and hate all around her.

They entered a high vaulted room that was the proper size and shape to be at the center of the dome. The gray plastic building material, though nearly indestructible, seemed aged, slightly worn, and uncared for. The judge nodded sleepily at his bench, and a few people slumped on the seats arrayed around him.

The administrator prodded Mischa in the back. They moved toward the Family's eldest member. His mane of white hair was yellow-tinged and limp, and the diamond hardness of his eyes was flawed. He shook his head slowly, Mischa thought for a moment at her. But the tremor was a manifestation of his age; he did not even seem to notice it.

"Sir."

His head jerked up, his eyes focused. "Bondsperson?"

Mischa said nothing, and no one else responded. She had not expected help, nor hoped for it.

"The Lady Clarissa sent her for punishment. Stealing in the Palace."

"I wasn't stealing."

The administrator shoved her.

The old man waited. No one intruded on the silence of his forgetfulness. Finally he looked up and around and seemed to remember his duties. "First offense?"

Mischa did not answer. The young man slapped her, grabbed the collar of her shirt, and pulled back and down. The fastenings caught against her throat; the shirt ripped open down the front and hung around her waist. The young man glanced at the scars on her back: an old knife wound, and clumsy beatings, but none of the narrow parallel marks of an official flogging. "First offense," he said.

"Standard . . ." the old man said. "And five for insolence." He leaned across his desk and peered down. "Do you understand, child?"

"Yeah."

The administrator hit her. Mischa stumbled with the blow, rammed into the desk with her shoulder but rebounded, turning, and kicked out. The administrator was not as vulnerable as a man would have been, but Mischa was almost halfway across the big room before she heard the lizard swish of a leather whip. As she leaped from one bench to the next, the lash curled around her neck, pulling her backwards. She fell, banging her head, and lay stunned, empty, removed from reality. They dragged her, groggy and unresisting, back to the judge, leaving the whip wrapped around her throat.

The old man shook his head, slowly, sadly. "You need taming, child."

"Standard first isn't enough for her," the administrator said. "She's been a thief for a long time to go for Stone Palace. She's just been lucky."

"And five for attempted escape . . ." The old man's voice trailed off, and he took another breath. "This is her first."

"We'll just have her back. She'll think she's got away with something."

"Punishments are standard."

The administrator muttered under her breath, but the old man did not notice. He seemed to notice her jealousy even less; he could not see what was obvious to Mischa, that the administrator wanted to sit in his place before her diamond eyes dulled, before her voice grew feeble, before her long, smooth muscles became weak and inelastic. She jerked the coiled whip and pulled Mischa half off her feet.

They took Mischa onto the plaza that fronted their dome. It was early: the ceiling lights were still brightening. Mischa wondered what day it was, if she had been in the deprivation cell overnight or longer. It seemed longer. Another of their Family was releasing the two people from the previous day's punishment. Friends waited for one, and helped him away, but the other was still unconscious, and alone. She was shoved off the plaza and left.

Six truncated transplanted stalagmites projected three meters from the deck. Their broken tips held metal rings; the attached thongs were stiff with blood and sweat. The administrator and her assistant lifted Mischa up and tied her. The cool stone pillar angled out a few degrees, partially supporting her. Her feet did not reach the ground.

They hung two other people up beside her. On her left was a man, an adult. On her right, a paid companion, not much older than she, did not resist as they took away his beaded vest and tied his hands. His face was marked with the tracks of tears. A long red scratch cut from the side of his chest down his ribs to his stomach, and under his low kilt. He would probably have to find another job, after this, or work at a much lower grade.

Someone stood at the front of the platform and began to read charges.

People gathered on the lower level to watch. Mischa rested her head against the stone and tried to shut out her perception of their hungry expectant feelings. They were anticipating this morning, reliving other mornings. Most were merchants with self-righteous auras; a few were Family people. The sound of a scuffle interrupted the concentration.

The charge-paper crackled when it was folded.

The older man was first. Mischa had not heard his crime and did not care what it was. His pain and his screams battered at all the defenses she could build. He possessed no anger, only fear, regret, remorse. Mischa neither understood nor shared his emotions; this punishment could not make her feel guilt. It would be guilt at her own survival. If those who punished her did not know that, she did.

The administrator's feelings came through. She enjoyed the power she held in the braided leather. The reactions of the spectators were approval and hate and vicarious pain and sexual excitement. The mixture had a mental odor of slime and decay and death. Mischa fought rising nausea and retreated within herself. The man screamed again and dragged her back, and that was the first time she really heard the whip crack and slash, and slither as it came away. Cool drops of blood spattered the shirt hanging around Mischa's waist, her side, her small breast, her cheek. She tested the thongs but they were tight on her wrists.

The smell of sweat was strong, mixed of exertion and excitement and fear. Mischa heard the man sob as his short punishment was completed. She tensed, involuntarily, and heard a laugh, very soft.

The man's filtered pain had not prepared her. The whip cut her back almost to the bone, crushed her against the rock, and rammed the breath out of her. She tried to inhale. The gasp was a shudder. The whip fell again. Mischa clenched her teeth. The blood-crusted stone pillar rasped at her forehead and her fingernails dug into her palms, but the sensations grew peripheral when she tried to concentrate on them. The lash always brought her back.

The administrator gave her twenty, and five for insolence, and five for attempted escape. She was an expert. She knew the timing so the pain did not black Mischa out; exactly the timing that could lure Mischa into believing that she had miscounted, that every one was the last.

Just before Mischa did lose consciousness, when the punishment was finished, she heard quiet, beautiful, horrible laughter.

4

Center shut down its radar beacons during the winter, for no one ever landed in the storms. This Subtwo knew, and planned for. The ship's instruments traced out the wide, flat desert, the high mountain ranges bracketing it, and the single anomalous flat-topped peak jutting from its dark expanse. Echoes and reflections hinted at unusual geology. Subtwo increased the magnification until the three-dimensional image of the peak filled his screens and he could see the tiny plot of the blockhouse off to one side. He was hypersensitively aware of everything in the control room of his ship, everything and everyone, all human-machine and human-human interfaces, his pseudosib next to him quite prepared to take over, the other people in the control room almost as superfluous as the old navigator's despondent young friend. All the instruments reported audibly, each on a different frequency: Subtwo could hear changes more quickly than his assistants could report them. But the crew was occasionally useful, and Subtwo did not begrudge letting them perform what they saw to be their tasks. Subtwo tolerated the trappings of leadership. He often thought Subone enjoyed them.

Subtwo's hands and feet moved against controls, his tongue and teeth guided pressure-sensitive switches, his eyes directed the functioning of photoelectric cells, as the ship fell through the upper atmosphere and began to decelerate. Wrapped in the framework of the control cocoon, Subtwo felt very nearly happy. All his senses were in use; no perception of waste impinged on his sensibilities. He was fulfilled.

The voices behind him whispered and exclaimed: his raiders lay in their acceleration couches and stared out the observation ports, watching the wisps of cloud as they whipped past the ship. The clouds thickened as the ship slowed, growing darker until the sunlight was cut off, and the only illumination came from within the craft, shining out against swirling iridescent grains. They could hear the particles scraping and skittering along the metal skin; the sound was of a thousand tiny fingernails against dry slate. Subtwo silenced the voices by allowing the ship a single shudder in the wind, and immediately regretted it, for he could pilot in worse conditions than this; he did not want his skill doubted by even the least experienced of his people. Still, his action produced the proper reaction, and the control room remained silent as Subtwo let the image of the ship sink toward the image of the plateau, very near the blockhouse. His instruments musically told him the characteristics of the ship and its surroundings, atmosphere and wind and approaching surface, engines, fuel, and personnel. The harmonics sang of earth, air, fire, water.

The ship touched and settled, powered down, vibrated at a frequency above that which most human ears could detect. But Subtwo heard it.

A brief hesitation, like a tribute to gods: do not rejoice too quickly. Then a quick laugh and the voices again, and a scatter of applause. That, not the hesitation, was for Subtwo. He thought all the people who followed him quite mad.

"A fine landing," Subone said. Subtwo saw that he had never integrated himself into the secondary controls, he extricated himself so quickly.

"Your trust is flattering."

"You seemed to want to bring the ship down yourself," Subone said, "so I let you."

Subtwo's absorption in the landing had protected him from Subone's annoyance, but he felt it now. It made him guilty and contrite. "Did you want to do it? I didn't realize—"

"Never mind. Let's go in."

Now that he had apologized, Subtwo realized that an apology had been unnecessary. Time and again he had asked Subone to communicate his wishes verbally, normally, instead of relying on the artificial biomechanical link between them. The link was no longer dependable, for which Subtwo was glad: he only wished it would finish dying and dissolve completely. Something must be wrong: he and Subone should have been free of one another long before this. But as they remained, they would always be too concerned each with the other; they would continue to have difficulty dealing with ordinary human beings, who could not and would never know automatically what another person was thinking. Something must be wrong: at times,

Subtwo thought he could almost feel the link, implanted in the primitive part of his midbrain, growing, not dissolving, binding him inexorably to Subone. But he knew that was a delusion.

Subtwo and Subone prepared to leave the ship. They went alone, only the two of them. The young raider who would give no name but Draco, Subone's assistant as much as anyone in their loose organization, stayed behind grumbling. He was only moderately pacified by having the responsibility for the second group. The pseudosibs were well over two meters tall, and Draco was a head taller, narrow, dark, fierce, with fluorescent flames painted around his eyes. He was a distinctive and intimidating presence. Intimidation was not yet their aim.

Jan Hikaru's Journal:
We've landed on earth, but I don't really care. The whole universe seems futile and ironic.

A few hours ago my friend called me to her. She could hardly breathe, and she was feverish and weak. I tried to go for help, but she stopped me. She wanted to go to the observation bubble, so I carried her. Once there, she leaned against me, turned toward the growing crescents of earth and moon as though she could see their light. It shadowed her fine old face, all the lines of character and time, her white hair, her clouded black eyes. The reflection seemed to give her warmth, as though it were the sunlight from which we were shielded. I tried to think of something to say, but there was nothing. I knew she was dying and I knew this was the closest she would ever get to touching her home again. We sat together, quiet and still, for a long time. Her breathing became easier. "Tell me what it looks like."

The moon was a sliver of silver and gray, and the earth was gray and dull brown. I lied to her. I never told her a word of untruth before, but this time I lied to her. I described a world more like earth when people first left it than when they last abandoned it. I told her that there were clouds, not that they looked filthy. That was when my voice broke. She touched my face and told me not to grieve, for she was close enough.

I embraced her, but there is no way to give a friend real strength. She began to fight for breath, and I couldn't stand by doing nothing any longer. I tried to leave, to get help, but she

gripped my hand and would not let me go. Then, quite suddenly,
she stopped fighting.

I didn't know what to do. I just sat there refusing to believe she
was dead until warm hands took her cold hands away, and led me
to an acceleration couch for the landing.

Now the ship sits in a desert, in the midst of a terrible storm,
and we sit in the ship, waiting, I suppose, for permission to enter
the city that is supposed to be nearby. All I want is permission to
bury my friend here, as I promised her I would do, and then
permission to leave.

The wind made a dreadful, destroying sound. The pseudosibs used
the airlock so the sand would not gain access to the more delicate
workings of the ship. As soon as the outer seal was cracked, they were
surrounded by a swirling cloud of dust and sand, as the wind filled
every empty space. It would have torn their flesh away had they not
been wearing vacuum suits.

They fixed a cable to the safety clamps and went out into the storm.

Subtwo found himself leading. His sense of direction was perfect, so
he had no fear of losing the blockhouse. He supposed he deserved to
break the path, to form with his own body a lee, a minor respite from
the wind for Subone, since Subtwo had taken the pleasure of landing
the ship for himself.

Even expecting the blockhouse, Subtwo was startled by its abrupt
appearance, as though it had popped up out of the ground. The sand
caused the illusion: one volume of its airborne granules was sufficient
to block all sight; one step, one increment less of sand-filled space, and
the wall of the blockhouse showed the curtain to be a colloidal suspen-
sion of sand in air.

Subtwo banged on the door with his gloved fist. Nothing happened,
and he banged again. The people within must have felt the ship land,
they must still have sufficient curiosity to wonder who could perform
such a feat.

The door crept open past him. He moved forward and stood in the
doorway, half-blocking the blowing sand. The interior of the blockhouse was almost dark, its instruments shut down, but several people
stood within, all dressed differently, as though they had been interrupted at leisure activities, except for one young guard in uniform,
with a cast on her wrist. Subtwo found the uniform amusing. He did

not understand trying to turn any such rabble as he had collected—as the Lord's shipowners must have collected—into even a quasi-military organization. He could not control his own followers completely, so he did not dictate to them at all.

"Gods," someone said, "don't just stand there."

Subtwo entered, with Subone beside him, in a leisurely manner. The storm-walk had not tired, only challenged him. The Lord's people stared. The guard gripped the handle of her laser lance, but did not draw it. The door squealed shut, forcing itself against sand. Subtwo realized from the reactions of those around him that the longer he stood hidden from them in suit and facemask, the more disturbed they would become, perhaps to his advantage. He gazed about the room until he was sure nothing had escaped his notice. The equipment was obsolete and worn.

He opened his faceplate. Subone mimicked his actions; they were mirror images. Subtwo took off his helmet and shook his head; his long black twisted hair fell out straight and free around his shoulders. He began slowly, silently, to remove his suit. Tiny avalanches of black sand fell to the floor around him. Beneath the suit he wore a simple coverall of a sturdy material, cool gray in hue. Subone wore the same, though the color of his was warm gray: tinged with red instead of blue. Around them Subtwo saw the usual reactions to their supposed similarities, though to Subtwo he and his pseudosib were very different, as different as the colors of their clothes: at opposite ends of a spectrum.

"Where is Blaisse?" Subtwo asked.

A ubiquitous tension filled the room, as though everyone there had expected the pseudosibs to remain silent moving statues for the rest of time. No one spoke until the attention finally focused on the uniformed young woman. She looked from side to side, and finally answered stiffly. "The Lord is in his Palace."

"Take us to him."

Someone snickered. Subtwo gazed in the direction of the laugh, drawing his eyebrows together. Subone still followed his lead and his actions. The snicker faded into a cough. Subtwo did not understand why anyone would laugh at such a simple request. It occurred to him, of course, that he might be violating some protocol. This did not disturb him, as soon all of them would be following his protocol.

"This way," the guard said abruptly.

She led them from the functional blockhouse into the Palace proper, down a long ramp, into tunnels covered wastefully in rich fabric and precious gems. Subtwo saw no use in upholstering hallways. The young woman moved ahead of them, walking fast and straight and steady, yet increasing her pace gradually, after looking back once and starting at the pseudosibs' proximity.

The passages continued on and on, until Subtwo felt their irregularities affecting him. His balance began to falter. He liked level floors and right angles; this was a place of bumps and projections and random curves. At first he sensed the same reaction from his pseudosib, and was comforted that he was not, at least, alone, but as they progressed Subone's discomfort decreased as his interest rose. Subtwo was upset and wished again that the lock between them would complete its dissolution. He felt increasingly these days that he was being forced to vibrate on a frequency not his own.

The young guard stopped and held aside a curtain. "In here."

Shoulder to shoulder and in step with Subone, Subtwo passed her without hesitation, though a trap might await. He felt the chance was low enough to take.

The immense room beyond was paneled with embroidery that followed rock curves ten meters upward to join a translucent dome that seemed to admit cold winter sunlight. A throne—a throne! Subtwo almost laughed aloud—stood on a golden platform at the opposite end of the hemispherical chamber, but it was empty.

"Where is he?"

The guard looked from Subone to Subtwo and back again, as though trying to determine which had spoken: not an unusual reaction. "He's coming," she said; Subtwo detected an uncertain bravado and was pleased that his arrival had caused consternation and confusion.

"I—" Subone said, and corrected himself. "We don't wait."

Subtwo turned with him; they crossed the throne room, still in step. They both had had trouble learning the first-person plural pronouns: such a strange usage, like verbal sexual intercourse. They climbed the steps to the throne and passed through the curtains beyond it. The young guard hesitated, then sprinted after them. "Just a minute—" She caught Subone's elbow. Using the whole force of his powerful shoulders, he swung back his arm and caught her across the ribs, tossing her against a tapestried wall. They continued; behind them, she cursed.

They had been told the layout of Stone Palace: Blaisse's suite connected directly to the throne room. Of course they met no stationed guards, coming as they did from this direction, in the winter. The young woman caught up with them as they entered Blaisse's bedroom.

Blaisse appeared to be asleep, but an alien humanoid sat up in his bed beside him and stared at the pseudosibs, terror in her face. Subtwo identified her species, her world, the customs of her people: parents raised themselves from abject poverty by selling their children into slavery. It was not a Sphere world. Subtwo realized he was probably looking at a slave, the first true, classical slave he had ever seen despite his travels. With difficulty, he controlled a wave of annoyance, directed toward the sleeping man.

"You'll have to wait in the anteroom."

Subtwo turned to the uniformed young woman. "But we never wait," he said, quite reasonably.

"You will now." She touched the cross-holstered laser pistol with her left hand. "No more games."

"What are you going to do?" asked Subone. "Shoot me and hit him with your cast?"

The jibe angered but did not fluster her: in her hand, the lance was steady. "In the anteroom."

Subtwo's wide peripheral vision showed Subone glancing at him, though he himself did not have to turn. He did not see any necessity for a confrontation with an underling. He shrugged—a gesture he had consciously learned and practiced—and followed the direction of her pistol. In the next chamber, a sitting room built on a comparatively modest scale, he waited, disturbed by the absence of doors, of privacy. That told him much about the people who lived here: the rulers did not impinge frequently on each other's living space, and the servants were not important enough for their opinions to matter. These facts conflicted grossly with Subtwo's roseate image of the way reality should be, an image that dulled and contorted as by successive approximation Subtwo altered it to conform to the way things were.

Subone began to wander about the room, opening drawers and cabinets.

"What are you finding?"

"Nothing," Subone said. "Alcoholic beverages. Dirty old books."

"Books—printed books?"

"Very amusing."

"What's the meaning of this?" The Lord held himself poised in the doorway, only partly dressed, wearing leather pants.

Subtwo did not react to the theatrical entrance. "We understood that your hospitality is granted to shipowners of a certain type."

"And you are shipowners? Of that . . . type?"

The slave, naked, knelt before Blaisse, fastened the top button of his pants, and clasped a silver belt around his waist. He seemed not to notice her, despite her unflawed form and the strange blue of her skin and hair, the sky-silver of her eyes. Gazing at her, Subtwo wanted to pull her to her feet and ask her if she had no pride or dignity. Then she fastened a stained, coiled whip to Blaisse's filigree belt, and Subtwo put aside his questions of dignity.

"Our ship is on the field," Subtwo said.

Blaisse looked past him to the turned-out drawers and disarrayed shelves. "What is this farce? Yale!"

The guard came in, scowling.

"I thought I made it clear: no one from Center is allowed here."

"They just landed," she said.

"Don't be ridiculous."

"They landed a ship. On the landing field. In the storm."

Subtwo watched the changes in Blaisse's expression as the Lord took his time putting on the leather jacket his slave held for him: anger, astonishment colored by skepticism, and finally curiosity. He took a sharp breath and straightened, as if to reprimand them, but suddenly stepped toward them. "In the storm?"

"Yes," Subtwo said.

Blaisse's attitude changed again. "I don't believe it."

Subone's voice was a sculpture. "You would be well advised," he said, "not to call us liars."

"Don't threaten me."

"We came to talk," Subtwo said. Blaisse was right, in his way: it was not yet the time for threats. "Merely to talk." This did not seem to be the man they had been told about; he had been described with contempt, but Subtwo was not facing a contemptible man. Unpredictable, perhaps, and distasteful, but there were power and assurance in him, though they blended strangely with childishness and cruelty.

"What did you come to talk about?"

"Division of power."

The young guard, Yale, caught her breath, and touched the handle

Vonda N. McIntyre

of the laser lance again; she, at least, was taking those words as threat. But Blaisse hardly reacted. "This is mine," he said calmly. "Here you take my orders."

"That's what he said you'd say."

Subtwo wished Subone had not spoken, but he could not do anything now; he was affected by his pseudosib's excitement at the prospect of violence. But Subone's excitement could not obliterate Subtwo's increasing perceptions of guilt.

"Who?"

"A shipowner allied to you. You did lose a ship, recently—?"

"You—!"

"Shut up, Yale."

Sullenly, she obeyed. Blaisse's developing anger seemed to have been dissipated by hers; he sat down in a soft chair and stretched out his legs. "We assumed Sphere officials had killed it." He waved toward misshapen hulks of furniture. "Sit down. Have you names?"

"I am Subtwo. My pseudosib is Subone."

Blaisse raised an eyebrow, whether from the strangeness of the designations or because he was familiar with them, Subtwo did not know. He sat down on a couch with room for Subone next to him, but Subone sat farther away, watching the young guard and smiling slightly so his teeth showed past his thin lips.

"We'll have a drink. Saita!"

Dressed in silver and sapphires, the slave appeared almost instantly. She served first Blaisse, then the pseudosibs, with a thick blue liqueur. She did not offer anything to the guard.

Blaisse sipped from his crystal goblet. Subtwo raised his, to sniff the volatiles: heavy, varied, incompatible with organic life. He did not drink; he did not choose to dissolve the nerve sheaths of his brain cells with ethanol. But nearby, Subone tasted the offering.

"Now," Blaisse said.

"You are undefended. We have our whole crew."

"I'm not entirely alone."

"Twelve people hardly make an army."

Blaisse raised his head, an involuntary minuscule motion of surprise. Subtwo felt sure that he now believed that the pseudosibs, not the Sphere, had killed his ship.

"They guard me adequately in the winter. When my ships return in the spring, my forces are more than sufficient."

"The crews—even the shipowners—would follow us."

Blaisse sat back in his soft chair, sipped his drink, and rubbed his forefinger back and forth across his upper lip as though in deep concentration. "I don't know about that."

"They would follow us. They would follow whoever controlled their sanctuary."

"Oh, that's quite true," Blaisse said easily. "Except a few of them, perhaps, but they could easily be gotten rid of."

Yale, behind him, shifted uneasily, as though she too could hear capitulation in Blaisse's words. Subtwo smiled, ready to accept a bloodless surrender.

"On the other hand," Blaisse said, "then you would have to fight the Families."

Subtwo made no involuntary movements of surprise, but this was new data, needing to be processed. "We are accustomed to opposition."

Subone seemed to be paying no attention at all to the conversation; Subtwo felt alone. He wished his pseudosib would stop his benign gazing at Yale: he understood her glare.

"You don't quite understand."

"Understanding is not necessary." Subtwo performed his shrug again. "If they oppose us, we will destroy them."

A small smile of pleasure began to form on Subone's face, and Yale's fingers curled around her belt near the holster of her lance.

"You'll destroy Center if you insist on total power." Blaisse did not sound perturbed.

"You dealt with these 'Families.' "

"No, that was my father, years ago. He was . . . a very ambitious man." Blaisse's expression was contented. "Your information is incomplete."

"Indeed?"

"My presence saves the shipowners from having to concern themselves with alliances in Center itself, you see, but my ties are indispensable all the same. An attack on me is an attack on the Families. And it's they, not I, who control the city."

"Ties may be cut and rewoven."

"Not ties of blood."

Subtwo thought of arcane rituals, the piercing of veins, vampirism. "Blood?"

44

"It was thought appropriate, since I control access to other worlds, that I be partnered with the eldest child of the Family which controls access to the rest of earth outside Center. My brother, in turn, lives with her people." As Blaisse explained, Subtwo slowly understood that he did not mean "blood" but genetics, and biological and social relationships. It was a most ridiculous way of forming alliances, though perhaps no more ridiculous than some he had witnessed. It was the way Center was ruled.

He saw that his choice was between dealing with the existing situation and engaging in an extended conflict. His and Subone's people could take over the Palace easily; they could even make it self-sufficient. But it would be exactly that, a closed citadel, lacking interchange with Center. They could build a citadel anywhere. But old earth was one place no official of the Sphere would ever come; and Subone had chosen this spot on the planet simply because of the city.

Subtwo's enthusiasm for this conquest flagged rapidly, for he saw that afterwards they would have to function within limits others had set. He wondered if this was what he had escaped to: a return to ancient history, with children traded between kingdoms for a joining of lineages.

"Perhaps," Subone said in a tone of preoccupation, still gazing on the young guard, "the partnerships could be rearranged."

Blaisse stared at him for a moment, then began to laugh, a loud, low, barking sound. He stopped when Subtwo half-rose from his chair, though he did not look afraid.

"There can be no 'rearrangements' of the Families," Blaisse said. "My blood is their blood. The ties are unbreakable. The Families would prefer suicide to capitulation."

"Then our problem would no longer exist."

Subone leaned forward, letting the motion bring his hand very close to his lance. Yale tensed at his actions.

"Neither would you, nor the city," Blaisse said. "Center is powered by a fission reactor. I understand that it is not difficult to make it—'go critical'—is that the term?"

Subtwo was disgusted by the very idea of a filthy fission reactor; that any human being, civilized or not, would even consider allowing one to explode was inconceivable.

The slave, Saita, lowered her head and touched a lock of her long silver-blue hair to Blaisse's instep.

Blaisse chuckled. "After all, I'm much more suited to the position than you. You'd be unhappy, confined to Center the rest of your lives. But I'm reasonable, and I'd be glad to be allied to anyone who can overcome our seasonal isolation."

"We will not be subordinates."

"The relationship could be arranged in a businesslike manner." He reached out and patted his slave's head absently, as he might an animal's.

In his mind, Subtwo rearranged images of the manner in which he had expected this meeting to proceed. As he was accepting the changes and making himself pleased with them, Subone stood up and strolled around the small room. By his carriage Subtwo knew he was neither pleased nor resigned. Subone paused next to the small grid of the intercom, and touched its controls. To anyone else, it would appear that he was fingering them absently, but Subtwo knew he was inferring the capabilities.

"Why should we believe you, about these 'Families'?"

Blaisse looked up at Subone abruptly, eyebrows arched, and his mood shifted instantly to fury as he rose from his chair and stood shaking. "Do you think I care if you or any other of your castoffs believe me?"

Subone spoke into the intercom. "Draco?"

"Here," Draco answered in his laconic manner. "All's well."

Subone observed Blaisse's anger calmly. "We are in control now."

"In control? My patience is ended. If you refuse the protection of my alliances, then try to make your own. I'll laugh at you from hell—and I'll welcome you there soon."

Subone smiled.

Subtwo understood abruptly what was about to happen. He stepped forward as Subone made one jerky, indefinite, deliberate motion of his hand toward his lance. Subone hesitated a fraction of a second while the young guard, left-handed, clumsy, pulled her own weapon. Yale had no chance against him. He shot her in the chest. Her spine arched backward at the shock, and she fell against the wall, collapsing to the floor. Her body convulsed once. The reek of burned flesh permeated the room.

"Stop—" Subtwo took the lance from his pseudosib's hand. A few months before, he would have known from the beginning exactly what

Subone was planning. Not having known this time, an indication of their growing independence, did not comfort him.

Blaisse sat heavily in his chair, but his voice was steady. "That was unnecessary."

"She would have killed me," Subone said. He pointed to Yale's weapon, flung into a corner.

This was the second murder Subtwo had been involved in so directly, the second by burning, and he did not like to be forced back to his earlier memory. He did not know how to expiate his guilt, yet he did not say that Subone had provoked the incident. They had not yet grown that far apart.

"This is unfortunate," Subtwo said. "To . . . disrupt us, just as we agree."

"Agree—!"

Clamping his fingers around Subone's bicep, Subtwo brought him to a sullen silence. Though their characters had diverged, Subtwo still led, and Subone had insufficient emotional leverage to affect his pseudosib in this matter. "We will be your equals," Subtwo said, "but you will retain your position."

Blaisse did not even glance toward the small crumpled body shrouded in his colors. Uncertainly, Blaisse said, "If she did something foolish . . ."

Subtwo spoke quickly, to deter the Lord from any thoughts of revenge. "Then we are agreed?"

"For the moment," Blaisse said, and sighed.

"Subone?"

Subtwo responded to Draco. "We've made an agreement with Blaisse. Did you follow orders?"

"Didn't hurt anybody," Draco said.

"They are not prisoners. We are not in conflict."

"They're kind of mad at us."

"Hold their weapons until they are calmer."

"Right."

Subtwo turned off the intercom. Subone glowered at him. "We don't need Blaisse. You're underestimating our abilities."

"No," Subtwo said. "Those are amply demonstrated. I took into account energy expenditures and our own preferences."

"And if Blaisse is lying?"

"What does he gain but a few hours?"

Blaisse, in his chair, seemed far from relaxed.

"We can benefit each other," Subtwo said, putting on his artificial, practiced smile.

"I'm sure," Blaisse said.

"Let us discuss terms."

They negotiated in another room. When they were finished, Blaisse reached up and pulled a silken rope. He was smiling again. Subtwo did not understand his good humor, and did not trust it.

"When you're settled," Blaisse said, "we'll have to get together. I'm . . . very anxious . . . for you to meet Clarissa."

A tall woman in black and silver entered and bowed. Subtwo had had to train himself to look for details of expression and to interpret them in a conscious way: the people around him, normal people, did it unconsciously. This woman showed no surprise; her gaze, quick and hooded, flicked over him and his pseudosib, though she seemed to keep her attention completely on Blaisse. She must have passed through the sitting room to reach this chamber, and the cloying scent of death hung close around them even here, but she did not react to that either.

"These gentlemen will be staying on the second level from now on, Madame," Blaisse said. The title was not one of respect, Subtwo realized, simply a habit, perhaps derisive.

The woman bowed slightly. "It is ready, Lord."

"They have their people with them."

"I will see to the arrangements." She spoke to the pseudosibs. "If you will come with me."

Blaisse stood up, rather lazily. "I think I'll come along."

Madame bowed again, without expression. Subtwo looked for signals of hatred or dislike or even distaste in her demeanor, but there were none. Neither were there signs of admiration or respect. The bow and the words were empty of feeling. Subtwo did not understand what the relationship between Madame and Blaisse could be.

She led the way out of Blaisse's suite, down a corridor, and into an alice tube. Subtwo experienced distress at the waste of the energy used by such a worthless toy, especially if Center's power came only from fission, rather than fusion or matter-antimatter.

Blaisse shrugged when Subtwo suggested that an elevator would be much more efficient. "I like it this way."

They descended.

The second level was similar to Blaisse's part of the Palace, and as richly appointed. Followed by his silent, obedient alien slave, Blaisse pushed back curtains and peered around corners and scuffed his sandals in the deep carpet. He found neither dust nor disorder; this level was as well kept as what Subtwo had seen of the other. Subtwo waited for Blaisse to give Madame the ritualized compliments the pseudosibs had been taught were proper. Blaisse said nothing; Subtwo felt the need to fill the vacuum of drilled-in courtesy, but remained silent.

"It stinks down here," Blaisse said. He made it sound as though they were breathing the rank odor of standing sewage.

"I regret that any uninhabited rooms gather a musty flavor, Lord. The situation will cure itself."

He grunted and forged ahead through the velvet halls. Subtwo felt himself becoming more and more unnerved. Nothing in this place was composed of straight lines. The curtains fell in waving gathers. The rooms were round, or irregular, or, worst, *almost* square. The angles were slightly flawed, the lines slightly crooked, the floors slightly uneven. Subtwo's feet touched minor irregularities. He felt Subone walking closer to him. He discovered a fantasy in which they walked across a rug that had nothing under it and it fell away beneath them. He shook himself out of the dream. Real people, ordinary human beings, lived this way. They did not demand living space built to the tolerances of a precision instrument.

Blaisse's inconsequential chatter infringed on Subtwo's determination to deal with the real world. Blaisse bothered him on a level even he could not analyze. He did not seem to be the same person his shipowner had told the pseudosibs about. Subtwo wished to be contemptuous, but Blaisse he could not discount.

"As you see," Blaisse said, "you don't need all of Stone Palace." Subtwo was not certain, for ordinary people were so changeable and contrary, but he thought Blaisse was amused. "Yes," Blaisse said, "we must have a party. I'm looking forward to introducing you to the Families."

They arrived at a foyer through which flowed a small stream bridged by delicate silver paths. Blaisse stopped. "If you want to inspect the barracks before your people move in—"

"The—'barracks'?"

"Yes. Separate quarters. For your people."

"Our people stay with us," Subtwo said.

"What, here?"

"Of course. There is ample room."

Blaisse frowned at them curiously, then shrugged. He slid his hand up Saita's back to her neck, and beneath her long hair. "If that's what you want." He glanced around, and suddenly seemed very bored by them and by his surroundings. "If you want anything else, speak to my steward. Don't bother me about it." He left them, without a word or glance of farewell.

" 'Madame'?"

"Yes, sir?" Her gray eyes flicked back and forth as she attempted to find from expression or word which of them had spoken.

"Is that your name?"

She caught Subtwo as the speaker, looked directly at him, then dropped her gaze and turned away. "It will do." She went down a corridor. Subtwo moved up on her right and Subone on her left to walk beside her. The programmed manners moved in. "Always learn their names," they had been taught. "Remember their names and impress them." That Madame was not someone they were required to impress did not occur to Subtwo. That she might not want to talk about herself was inconceivable.

"But it is not a name."

"I will answer to anything you care to call me, sir," she said. Subtwo noticed the tension in her. He was interested; this was the first indication of any feeling she had revealed.

"I'd rather call you by your name," he said, pushing her for the interest of it.

"I was eight when I was captured," she said. "I have not had a name since my freedom and my childhood were taken from me."

As the mind so often works, in defiance of entropy, bits of information were shaken randomly by her words and came down in a pattern that evoked memories Subtwo would have preferred to avoid. He pulled himself back to the present. The dark woman looked away from his face when she saw that his attention had returned.

"A person should have a childhood," Subone said. The slave woman started at his voice. Subtwo composed his own expression, as he realized it must show the same emotions as his pseudosib's: a faraway look with none of the pleasant nostalgia of usual reminiscence.

They walked in silence for a distance, until they reached another alice tube. "This leads to the first level," Madame said. "One of the corridors there goes back into the Palace, the other goes upward to the blockhouse."

"Our crew will be hungry and tired," Subtwo said.

"I will have a meal prepared," Madame said. "The rooms are ready. Will you require special services?"

"That's up to them."

"Do you require slave quarters?"

Subtwo almost snapped at her, but calmed himself. "We have no slaves," he said. "Slavery is an inefficient use of energy, and a waste of human potential."

She bowed to him, from the waist, a very slight inclination.

"Come in the morning. We'll want to acquire some building materials."

"I will be available when you are ready, sir."

Subtwo led the way up the alice tube.

5

It was Dim, the scarlet time just after the brightest lights went out, just before dark. All the thirsty spectators had gone home long before. Mischa moved, and that was a mistake. She almost fainted again. On one side of her, the older man was a storm of guilt and remorse; on the other, the companion was a quiet pool of desperation.

Without thinking about it, Mischa worked her wrists against the thongs that bound her. Nothing intelligent and nothing human drove her, only the need to be free. The thongs began to rub her skin raw. When her wrists bled, the dry leather around them grew damp and started to stretch.

The companion looked over at her, slowly, painfully. "Don't, girl," he said. "They'll let us down in the morning. If they catch you—"

Mischa made an animal sound. Her hands came free and she slid down the stone and fell to her hands and knees. She felt completely empty, of emotion and of strength. The pain was a part of her; it ate into her, like a malignancy. Her back was crusted with blood. She got to her feet, stumbled forward, and almost fell off the edge of the plaza. Raw flesh scraped a corner and she crouched shivering until she could move again. Her throat burned, and her eyes. Blood began to ooze from newly opened welts.

She crawled and stumbled toward the alpha-helix. She neither saw nor felt the few people still out, who watched and avoided her. She knew only a feral and desperate need to escape. The alpha-ramp rose under her feet, and she climbed.

Someone touched her arm. She reacted violently, reflexively, pulling away, reaching for her lost knife, stumbling again, into sand. She froze with the pain of it. Her breath came out rough, almost silent.

"Mischa, it's all right, it's me."

She heard the words, but they meant nothing. She pushed herself up, leaving blood in droplets in the sand. Her arm was touched again. She tried to push the hand away.

"Let me help you, dammit."

Mischa did not ignore the voice, she simply did not understand what it was saying. A few more meters above and ahead was the radial tunnel leading to her niche. A thought wandered into her mind: she might not make it. One more step, another. The muscles of her calves hurt so badly they trembled.

The person following her touched her again. Startled, Mischa pushed out. After that the footsteps stayed farther back. At the edge of the radius she held herself up against the wall for a moment. The follower took a hesitant step toward her. Mischa plunged away into the blood-red darkness.

The tunnel floor was a quagmire, the dimness a filmy curtain across her eyes. She stumbled on.

More by feel than by sight she knew she had reached her home. The tunnel walls were rough and natural instead of smooth and finished. Her fingers scraped over stone to the fissure.

She fell inside, like a toy with all the joints bent backwards.

Mischa began to come to, fighting to reach the surface of consciousness. Her struggle became an actual physical effort of grasping and twisting and climbing upward from a deep abyss. Survival drove her; not knowing what surrounded her, she had to make herself safe.

"It's all right, everything's all right, Misch. Go back to sleep."

She finally heard the voice and felt gentle hands on her shoulders, holding her down. She fought for a minute before she identified the voice as friend-not-foe, no more, and the words hardly far enough to grasp their meaning. She almost continued the long impossible journey but the voice soothed and reassured her, and she slipped back into the crevasse of unconsciousness.

She lived an endless sequence of fever dreams. Later, the details were never clear. Time stretched out, and every dream drew her deeper, farther from light and air and iridescent sand and sun and ships and stars.

Then she was trapped in true darkness. Like a wounded cat, she slept. A barrier stood before her, but when she tried to pass, it was too slick and high to climb. When she tried to go around it, she traveled in an unchanging straight line that returned her to her starting point, which was unmarked but which, somehow, she recognized. The anger of frustration welled up inside her. She used it to beat at the barrier. It exploded, silently, leaving dense fog and smoke. She walked through the debris for a long, long time.

The fog dispersed slowly. Mischa lay on her stomach in her bed. She was alone in her niche, and she could not remember when the aura of friend-not-foe had dimmed and disappeared. She sat up. On her side, heavy scabs were beginning to flake away over shiny scar tissue. The wounds had been washed and carefully tended. Her time-sense was thoroughly skewed. She thought she had been unconscious for a couple of days at least, but she was not hungry.

She stood up. She was stiff, weak, a little shaky. Her pants and torn shirt lay on the floor in a corner, filthy and ruined, so she put on a clean pair of pants from the big wooden chest, and laid aside a jacket of the same smooth-worn material. Then, feeling foolish, she had to sit down and rest.

Mischa heard a noise and scraping outside her cave. She slipped aside, next to the entrance, but did not have time to cover the bright and well-fed lightcells. Someone pushed the curtain away and dropped a bag inside. Kiri slipped in and slid to the floor. She stood up awkwardly, saw that Mischa was not in her bed, looked around with alarm, and found her with relief.

53

"You're losing business," Mischa said.

"You shouldn't be up."

"When is it?"

Kiri told her. Her estimate of two days was a day too short. Mischa sat on the wooden chest and started to pull her knees up under her chin, but stopped when she found how much it hurt to bend her shoulders forward. "Listen," she said. "Thanks."

Kiri shrugged, and turned away. "Old debt." Her voice was soft. Mischa let the subject drop. Kiri owed her nothing. If she owed Chris, then she must know he could never be repaid.

"How do you feel?"

"Pretty good."

Kiri pulled a hot bottle out of her bag and opened it. The odor it released was pleasant, and while Mischa could not remember a particular time of having smelled it before, it was familiar. Hungrier than she had realized, she accepted the steaming broth and sipped it. "Did you get in trouble?"

Kiri shook her head. "But I didn't find out until too late to get a bondsperson." She brought Mischa's knife out of her pocket and handed it to her. "Nobody'd stolen it when I got there." Mischa valued the knife, and had not expected to get it back. "Hey, Kiri . . ." She could not think of anything to say that did not sound silly.

"Eat your soup," Kiri said.

After Kiri left, Mischa slept for a few hours, but when she awoke she was too restless to stay in bed. She eased into the jacket and walked slowly down the radius. When she reached the helix she sat on the edge of the path and looked out over Center. Stone Palace was like a slash in the wall, bare and uglier than the shanty-hut units and crowded people and everything else that made Center what it was. She knew she could do nothing, right now, but she swore to herself that someday she would bring the extravagant appointments of the Palace down around the elegant Lady Clarissa's head.

In that instant, an explosion crumbled a section of the Palace wall. The cavern shuddered. In the moment before shock wave and sound and bits of debris reached her, Mischa threw herself around and down. Dust and rubble fell on her back. She winced and turned on her side, shielding her face. The blast echoed back and forth, slowly, like ripples in a long pond.

All the lights went out.

People began to scream. Mischa had realized several years before that she could see better in the dark than most people, that she could see in some places where other people could not see at all, but she had not realized that the ability had protected her from a primeval fear. From every direction, fifteen seconds of terror washed over her: few in Center had ever experienced total darkness. Mischa compared the deprivation cell to what the people around her must be going through, and understood their panic.

The lights flickered on, dimmed, brightened. The feeling of terror faded much more slowly than its sounds.

The results of the blast seemed hardly to justify its force. There was a new opening in the Palace facade, at ground level. Workers swarmed around it as soon as the dust had cleared. Mischa sat up, brushed herself off, and watched. As she scrambled to a better vantage point, the change in the cavern wall kept catching on the corner of her vision.

The workers began to smooth the blasted edges, forming a new doorway to the lower level of the Palace. People on First Hill, which faced the Palace, stood on their balconies pitching stones and gravel out into the Circle. Mischa saw no bodies or blood, which was on the order of a miracle.

She began to notice other, more subtle changes: an undercurrent of excitement, more people along the arc where the bars were clustered. It was like early spring, when several of Blaisse's ships came in at once. Mischa was beginning to tire, but her curiosity kept her going. She started down the helix and met Kiri coming up.

"You do get around."

"What's going on?"

"I guess the new people decided they needed a private entrance in Stone Palace."

"What new people?"

"A ship landed while you were healing."

"In the storms—? And you didn't tell me—"

"I thought I could keep you resting," Kiri said. "I yield."

"Who are they? How—?"

"Come back home and I'll tell you what I know. Which isn't much."

They returned to Mischa's niche.

Jan Hikaru's Journal:

Earth: clouds, a walk through a sandstorm that would kill an unprotected person, a maze of caverns, trapped human beings. I believe that the city we are in grew up inside one of the huge bomb shelters built here before the Last War. We are in gaudily appointed rooms that I find irritating, but they seem to suit the other people from the ship.

I haven't buried my friend's body yet; I can't until I know the customs. I'm acquainted with no one. Whom should I ask? Beggars? Slaves? (There are slaves in this society. How can I do nothing, knowing that?)

I can't stay in the Palace, I can't stay with the pseudosibs and their people. I have no place here, I want none. But I haven't any other place either.

Am I just afraid? When something happens that I can't accept, that I as an individual could protest, will I rationalize inaction?

I went outside Stone Palace today. I had to get out. I walked along a street of bars and pleasure houses, where people sell services, their bodies, drugs in any form or effect. And beggars—I have never been approached by beggars before. People used to try to press coins into my hands when I helped my poet through the streets. I regretted not having money or anything else to give the crippled children in the city, until I realized that their deformities are induced, not congenital. They have mutilated themselves, or they have been mutilated.

How could we leave earth to this?

During the following days, Mischa watched the pseudosibs from a distance and found out all she could about them from the people with whom they dealt. She saw that their section of Stone Palace was much less guarded than Blaisse's, and that they seemed not to have such a pathological fear of the city. This encouraged her. Yet time had passed; she was forced to take note of it: her immediate need was to replenish her store of tribute before her uncle and Gemmi called her again. She spied on Stone Palace from the alpha-helix all one day, but did not approach it, and when the lights above began to dim, she left her own shabby section and climbed down to the Circle.

She had been watching one of the bright little import shops facing the Palace. A recess one level above the shop gave her a place to sit where she was not obviously spying on it. The climb had tired her; she kept dozing off as she waited. When the ceiling lights faded to their lowest intensity for the night, the merchant pulled heavy curtains across the multicolored sparkles in the windows and locked his door. Mischa already knew that he lived behind the shop. That was not in itself a hindrance; she was by training and preference a sneakthief, and quiet. It only remained for her to watch his place throughout one night, to discover whether he had a companion contract or a security subscription.

The patrol did stop once, early on. Mischa inspected the Family people hopefully, but neither of the pair was the ice-eyed administrator. She must be long since promoted from foot patrol, but Mischa would have liked to rob a place whose protection was that one's responsibility.

Mischa waited until the night was half over. Finally, doubting her ability to stay awake another four hours, another one hour, she walked slowly home.

The next night, the hours passed slowly. Mischa watched from a higher vantage point. The security patrol stopped only once, at the same time as the night before. Mischa knew it was good: she knew she could walk in and take what she wanted whenever she decided to.

Perspiration broke out on her forehead. She held out her hand and found it trembling. She clenched her fist and the new scars on her wrists turned white. Her body tried to tell her that she had been too badly hurt too recently, that she was still weak, that she was tired from her vigil. She climbed down across the roofs until she was over the shop. Her knees and her stomach felt the same, frightened. When she drove the shaking out with anger, it was anger at herself and at her fear: tomorrow when the time came to return, would she find some excuse against it? She might fool herself into being too tired, too weak, any of a hundred things. The possibility of that much self-deception scared her as much as the possibility that she was losing her nerve.

There was no motion nearby, little sound, an aura of life, but sleeping life. Lying flat on the roof, she listened, and received a reward of silence. Looking over the edge, she found the windows dark and curtained and the door firmly closed.

Chris had taught her to pick locks so early that she could not remember the lessons. He had been a good thief; she was better. She swung down to the next level. The shop door was recessed, putting her in deep shadow. With her lockpicks she gently probed the double locks. Opening them took longer than she liked, but the door finally clicked open, with neither the shrill scream of a scare-alarm nor the low reverberation of a warning device in the merchant's sleeping quarters.

Mischa eased through the doorway. Inside the shop, semiprecious stones glowed deep black or glinted brightly. As Mischa shut the door, the outside lights flickered. For half a second the shop was a shattered rainbow. It would soon be light in Center.

The single doorway at the back of the shop was closed only by a curtain. Mischa crept quietly about, checking for silent-alarm wires, finding none.

The glass cases were locked and uninteresting. Everything on display was semiprecious or artificial, and set. Unset stones were less trouble, harder to trace.

Beneath the cases, shallow drawers in tiers of four each opened toward the back. Narrow panels separated them. The drawers were locked, but no more securely than the front door. They held boxes of pendants and rings and anklets of no higher quality than the jewelry already displayed. Unperturbed, Mischa stopped actively searching, sat back against the wall, and simply looked, as she did for the moon on the nights she was outside. The sky-glow behind the clouds would catch on the edge of her vision, not where her sight was sharpest. This search was similar, but she made her mind act, rather than her eyes.

She knelt again before the drawers and slid her fingers beneath their lower edges. She tapped the panels between them, listening for any hollowness, and tugged at them gently. One opened, swinging upward and outward smoothly and quickly. The hinge clicked faintly; the panel remained open.

A flexible coil of thin insulated wire, badly balanced on a narrow shelf, slipped out. Mischa caught it before its attachments clattered on the floor. She sat back on her heels, holding the lock leads. Outside, the lights flickered again, casting a quick streak of gold past the shop's window curtains. The radiance caught on the tips of the paired electrodes. The light faded, and the shop was scarlet and ebony once more.

Mischa placed the cold electrodes against her temples. They attached themselves, pushing fibers into her skin; they drew her out, and sent her along the thin silver wires. She could feel the resonances of the man sleeping in the room behind the shop. His recorded essences formed a barrier; the lock should open only to him.

Mischa did not like being forced so close to anyone; with the lock recording on one side and the merchant on the other, she could perceive him better than she had ever been able to perceive any ordinary person, anyone but Chris or Gemmi. The usual faint aura took shape, clarified, solidified. Wanting to fling the contacts away and leave, Mischa touched the wall of a simulated consciousness, and reached out for the true being. She became a channel for thoughts; she could not shield herself. They washed in, unfiltered, amplified, but she took them and molded her own patterns to fit, and ran up against the barrier. It resisted, yielded, but did not open. She shifted and tried again, racing through the spaces of several independent variables. Mischa struggled to stay afloat and aware in an inundation of hidden, half-controlled fears and desires.

The barrier shuddered and dissolved; the lock on the hidden compartment fell open. Mischa pulled away the sticky contacts and threw them down. She was dripping with sweat, but steady.

The secret drawer slid open to gentle pressure. Mischa lifted out one of the fist-sized leather sacks that filled it.

The stones, poured into her palm, glowed as though ready to erupt with light and heat. Each was all colors, one at a time. They shifted and moved in her hands like living things.

Mischa put the first bag under her jacket. The others were filled with set stones, but set stones worth stealing. She took as many as she could comfortably and unobtrusively carry in her inner pockets. At the bottom of the drawer lay a flat black box with a pebbled leather surface. She opened it slowly.

Even in the darkness the eyes glittered out at her. The size of a fingernail, or a thumbnail, or the entire exposed area of an eye, they were small multicolored multifaceted concavoconvex discs that fractured light through the planes of precious stones or reflected it from polished metal. The opaque iris enhancers had openings for the pupil, but many of the even minimally transparent ones were a single expanse of decoration. In a person's eyes they turned the world different colors or broke it into pieces or turned it upside down. They were hand-made, hand-designed; no two pair were alike. One pair was pink roses with an effect of three dimensions. Another held spirals that could drink a soul. Mischa shut the box and kept it.

Since the eyes were not displayed, they must be contraband, smuggled in past the Family of the gate without duties or taxes. And that meant, in turn, that Mischa was almost safe in taking them; the theft could not be reported to security, and the merchant had little other recourse. She was almost sorry to steal from a man who cheated the Lady Clarissa's people.

The drawer stuck when she tried to close it. She eased it out and pushed again. It squeaked against its runners. She froze, but behind her the merchant came groggily awake, broadcasting the desire to pretend he had heard nothing. He was indecisive and afraid, and without being aware of the cause, upset by the remnants of Mischa's intrusion into his mind.

Mischa heard him get up; his attempted silence was marred by his weight. Even on tiptoe he sent vibrations through the floor. Mischa moved back and waited beside the curtained doorway. In a moment the naked shopkeeper peered out, his blanket wrapped around his shoulders. Only the needler in his hand made him dangerous. When he reached for the light switch Mischa grabbed his wrist. For all his slothful appearance, he was strong, but he had no training and no practice. Mischa got the needler away from him and kicked it across the room.

"Lie down."

He made a sound of protest. Mischa flicked out the blade of her knife. The sound silenced him, and he lay down quickly, still clutching his blanket. Mischa took it away and cut strips from the woven synthetic.

"You can't do this." His voice squeaked in the middle of a word.

"Okay," Mischa said.

As she twisted the slices of blanket he gathered himself. "Come on," Mischa said. The sarcasm in her voice seemed to keep him still more than any real warning might have. She tied his wrists behind him, made him bend his knees, and tied his feet to his hands.

"My arms—"

She ignored him, but he took a quick breath. Mischa grabbed his chin and pulled his mouth shut. The clack of his teeth was louder than his single croak.

"I lose my temper so easy it makes me mad sometimes." Mischa did not like to frighten people more than absolutely necessary to keep them from forcing her to hurt them. She was a thief, not a terrorist.

The jeweler blinked, trying to see her, trying to find any way to identify her in the dark. Mischa opened the hidden drawer again and used one of the small suede sacks to gag him. He struggled when he realized what it was. Mischa grinned, but waited until she was sure he would not choke on the leather, vomit, and suffocate himself.

The shadow in the doorway was paler now. The lights flickered more often, almost regularly. Mischa waited, holding the door ajar, and slid outside between two washes of light. She left the shop closed but unlocked. Eventually a customer would come in, or the jeweler would work the gag free.

Mischa was drenched with sweat, but the residual weakness had disappeared and she felt good for the first time in much too long. She headed home, laughing quietly. The exhaustion she felt was a satisfying kind, the result of long vigilance and a good job, and knowing, not just hoping, that nothing her uncle or Stone Palace or the Families could do to her could destroy her.

6

Entering his newly finished rooms for the first time, Subtwo allowed a sense of well-being to flow around him. The environment lessened the tension under which he had struggled since arriving on earth. In his rooms were no velvet tapestries, no embroidery, no rough-worked stone. The lines were straight and the angles square. His apartment consisted of pleasing rectangular shapes and volumes. The proportions were geometrically and aesthetically perfect.

The walls and floor and ceiling were formed of white plastic, Subtwo's desk module held a three-dimensional representation of a complex mathematical function (the only decoration he needed or wanted), and the spare shipboard computer was already installed. He had access to anything and everything he had ever needed before.

Throughout the remodeling, Subtwo had worked with Blaisse's steward: Madame had executed his wishes with flawless efficiency. Subtwo admired her abilities and appreciated the speed and ease with which the transition had been accomplished, yet now that he was physically comfortable again, he was not settled in his mind. It took him much thought and analysis to realize that his unease resulted from having no more work to do with Madame.

He wished others of his people would ask to have their rooms changed so he could feel justified in requiring her presence. He could not understand their preference for plush and velvet.

A few flaws still marred his place. Eventually they would prey on him, catch his eye, enrage him, but he wondered if Madame would take his insistence on perfection as criticism. He had never worried about making criticisms before, and had always insisted on perfection. Yet this was tolerable: no simple pattern of flaws could upset him more than had the raw stone caves and useless ornamentation. He saw the precious stones and metals in electronics, guidance, fine mechanical constructs; their misuse in mere decoration sent him into periodic rages that he almost failed to conceal. In this castoff place there seemed no way to convert them to any useful function.

He had been on earth only a short time and already he was bored. With the boredom came loneliness, which he had never experienced before. He had never needed anyone, even Subone. Though the pseudosibs seemed united against outsiders, they had never gotten along well. They simply tolerated each other; and they knew each other so well that they were interchangeable in any action. This had nothing to do with liking or empathy or love; it was a purely physical leftover from their upbringing as isolated behavioral duplicates, each influenced as much by the other's responses as by his own.

Since they arrived on this world, Subone seemed to be growing apart from him. Subtwo's pseudosib spent more time with the squad members than working; he wasted his time in dissipation. Subtwo had gone into Center only once: the noise and disorder were more than he could stand.

"Come," he said, in response to a scratch on the door. It was Madame, who did not knock, whether because she had no experience with doors or because she was reluctant to make so much noise, Subtwo did not know. The sensor which controlled the opening mechanism was clumsy and makeshift, slapped together by a technician on his crew. It was insensitive: it would open to Subone's voice as well as to Subtwo's own. It was one of the small flaws that would begin to annoy him soon.

He turned to face the steward. She was a handsome and elegant woman, and he still did not know her name.

"My rooms are finished now. How do you like them?"

She looked at him with what seemed genuine surprise. "Why do you ask my opinion, sir? It is of no merit."

He had not yet decided if she were serious in her self-deprecation or if she were mocking him. He believed she was too intelligent to believe her thoughts were worthless, but in the days they had been working together, she had never deviated from the role she played, if role it was.

His sexual experiences had been experiments, exploratory for him, casual for his partners. Memories of them did not linger unbidden, as did Subtwo's thoughts of Madame. She performed her duties with exquisite correctness but was never servile. Nor did she ever assert her individuality or her opinions, which disturbed Subtwo deeply, but he had realized that such self-repression was essential for survival in a place where a free person literally held the power of life or death over a slave. He thought, though, that by now Madame should know that he would never take advantage of such a situation. He thought she should trust him. He did not understand that Madame's situation required either an erosion of spirit or an erosion of trust.

"Come now," Subtwo said. "I'm not Blaisse."

"You are his guest."

"I'm used to being thought peculiar for my tastes. I could hardly be offended if you agreed with the majority."

"By the rules of the Palace, you may correct any slave whose behavior you find offensive."

"No one should be offended by honesty." He smiled, a cold expressionless smile that was in his terms meaningful.

"I find your rooms somewhat strange but not unattractive," Madame said abruptly. "Strange . . . yet somehow familiar."

"A few places in the Sphere build in this style," he said. "Perhaps you—"

"There is no way of knowing."

"Civilized planets keep records."

She smiled at him ironically, and needed to say no more to indicate the futility of his curiosity. "Is there anything you need, sir, before I go upstairs?"

He hesitated, gazing at her, until he realized she had looked away from him and was standing rigid and withdrawn.

"No," he said. "Nothing."

Jan Hikaru's Journal:

Today I had a long, strange conversation with Subtwo. I think my presence upsets him. He knows I'm not a raider, he knows my interests and my areas of competence, he knows my background, but he doesn't know what I am. And how could I tell him, when I don't know myself?

I did tell him that I don't plan to join his group, and never did, that I'm here by chance, that I'll leave as soon as possible. Whatever happens, I doubt I'll be stranded here. Subtwo was not, I think, brought up with starship traditions, but he respects (or indulges) his people's customs. And the raiders have enough regard for my poet to give me a ride off earth.

I think Subtwo knows more about me than I know about him and Subone. Something unusual: I used the computer link in the common room and tried to key the memory for the pseudosibs. I didn't get a null, so there should have been information in the news-storage banks, but the terminal couldn't—or wouldn't—produce the data. I wonder what terrible things the blank spaces held to make a perfectionist like Subtwo erase a whole segment from his precious files?

When the invitation from the Lady Clarissa arrived, Subtwo had to send someone into Center to find his pseudosib. Subone had been spending more and more time in that morass of irregularities and inconsistencies. He seemed to like it, while it drove Subtwo to distraction. Subone would sit with his people, with sellers of sexual oddments, with anyone, with no one, drinking and laughing, forgetful of propriety and oblivious to his training, his position, his intelligence. Subtwo was pleased with the growing apart, though he wished Subone had chosen a different way of manifesting the change. Perhaps, with his increasing ingestion of narcotics, depressants, hallucinogens, and stimulants, Subone was trying to drive away what reactions he felt from Subtwo. The experiment of their upbringing would not be completely finished until they stopped feeling the occasional resonances of each other's muscles in their own.

When Subone returned, he was wearing a smelly tunic of animal fur and he had animal teeth tied in his hair. He smelled of ethanol and sweaty sex.

"Yeah, what?"

Subtwo disliked the imprecision that had crept into Subone's speech, but could think of no way to correct it. "We're dining in the Palace tonight," he said. "At the request of our hosts."

"At their orders, you mean."

"We are partners."

Subone sneered. The expression fit badly on his smooth, bronzed face. "All right," he said. "Let's go."

"Are you going like that?"

"Of course. Why not?"

"It offends me."

"Ahh," Subone said in disgust.

Subtwo shrugged; they walked together to the alice tube and allowed themselves to be pressed upward into the Palace.

Subtwo had not expected a banquet. Clarissa's communication had made no mention of other people, but when the pseudosibs reached the top of the alice tube, they were conducted to a large hall lit by chandeliers and guttering flames in cages of brass wire. Multiple flickering shadows, like electromagnetic auras, surrounded all the people: forty-one, Subtwo observed, and he and Subone made forty-three. Both prime numbers. Subtwo knew of omens, numerical omens based on primes and perfect squares and triads, but he did not know if this might be an omen, or what kind. He did not like prime numbers: no formula could predict them.

The Lady Clarissa reclined at the end of the table near the doorway by which they entered. She was wearing a series of metallic strips that twined around her body, changing hue and intensity with the temperature gradient. She stretched out her graceful jeweled hands to the pseudosibs. Her eyes mimicked the flash of diamonds. Subtwo wondered how she could see through the multiple facets; he wondered if she saw, with an insect's vision, numerous minuscule shifting images.

"It's good of you to come," she said. "Everyone's anxious to meet you."

"We are pleased to be invited," Subtwo said by rote, as Clarissa inspected first him, then Subone, with an unhurried gaze. The iris enhancers gave her a strange appearance of blindness.

Clarissa released Subtwo's hand, and stroked Subone's furry tunic. "How exquisite," she said. "It must have been very expensive. It suits you well." She let her hand rest just above the hem, which reached barely halfway down Subone's thigh. Subone smiled at her; his teeth were as white and shiny and sharp as the fangs strung in his black hair.

"In such a historical place, what else should I wear but fur?"

Clarissa laughed. "But what does one wear under it?"

"Why, nothing. That would reduce its barbaric impact."

The guests in range of his voice laughed uneasily, unsure of Subone's aim, compliment or insult.

"You must let me wear it sometime," Clarissa said. "It would make me feel primal."

"You may wear it now, if you like," Subone said, and reached for the lacings. Shocked, Subtwo reached out to stop him, but Subone's quick glare held him back. The Lady Clarissa watched until Subone had unlaced the tunic past his groin. "Ah, no," she said. "I spent too much time on my own garments, and they might not flatter you."

"Another time, perhaps."

Clarissa introduced them to the nearby guests, and pointed out each individual of the assembled company, who lay on thick cushions around the long table. Subtwo made appropriate sounds of greeting, filing their names and faces away in his mind should he ever need the information. They were all related to Clarissa in one manner or another, and each was served by at least one personal attendant. The attendants were not introduced, though Subtwo had included them in his original tally.

He involved his full attention in the social ceremonies only when Clarissa announced Blaisse's brother Kenton, who had been sent to Clarissa's people to seal the alliance between the Families and Stone Palace. A few years younger than Blaisse, he was a sullen man who muttered an unintelligible response and turned back to the ministrations of the youth behind him. Subtwo shuddered and averted his gaze: the slave's hormonal balance was disarranged, Subtwo supposed purposely. The result was not pleasing to his eye. But Kenton both interested and repelled him, for Subtwo had found that all Blaisse's statements about the Families were true. If the pseudosibs had tried to carry out their original plan, one of them would now have been in Kenton's place, dissipated, trapped, turning in boredom to perturbing other people's lives.

Clarissa finished the introductions and grasped Subone's hand. "Sit here by me." He sprawled next to her, his bare thigh against her leg.

Clarissa glanced up and spoke to Subtwo, as though in afterthought. "Blaisse wishes you to take the place to his left."

Subtwo walked to the other end of the room, aware of the stares of the other guests. They reminded him of another uncomfortable entrance he had made, when he was first presented to the outside world as a successful experiment. The world's first experience with him was his first experience with the world, and he had wished only to flee back to the safe and constant environment in which he had been raised. That day had held the beginnings of his guilt.

He looked around. These people were nothing to him. He would not even remember their names. If he refused to remember, their pitted stupid faces might blur together in his memory. Except for their foolish dress, they looked ordinary enough individually. But collectively, their physical similarities revealed so much inbreeding that Subtwo felt distress, with simultaneous relief that he had prevented Subone from completing the Palace takeover. Subtwo knew that he could never have considered a permanent sexual alliance with one of these high-bred, inbred, radiation-exposed people. He could imagine their chromosomes leaping and twisting and breaking and rejoining in some mad intoxicated dance, to a rhythm counted by free subatomic particles. The possible results of a partnering were too disgusting to contemplate, though Subtwo did not doubt that their gene pool would benefit from an infusion of new traits.

He reached the end of the table, shuddering, but having avoided touching anyone, slave or lord. By then, they had all gone back to their pleasures or their duties, and Blaisse's alien consort was the only one to observe Subtwo's approach. She watched him, wide-eyed, frightened.

Blaisse looked up languorously and gestured to a pile of cushions. He was already under the influence of some drug, Subtwo did not know and did not care which one. "Sit down, sit down," Blaisse said, motioned for a drink to be poured, and turned back to his conversation with the gilt-gray-haired woman on his right. The serving slave moved forward, sidling very close, and poured three layers of different colored fluids into a heated goblet that mixed them slowly. The effect was revolting. The slave rubbed her naked hip against Subtwo's shoulder. Subtwo ignored her and she went away. A male slave replaced her, but Subtwo ignored him as well. At the other end of the table, Subone and Clarissa whispered and laughed together and put their hands inside each other's clothing.

Subtwo sat in the midst of golden cushions, still with distaste, hiding his dislike with rigidity. The people nearby began to watch him covertly, but none addressed him. The noise of conversation became almost white in its meaninglessness. The crystal chandeliers broke the light into spectra, giving the impression of underwater illumination. The serving of food began. Accustomed to artificial fare, Subtwo had no taste for natural products. Unruly textures disturbed him; chewing the meat made his jaws ache. The probable cost of the banquet did not impress him. He ate slowly and cautiously, tasting every mouthful of each course for suspicious inclusions, wishing for distilled water to wash away the taste of spices. He looked for Madame, but she was not in the room. He knew she must be within calling distance, but he did not know how to call her, and she was one person, perhaps the only one, whom he did not wish to command.

As the evening progressed, the clamor made by the revelers rose toward his threshold of pain. Subtwo was bored, but too uncomfortable to let his thoughts take a path away from this gathering of animals. He noticed Blaisse's slave girl watching him again, always watching, with those round, jeweled, silver-blue eyes, with her hair brushed back like a mane, with her breasts only half-covered, lying behind Blaisse, peering over his shoulder.

Blaisse turned to Subtwo and smiled as though his guest had just arrived. "Do you have what you want? Does your attendant please you?"

"I can feed myself," Subtwo said.

"Ah, but we all need someone to watch over us at these gatherings," Blaisse said. "In the event that we are incapacitated in our play." The beverage he sipped sparkled with a silver drift of some compound Subtwo assumed would work synergistically with alcohol.

"I prefer not to submit my body to such indignities, even in play."

"What difference does it make? What else is life for, but to play with? Others understand that. Your brother—"

"We are not brothers," Subtwo snapped.

Some rare spark of curiosity seemed partially to sober Blaisse. "Not brothers? What, then?"

"The correct term is 'pseudosib.' We were raised identically, separately, without human interference. Our reactions were linked."

"I would have thought you were twins."

"No, we are only distantly related. We were intended to represent the behavioral equivalents of genetic twins." Subtwo knew, but thought it strange, that people found distinguishing between himself and Subone difficult; he saw only general similarities. Still, he was trained to observe minute detail, while ordinary people fumbled through their lives with generalities. He glanced down the table at Subone. "Obviously, the same parallels do not hold."

"I see," Blaisse said, and yawned. "That's very interesting." But he asked no more questions; he reached for his silver-laced drink, swirling the liquid before putting it to his lips. Half the people in the room had gone to sleep over the last course. Their clothes disarrayed, they nestled in the cushions, while the rest pleasured themselves with their attendants. Subtwo felt pressed down and smothered by the glutted snoring bodies and the pumping flesh. He wanted to leave, but he did not know the protocol; he wished he could overcome his early training all at once and become rude and thoughtless and sloppy, stand, shout imprecations, overturn the table, and stalk away. But he sat for another hour, stiffly, disapproving, while the activity ranged around him. It could not be called an orgy; it was closer to mass communal masturbation. None of the free people caressed or even touched each other. They lay supine and allowed their slaves to work over them until involuntary reactions set them into motion. It was as though they considered each instant's personal pleasure so important that they would not give up any of it, not to give pleasure to another human being, not to communicate, not to love. They seemed to feel the rewards would not be worth the cost. They threw away what Subtwo sought, and he despised them for it.

In the whole huge room of jeweled and perfumed people, only Subtwo was alone, and only Clarissa and Subone were together. Subtwo could hear their voices; he could not avert his ears as he averted his eyes from the Lady's bare white skin and his pseudosib's darker nude body. He could hear their commands to each other, and he reflected both that Subone had learned a great deal since their release and escape from their solitary, sexless beginnings, and that Subone and Clarissa were really no different from anyone else in the room.

He waited until almost everyone had fallen into exhausted sleep, and even the slaves dozed, awakening and glancing covertly at him every so often to see if he had left them without observers. He started to rise.

"Is there nothing you wish?"

Startled, he glanced down. Blaisse's alien slave peeked past her lord's body. She cringed at the sharpness of Subtwo's look. Almost naked now, she wore only the jewels on her eyelids and the armbands of silver and sapphire. Subtwo realized quite abruptly that she was very young.

"How old are you?" he asked gently. He remembered her name: Saita. He was almost surprised that she was not called by some animal's diminutive, like a pet, for Blaisse had not treated her as an intelligent being, but used her as an animal.

"I don't know, Lord."

"How long have you been here?"

"The Lady Clarissa has said three years, Lord."

He saw that she had never been taught anything but how to induce erotic pleasure. Wasted potential always enraged him. There was intelligence in her face; she was not stupid, only naive and ignorant, ignorant of the meaning of her status and surroundings, somehow untouched by them.

"No," he said. "No, there's nothing I want that you can give me."

He made his way past sleeping and unconscious bodies, stepping over and around them with revulsion. At the other end of the table Subone stretched on his cushions. The Lady Clarissa lay with her head pillowed on his belly and her sparkling eyes closed.

"You don't know how to enjoy yourself," Subone said.

Subtwo hesitated, looking down at them. Subone's muscles seemed slack, his expression greedy and foolish. Abruptly, Subtwo departed, making no response.

7

Mischa climbed through the narrow hidden fissure that connected her cave to the larger cavern behind it. The jewels were locked away, she was well rested, she had eaten. Tossing her clothes onto the sand, she plunged into the still, dark pool and came up sputtering from the cold. The second chamber was so cool that the floor and the shadows were black, while the ceiling, warmed slightly by air currents from Center, glowed deep maroon. Mischa found this rare near-darkness restful. She floated on her back for a few minutes, until, growing chilly, she paddled closer to the edge of the pool and stood up. The bank was of fine-grained black sand, carried in from the desert outside, bit by bit, over many years. Mischa scooped up handfuls of the sand and scrubbed her body, vigorously until she was warm again, slowly until she felt clean.

It was evening when she went out again into Center. She wandered along the Circle, covertly studying the new offworld people. They did not wear uniforms, but they were readily distinguishable. They were taller and darker than Center people, most of whom had never in their lives been exposed to sunlight. All offworlders gave an impression of bigness and of solidity, but these also spoke and laughed loudly and frequently. The looming stone sky had subdued other offworlders. Mischa could understand this group's lack of fear: they had come in through the storm. They must feel special, chosen, knowing they were the only ones ever to live through that trial.

Mischa climbed the side of First Hill, and watched the activity below and around Stone Palace. When the lights dimmed, the new doorway remained open. This Mischa did not understand: fearlessness or even contempt seemed an insufficient reason for the new people to leave themselves so vulnerable. Her suspicion was aroused.

She waited until the traffic into the new entrance ceased, until it seemed that those who were returning to bed had done so, and those staying out had settled into their pleasures. Then she climbed down to the Circle and crossed the trampled, littered black sand. The beggars watched her, and she thought she heard them whisper and titter when she stopped in front of Stone Palace.

Slowly, they grew silent. When Mischa stepped over the threshold, no one outside or in spoke to her.

The tapestries and the velvet had disappeared. The corridor was lined with flat panels of light brown plastic that reflected no echoes. The lines were clean and sharp and the corners right-angled. The air smelled curiously flat; the tang of stone was gone. The carpeting had been replaced with a cushiony tile.

The hallway projected a long way back, without branches or adjoining rooms. Mischa felt uneasy in a space so regular and devoid of hiding places. She reached a foyer in which, if a fountain of water had existed, it had been replaced by one of light. Self-luminous panels regularized the chamber's shape into a polygon with alternate empty faces of hall entrances. The tapestries began again in all the halls but the middle one. Mischa moved toward it. The faint air currents of her passing disturbed the fountain. Its fibers shivered, and their hue changed slowly from red to soft blue.

The aberrant hallway was square and straight, and built to appear longer than it really was. The ceiling crept down, the walls in, the floors up. The perspective was exaggerated, yet the huge double doors Mischa approached were almost three times her height.

And still she saw no guards. She touched the left-hand door, and it swung silently, easily ajar. By every criterion of suspicion Mischa had ever used, she should turn and flee this place. She moved one step closer, so she could see inside the room beyond the doorway, and she expected an outcry, an alarm, the touch of a captor's hand. She could feel the scars on her back; she could always feel them on some level of awareness, and she knew she always would.

She hesitated with her hand on the door. If she went away now, she would be safe for a little while, but the inevitable results would be the same as if the pseudosibs drove her away. Her sister's insanity would affect her until she was as helpless and pliable as the little girl. As well be dead . . . and Chris *would* die, for nothing in Center could ever help him.

Mischa slipped inside.

Cold and cubic and mechanized, the room beyond was so completely different from anything else in Center that Mischa needed a few seconds to orient herself. She began to recognize pieces of furniture, decorations, electronic equipment. The furniture looked uncomfortable, the decorations unartistic, the equipment incomprehensible. From deeper inside the suite a kind of frighteningly frigid passion crept out. It rose to a peak, like an almost inaudibly high noise at the threshold of pain. It fell off abruptly. It was still present, still alien, but less intense.

The next chamber was a bedroom. In the bed a companion sat half up, back to Mischa, trying to caress the pseudosib lying beside her. He stared at the ceiling, not responding. She whispered something and stroked his smooth chest, stroked her hand down his cheek, and twined her fingers in his long black hair. He slapped her, roughly, and turned over, hunching his heavy shoulders.

The young woman stared at him, touching her face in disbelief. She flung away the bedclothes, reaching for her dress, and stood wriggling into the tight openwork knit. Mischa knew her slightly: the companion was recently turned to the business, highly paid, well respected, with every right to expect better treatment. Other classes hired themselves out for beatings.

The companion saw Mischa, and did not recognize her. "Who the hell are you?" Anger and frustration burst out. She glared for half a second, whipped around, and dragged the rest of the blankets off the pseudosib. He sat up, finally roused. His eyes were bloodshot. "I told you—" He broke off when he saw Mischa.

The companion threw the blankets on the floor. "There he is," she said to Mischa. "He's all yours." She left the room, taut with fury.

The pseudosib glared at Mischa without speaking. She did not know which brother he was, and she did not like the feel of him; her wish to leave increased, but it was still less strong than her reasons for coming.

He swung his legs over the bed and stood up. He was massive, two meters tall or more, and half that, it seemed, across the shoulders. His smooth tan hairless skin was so perfect, so glossy, that Mischa almost expected his nude body to be as mechanical and sexless as the strange sculptures hulking in the corner.

"Now," he said. "Who *are* you?"

The blank white wall-screen lit up with the image of the second brother. Mischa looked from one to the other. She had never seen them before, and their similarities were quite singular, but the man in the screen seemed more serious, less dissipated. The room behind him was the same, but he had one tiny, faint line between his eyebrows, while the forehead of the pseudosib beside her was completely smooth. "Go plug yourself into a computer," he said to the image. When he spoke, the flesh beneath his jaw seemed very slightly loose: the beginnings of fat over tight muscles.

The image looked Mischa over. "She's rather young for your tastes, isn't she?"

Mischa said nothing, though she was tempted to mention that the companion who had left was almost the same age as she. The two brothers together were more than twice as unpleasant as one alone.

She noticed the small camera tracking where the image gazed. She felt acutely uncomfortable in its range. It swiveled away when the image looked back at his brother.

"She's uninvited." His cheeks were flushed and his voice defensive. "What happened to the alarms?"

"I was curious about her," the image said.

"You watched her come in? You let her come in?"

"You have your own alarms. If you choose to leave them disengaged, that isn't my worry."

"She might have killed me!"

"Don't be ridiculous. I scanned her. I'd hardly allow her to come so far if she were armed. What can she do?"

"She can get out of here."

Very deliberately, Mischa hitched her hip up on the low storage cabinet behind her. She refused to reveal how shaken she was to learn she had been watched all the way in without her knowledge, though she had looked for scanning devices. Still, they had not detected the crystal knife, or they had discounted it as useless.

"Are you deaf, or stupid? I said get out."

"Just a moment," said the image. "What do you want?"

"I want to go offworld," Mischa said.

"That's very interesting," the image said. "Come over here. We'll talk."

"Wait a minute," his brother said with instant covetousness. "She came here first." He looked at Mischa as though he had not even glanced at her before. "You're a funny kid. Stay here. I'll find something for you to do."

Mischa said something untranslatable in an offworld language, the choicer parts of which Chris knew and had taught her. It expressed her opinion of funny kids and funny kid jobs in two main words, a handful of prefixes, and one very emphatic suffix.

"Get out of here!" His voice and emotions crept up into rage. He glared at the image in the screen. "I hope she takes a scalpel to you, you walking tissue culture."

Mischa entered quarters that were a mirror image of the first except in color: the neutral hues were tinged with blue rather than red. The second pseudosib met her at the door and waved her to a couch; she sat on it cross-legged and he sat across from her, appraising her.

"Which one are you?" she asked abruptly.

He raised an eyebrow and smiled slightly. "I am Subtwo. And you?"

"My name's Mischa."

"What can you do?"

"Anything," she said. "Show me once."

He nodded mildly. "Have you had any schooling?"

"All the name I have is 'Mischa.'"

"I don't understand."

"Only people in the Families have a last name, and only people in the Families have a school."

"Ah, the Families. . . . Surely you can read?"

"Yes."

"But how did you learn?"

She shrugged. She could no more remember learning to read than learning to pick locks. Chris had, perhaps, taught her that too, but she had no idea where he had learned. "I don't know."

"What do you want to do?"

"Leave Center. Leave earth. Go to the Sphere."

He leaned back. "You don't like earth?"

"No."

"Why not?"

"Because . . ." She did not know how to tell him, and she did not want to talk about her relatives. "It's dying, it's stopped. It—" But Subtwo was nodding, and Mischa fell silent.

"What do you do, in the city?"

She was unsure exactly what he was asking. His expression was impossible to read and his emotions were clamped tight. But she looked directly into his eyes and said, "I'm a thief."

His features tensed in a quick and automatic grin, a response to what he seemed to think was a joke, but Mischa remained serious. Subtwo's expression sobered. "Are you good?"

"I'm good at anything I do."

"Don't you think it's wrong to steal?"

"No."

"Why not?"

"Have you seen the beggars?"

He glanced at her sharply. "Yes—?"

"That's my other choice. To sell myself—"

"I see." He cut her off; Mischa could see that he did not want to hear any more. "What if you're caught?"

75

Mischa shrugged. "They punish you."

"Have you been punished?"

"Not for stealing."

He looked at her so long without speaking that she grew nervous. Finally sick of the tension, she asked, "What's the matter?"

"I am trying to decide what to do with you."

"Teach me to fly ships."

He raised his eyebrows and forced out a deep laugh. "My time is worth more than that. You'll need several years of preparation first."

Mischa flushed, resenting the laughter. She hunched her shoulders and let her hair slide across her eyes, but still watched him.

He touched buttons in quick succession on the console intercom behind him. After a few moments, Mischa heard a voice from the speaker, but the volume was too low for her to make out the words.

"I have a task for you," Subtwo said. "I do not think it will conflict with your ethics." The statement could have been sarcastic, but was not.

The response sounded tired, but not sleepy; not bored, but affirmative. Subtwo shut off the intercom. "You should have come during the day," he said.

"I didn't think I'd get in."

"Hm." His expression seemed slightly amused. "Would you have come if you had known I was watching?"

"I don't know. I guess so. You'd've had to see me sooner or later."

They waited in silence until a barefoot young man came in. He wore black pants and a black robe with a green and gold embroidered dragon crawling up the shoulder. He glanced at Mischa and faced Subtwo with something of a defiant air.

Physically, he resembled a few other offworld people Mischa had seen: pale tan skin, very dark eyes that appeared slanted because of the structure of the eyelids. But his uncombed hair, instead of being black, was bright gold.

"Yes?" If he had been awakened, he did not seem annoyed by it, but he looked very tired.

"I have a new crew member. I would appreciate your teaching her as much mathematics as you can. Start her in xenobiology. And the other basic subjects—her education has been neglected."

"All right."

"Very good."

Subtwo turned to his console, and they were obviously dismissed. The young man gestured toward the doorway with his head, not peremptorily but pleasantly, without taking his hands from his pockets. They left Subtwo's quarters and walked together down the hall to the foyer.

"I'm Jan Hikaru," the young man said, sitting on the edge of the fountain. The light-fibers brushed his shoulder and shimmered into orange.

"My name's Mischa."

He took his hands from his pockets and rested his forearms on his knees. His hands were narrow and bony, and, like his movements, graceful and strong. Mischa admired the lines of his body.

"What do you want to learn?"

"Everything."

He smiled, pleasantly enough but superficially, preoccupied. "Calculus, then, to give you the feel of things. Number theory and machine communication and enough astronomy to get you around. And the xeno. Do you know any of those?"

"No." If he had not been so serious, she would have believed he was mocking her and she would have grown angry; even so, her tone was sharp.

He glanced up, paying real attention for the first time. "I'm not fit to be a teacher," he said. "I know too little. But I will do the best I can."

Mischa followed Jan Hikaru; he took her to a room across the hall from his own. It was less garish than most of those she had seen, for which she was grateful. The tapestries were blue and the thick rug a deep dark green. Jan showed her around briefly and left her alone to sleep. She found herself prepared to like him.

Mischa could not sleep under the ornate blankets or on top of them or even on the floor. She lay in darkness for long slow minutes that seemed more like hours. The silence was alien after the echoing exchanges in the corridors where she had lived. Half-awake, half-dreaming, she imagined herself already on another world, one peopled by figures from the drapes in the Palace, clothed in precious gems and metals or in more precious furs and leather, passing like silent spirits between the curiously substantial ghosts of trees that had not been seen on Mischa's part of earth in centuries. She walked toward them, but they receded, beckoning, smiling. Leaves brushed dew against her face. The sky was purple-black; stars crowned one horizon while the clear streaks of dawn cleansed the other.

A feeling like terror, a cold draft in a wave from her face to her stomach, drove her out of her fantasy. She sat up with her fingers clenched in the carpet. The visions disappeared.

So had ended all her dreams, real or construct. She feared for the one she lived in now, for if it shattered, it would be the last.

Mischa rose and looked into the hall through a narrow gap in the curtains. She could detect no one, so she crept out to explore. The corridor into which her room opened continued for a short distance, then, after a short purposeless curve, stopped. For a moment she thought she would ask for a different room, one not on a dead-end hall, then she shrugged. If Subtwo neglected to keep his word and she had to flee again, she did not think she would care if she had escape routes or not. There was nowhere to escape to.

At the open end of the hallway the light-fountain was dimmer, as though it, like people, needed rest. It glowed softly. Mischa walked across the softly lit central node and brushed her fingertips against the strands. They sparked brightly and faded again.

"You—"

Without thinking, Mischa fled from the voice of the slave steward, who came without warning, sound, sight, or aura. She ran until she reached her room, stopped outside it, and turned to face Madame. "Stay away from me. I'll kill you this time."

"You are persistent," Madame said. "There is no need to speak of killing. Put away your knife and I will take you out of here."

"I'm working for Subtwo. You can't touch me."

Madame arched one eyebrow. "We must go to him, and he will confirm or deny you."

"That isn't necessary."

The door-curtain of Jan Hikaru's room draped across his shoulders like a cape as he leaned against the wall with his legs crossed at the ankles and his arms folded on his chest. "She's telling the truth."

"Do you take responsibility?"

"I already have it."

"Very well." Absently, she flicked her short whip against her skirt and started away.

"I told you I wasn't here to steal."

Madame looked back skeptically. "That," she said, "remains to be seen."

Mischa reddened; her pride was hardly salved by Jan's enigmatic half-smile. It was as though he knew everything that had ever happened or ever would happen, as though he were just observing the motions for his own amusement.

"What's so damn funny?"

"Nothing," he said. "It doesn't matter. I'm sorry. Since we're both up, do you want some tea?"

"I don't know what that is."

"Subtwo was right," Jan said. "Your education has been neglected."

Mischa sat on the carpet in Jan's room, sipping hot tea and staring down into the cup at the small remnants of the leaves from which it was brewed.

"Couldn't you sleep?"

Mischa shrugged. "I like to know what's around me."

He swirled his cup slowly. "Ah."

As they drank together, Mischa could see him watching her through the steam of his tea. The wall-curtains of his room were brown and unadorned; against them, sitting cross-legged on the bronze-colored rug, he was for an instant a mysterious and very alien figure. All Mischa could feel of him was a deep, sad quiet; there was much more, but she could not reach it.

"Do you know what you're doing?" he asked abruptly.

"Yes."

"Is it what you want?"

She could not answer immediately; he had asked exactly the right thing. "It's the only way I can leave earth."

He sipped his tea. "Is it worth it?"

"What do you care?" she snapped, but the familiarity of the exchange sprang up and hurt her. "What gives you the right to talk? You're doing the same thing."

"Well, not quite."

"You're with Subtwo—what else can you be but a raider?"

"I was with a friend who wanted to return to earth. This is the only way to get here or to leave."

"What happened?" She felt she already knew, because though she could not feel his pain, she could see it in his eyes and in his face, too new and too deep to hide.

He finally answered. "She's dead."

Mischa could only sit silent and uneasy with her inexperience at consolation.

"She wouldn't have been happy here," Jan said bitterly. "Go back to bed."

He stood up, but Mischa reached and stopped him with a touch. "That's what I mean," she said, and left him, alone.

8

Subtwo heard the faint scratching on his door and turned from the bright twisting figures on the console screen. "Come."

Madame entered and stood before him. He smiled to see her; it had been only a few days since he had talked to her, but seemed much longer. "Good evening."

"Sir."

"What's the matter?" He had learned the subtleties of her voice, the tones that meant she wished to ask a question or make a suggestion, but was restrained from doing so by protocol and training. He was accustomed to directness, but directness was denied her. He wished again that she would tell him her name.

"There is a young girl—"

"It's all right. I said she could stay."

"She is a thief, sir."

"I know. She told me."

"You trust her?"

"She wants things I can give her more than she wants anything she could take. Has she been here before?"

"Yes, sir."

He waited for her to continue, but she did not. She had trained herself to answer only questions asked, not questions implied. It was a small defiance that could neither be identified nor objected to on any level of rationality. This similarity of a human being to a computer might have pleased him some time before, but now, with this human being, it did not.

"What happened?"

"The Lady Clarissa sent her to be flogged."

"Flogged!"

"Yes, sir."

More and more often these days Subtwo felt the need for profanity, but he had not yet found words that comforted him. "Fools," he said. "I'll tell them she's to be left alone."

"If—"

"Yes?"

"It might be safer . . . for the child . . . if she stayed out of the Lady's sight."

"Is she that vindictive?"

Madame did not answer.

"All right," Subtwo said. "I'll warn Mischa to avoid Clarissa."

Madame bowed her head to him.

He wished she would drop her deferential pose: he was sure now that it was a pose, a self-protecting wall that hid her intelligence and her pride. He had known many people, but he had never been more than superficially and physically close to anyone but his pseudosib, and that closeness had been forced on them. He had begun to hope for, to need, a relationship with commitment and responsibility.

"I regret disturbing you for such a trivial matter."

"I don't mind."

She took that as a dismissal and bowed again. As she turned to leave, the glow of his display screen brushed the smooth skin of her cheek and her bare hip. He leaned forward, reaching toward her, and she heard him and turned back. "Is there something you wish?"

He let his hand fall, suddenly abashed. "I have been . . . lonely. . . ." He could think of nothing more adequate to say.

"If you would tell me your preferences, sir—"

He stood; she became silent.

He went to her, stopping very close, looking down at her. "I have been lonely," he repeated.

She almost fled; she whirled and ran three steps before she stopped, he hoped for some reason more than fear. She did not turn. He followed, and stood behind her. The tendons in her neck were taut. He wanted to touch them, kiss them, feel her pulse against his lips; he wanted her to turn suddenly and embrace him; he wanted to feel her tongue against his teeth and her silver fingernails in his back. He wanted to explore her while she explored him; he wanted to writhe with her in warm darkness. He lifted one hand, but stopped himself when his fingers brushed the soft fibers of the black velvet she wore. He was shaking.

"Sir—" Her voice trembled. She cut herself off and stood, silent for a moment, her breathing slow and deep. "There are others in the Palace. They are trained." She was distant again: the perfect servant, and her voice was hard.

"I can buy that in the street. I can trade a moment of pleasure with any member of my crew."

She did not respond. For a long time, neither of them spoke.

"I have wanted . . . something more."

"Something like love?" she said abruptly and sardonically. He might have killed anyone else for mocking him.

"Is that so ridiculous?"

She flinched from his touch, but turned and faced him. Her dark-painted eyes glistened. "If you summon me to your bed I will submit to you," she said. "That is your right and my obligation. But I am a slave and I cannot love."

He touched her cheek very gently, then stepped back and folded his arms. "Good night."

She bowed. "Good night, sir."

It was not until she had opened the heavy door that he spoke again. "Or will not?"

She looked back at him, and her voice was again self-contained. "As you please."

The door closed softly behind her.

Jan lay on his bed in the darkness, staring toward the ceiling. His feelings of depression were heightened by his being in this deep cave with tons of rock overhead. His reactions had little to do with fear, a great deal to do with isolation. In a detached way, he observed himself, his recently acquired ability to waste time, his indecision. He was not happy with himself. He had nothing he wanted to get up and do to use the time until he might become sleepy. The prospect of talking with Mischa was the only spark of interest he could find. She might be as awake as he, lying in the night, anxious, wondering what the next day would bring. Mischa would give Jan his first chance to talk about the city with someone who knew it. But he stayed where he was, in the oversoft bed; he did not want to disturb her if by chance she had managed to sleep. He felt for the pulse in his left wrist and began to breathe slowly to its count, twelve beats, in, twelve beats, out. Finally, fitfully, he dozed.

It was still early when he got up, washed briefly, and dressed. He had stopped suppressing his facial hair, and his red-gold mustache was beginning to show across his upper lip. Previously, he had seldom let it grow. His father had been able to reconcile himself to, or ignore, Jan's blond hair, but Jan had always felt that expecting Ichiri to accept a reddish beard would simply have been cruel.

Jan crossed the hall. He had never entered anyone's room in the Palace—that realization struck him abruptly—so he had not noticed before that there was nowhere to knock.

"Are you awake?" He kept his voice low, in case she might not be.

Mischa pulled aside the curtain. "Yes."

He looked at her more carefully this morning. Her dark pants and jacket were worn, short at wrist and ankle, and did not quite meet at the waist except when she stood still. Her feet were bare. She was only as tall as his shoulder; though she was thin, she gave no impression of frailty. She was not beautiful, but the lines of her face were cleanly sculpted and strong. Her fingernails were broken and chewed, and her wrists—her wrists looked scarred.

She regarded him with some wariness. After last night, he supposed he should not be surprised at any suspicion she showed of anyone. Her eyes were so green they fascinated him. He realized simultaneously that he was staring at her, that she did not flinch from his gaze, and that she did not like being stared at. He glanced away, self-consciously, and looked back, but without the intensity. "Would you like breakfast?"

"Sure."

Their corridor was deserted, but they saw a few other of Subtwo's people when they arrived at the dining hall. Jan took a table across the room from them. Their occasional laughter drifted to him, and their half-amused opinions of the Palace food. They only glanced up when he arrived, and afterward paid him no attention.

"You really aren't one of them, are you?" The tension and suspicion of last night had left her voice.

"No," he said. "I'm really not." That was his choice; he had not been ostracized. He had isolated himself; he had avoided even personal relationships. Or perhaps he had not avoided so much as been oblivious to them.

He showed Mischa how to get food and drink. An area had been hastily reworked in cafeteria style and the spare ship's cook assembled and stocked with local food; Subtwo would not permit slaves in the public rooms. Jan was grateful for that. He was not yet ready to face the situation in which he found himself.

The nervous tautness Jan had noticed in Mischa's stance and movements was somewhat relaxed. She sampled coffee and did not like it, so he brewed the tea he had brought from his room.

She accepted the cup he offered. "Who are they?"

"Subone and Subtwo?" She nodded. All he could have told her was the gossip he had heard, none of it pleasant. Had Mischa planned to join Subtwo's crew permanently, Jan might have put aside his disinclination to repeat unfounded tales; but, the situation being what it was, he saw no point in making the pseudosibs into monsters. "No one knows much about them," he said. "They're very reticent about their past."

"They're not like anybody else who ever came to Center."

"They're not like anybody else at all. They're said to have been experimental subjects. There's no telling what kind of conditions they grew up under." He did not tell her that they might or might not have murdered the man responsible for the conditions.

Jan took a bite of the food. He was not very hungry and did not like the taste or texture any more than did the raiders. The flavors were artificial, either too strong or not strong enough to screen out the taste of yeast or bacterial chlorophyll. He pushed the mushy portions around on his plate.

"Are you okay?"

He put down the fork. "My body doesn't approve of so much traveling, I suppose."

"You can get outside food some places. It's expensive but a lot of offworld people seem to think it's worth it."

"I haven't felt hungry recently," Jan said, and shrugged it off. "I'll be all right."

She seemed about to say something more, but did not. Her manners were far from elegant, but neither were they uncouth. Her restraint and her composure gave her a sort of untrained natural grace and consideration that Jan appreciated, even while noticing it only peripherally. Realizing she had finished, he dragged himself out of his mental and emotional circlings. "Let's get started."

They returned to Jan's room. He gave her his library extension. She took it carefully, as though it might shatter when she touched it.

Jan said apologetically, "Real books are more emotionally satisfying."

Mischa glanced up at him, her expression half-amused, half-curious. "Do you really think it matters?"

"Perhaps not." But he had always felt that the word "book," in standard English, was very nearly onomatopoeic. Having been raised with rooms full of dusty, leatherbound, fascinating books, he found that the fluorescent green words on the dark blue screens of library extensions came between him and the writer. Still, he understood the need for conservation of space in a ship. The general memory bank of the pocket-sized device Mischa held was extensive, and had exchangeable banks for specialized subjects. Jan showed her the codings. Mischa listened with little expression, but Jan had seen her quickly hidden flash of interest. He never had to repeat an instruction.

Aware of her eagerness, he kept his explanations brief. He realized suddenly how few written signs he had seen in Center, and how easily he might have shamed Mischa if she had not been able to read. He said nothing, but felt great relief that he had by luck avoided a blunder.

He pointed out the title of an elementary book on xenobiology. It was somewhat out of date, but it had begun his own interest in the field, and he had never found one better for that purpose. "Read this, and when you're finished, come back and we'll talk."

She left him alone in his dim room. He felt a vague sense of disquiet. His time-sense was deceived by the lack of diurnal rhythm in the Palace. He felt as though he had been on earth much longer than a very few days. However short the time was since the pseudosibs' ship had landed, Jan had no rational excuse for his neglect of his single responsibility. The promise he had made, to bury his friend here, was unfulfilled; she lay cold and shrouded on the ship. Jan did not want to consign her body to dust and decay; he did not want to admit she was dead. His sleep had been troubled since her death. He reached for her in the darkness, and grasped only air; he heard her voice in the night, and awoke to silence. He had given too little thought to death in his lifetime. Lately, the possible solace of belief in an afterworld had become very attractive.

He slid out of his dragon-robe, pulled off his boots, stood in the center of the cool room, and began to do isometric exercises. Moving only to change position, he showed very little evidence of the violence of his exertions, but sweat soon ran down his sides and soaked into the waistband of his pants. His hair stuck to his face with perspiration that slid into his eyes, stinging. Only when he finally began to tremble with exhaustion did he stop to rest. He lay down on his bed for a moment; without meaning to, he dozed.

"Jan?"

He sat up abruptly, startled by the soft voice. "What?" It was more an expression of surprise than query.

"I'm sorry," Mischa said from the doorway. "Go back to sleep. I'll come later."

"No, wait." He combed his sticky hair with his fingers and swung his legs over the edge of the bed. Stiff with abrupt activity and cooling, his muscles ached fiercely. He kneaded his biceps with his thumbs. "I didn't mean to go to sleep. Is anything wrong?"

"No, you just said to come when I was finished."

"What time is it?" He did not feel as though he had slept so soundly so long.

"Almost midday."

"You're done?"

"Yes."

"Very good." He ran his fingers through his hair again. "I'll be right back. I don't make sense before I wash my face."

When he returned, with clean water dripping slowly from the hair at the back of his neck, he felt considerably more awake and slightly less dirty. He sat down on the rug and gestured for Mischa to join him. She put the extension on the carpet between them, as though returning a loan.

"What did you think of it?"

"Is that all real?"

"Yes," he said. "Of course."

"I had to ask," Mischa said. "It's just that compared to the places in that book, it's empty here . . ."

"Yes, well . . ." Empty: most of earth, but not all of it. He smiled a little. "I'll be giving you things to read that are true or not depending on your point of view, but I won't try to fool you."

They began to talk, and Mischa spoke without self-consciousness, without first probing to see what Jan believed, with a kind of directness that revealed self-confidence lacking egotism: undidactic and able to consider alternatives. Jan had not known quite what to expect. He knew Mischa must have a considerable amount of innate courage and cleverness; her lack of information on subjects he considered basic had appalled him. He had not expected the keen and logical and perceptive intellect she revealed. He was astonished.

Their conversation did not cease until they realized, almost simultaneously, that they both were hoarse. Jan stopped talking; Mischa said something that came out as a sort of croak. They looked at each other and suddenly laughed. If Mischa laughed seldom, she laughed well; Jan liked the sound of her delight.

"Are you hungry?"

"Yes," he said, with some surprise. "Yes, I am. Let's go."

It was quite late; Jan and Mischa were the only ones in the dining hall.

"You argue well," Jan said, straining tea into two cups. "I don't know about you, but I'm tired."

"You don't seem as tired as you were last night. Or this morning."

Steam from the tea swirled around Jan's face with the exhalation of his breath. "A different kind of tired," he said. "Better." He leaned back, staring up at the rock ceiling. "No one in the Sphere thinks about earth anymore. They've put it out of their minds. It's quite a shock to visit a place you've always been taught was dead."

"No," Mischa said, and Jan thought he might have offended her, but she continued. "It isn't dead, it's dying. And that's worse."

"I'm going to take a bath," Jan said abruptly. "Want to come?"

"Sure."

Jan had been pleasantly surprised to find a Japanese-style bath in the Palace. He had spent so many years at school, avoiding going home for any reason, living in places where the only bathing facilities were small showers, that he had almost resigned himself to giving up the luxury of soaking in a deep, hot tub of water. Since leaving school, living in cheap and sometimes squalid places, he had done most of his bathing from the basins of public washrooms.

In the dim, steamy bathing grotto, he and Mischa stripped, soaped and rinsed themselves, and slid into the sunken pool. Mischa was even thinner than he had thought. There was a deep, old scar on her left forearm, and a newer one across her ribs beneath her left breast. He wanted to ask her about the scars, but did not know how. He lay on his back, floating. The water filled his ears; he could hear the circulation, the faint low splashes of wavelets against the side of the pool, his own heartbeat. The heat soaked into him, producing a pleasant, languorous feeling.

"Can I ask you something?"

"That's your job," Jan said. "Mine's to answer."

"Where are you from?"

Jan raised his head and was momentarily startled by the illusion that her eyes reflected the light like a cat's. He shook the water out of his face; then Mischa's eyes simply seemed black in the dim light.

"I come from a planet called Koen," he said. "It's very beautiful." The very name meant "park." Nearly the whole world was parklike, in an infinity of ways. Recalling it, he described it and its inhabitants. It had been colonized by people who had for centuries felt a comradeship with the land; they did not violate their new earth. But the world was in some ways too pleasant, and too easy; it provided insufficient challenge, and the people grew self-indulgent and too concerned with the minute details of life. "My father used to spend a lot of time trying to grow bonsai trees," Jan said. "They're supposed to stay very small, and grow as you direct them, but his always kept growing until he had to plant them outside." This far away, this removed in time, he could even smile about his father's eccentricities. "He used to write poetry too. It was terrible, whatever language he tried."

"Why did he keep on with it?"

"He doesn't realize it's bad. And there's no point in telling him. If he believed it, he'd be hurt, but he wouldn't believe it in the first place."

"Oh."

"He's quite . . . unusual." Jan took a deep breath of the damp air. "He sometimes thinks he's a character from a very old novel. Genji Hikaru wrote poetry, so Ichiri does too."

"You don't have to read it, do you?"

"There are days when it's the only way he'll communicate."

Mischa laughed softly and Jan found himself smiling. On this level, it was amusing. "The poetry's not all of it," he said. "Mixing perfume was a social grace when the novel was written, so of course Genji excelled at it. But sometimes our house smells so bad you can't sleep in it."

"That must be uncomfortable if you have storms in the winter."

"There isn't any winter on Koen."

"No winter," Mischa said, with some wonder. "I wish it was like that here." She slipped underwater like a young otter, and came up behind him. "Have you got any other family?"

"No," Jan said. "My mother died about a hundred years ago."

"Oh," said Mischa, with the beginnings of sympathy. Then, *"What?"*

"She died—" Jan stopped. There were no germ banks in Center, so the manner in which he had been produced was unfamiliar to Mischa. "She lived a hundred years ago," he said. "A hundred years before I was born." He told Mischa about the banks on many places in the Sphere, where genetic material was kept frozen for anyone who cared to deposit it, where anyone who fit the terms of the donor's will could make a withdrawal. The means of reproduction were theoretically simple, technically rather complex and expensive. It was undertaken on Koen perhaps more often than in other places. The people were rich and the past important: on Koen, one was more likely to become infatuated with a historical figure and wish to reproduce with one.

"Why do people go to so much trouble?"

Putting his feet against the side of the pool, Jan pushed himself through the water, feeling it flow through his hair, across his shoulders, between his toes. He had never thought about some of the things people could do on the innumerable and variegated worlds of the Sphere. He was not sure he could answer Mischa's question.

"It's difficult to explain. When you get out there and see more, it'll be easier to understand. People don't have to work as hard; on the other hand, there are more things they can do."

"You mean they can do nothing but play. Your father made you—" She sounded shocked, and a little angry. "Is the Sphere just like Center? Do they play with each other's lives too?"

"No—" Jan hesitated. No one had ever expressed his own questions in those words and those sentiments. He did not like the idea of himself as a complicated plaything, though he had long before accepted that his father would always try to direct his life in ways that ordinary families would not. "Yes, I guess they do, to a certain extent. People always do. On Koen at least the manipulation is less likely to be tyranny than overprotection." From what he had seen of Stone Palace and the city, most controls in Center were built on pain and fear. Jan's father had never hurt him, and Jan had never been afraid of Ichiri. "My father makes people feel they've tried to injure him deliberately if they don't do what he expects." He glanced toward Mischa through the steam. "It took me a long time to figure that out. It's quite effective."

She nodded. "I understand." From her tone, Jan felt that she had experienced control by manipulation as well as control by force, that she did indeed know how hard it was to defy someone who continually expressed love.

"You must wonder what your mother was like."

"I've read her journals, and there's a good deal of documentation about her life. Murasaki was quite extraordinary." Jan envied her; he wished he had inherited more of her decisiveness and flexibility. She had been an explorer, one of the few with a first-contact clearance, until an accident almost killed her and ended her first career. Her second was benthic architecture: thirteen worlds held undersea cities she had designed.

"She sounds like a good person to have for a parent," Mischa said. "Even if you never got to meet her."

"Yeah," Jan said. "But, you know? That didn't have anything to do with why Ichiri picked her."

"What, then?"

"Her name. Just her name. The old novel I told you about—it was written by a Japanese noblewoman named Murasaki, who used herself as a character—Prince Genji's wife."

"You're right. Your father really is strange."

Jan allowed old memories to overtake him for the first time in a long while. Once he and Ichiri had not spoken for weeks because Jan would only answer to his own name, the name Ichiri was required to give him by the terms of Murasaki's will. It was the name of her father, a man pictures showed as pleasant, large, square-faced, and very blond, one of the original settlers of Koen. Half the original colonists had been

Dutch, and the other half Japanese; Ichiri's own descent was not as pure as his strange ideas made him believe.

"He always wanted to call me Yugiri," Jan said. "But Yugiri wasn't Murasaki's child, only Genji's." He laughed, without much humor. "He never gets anything right."

Jan shook back his wet blond hair and returned himself to the present. Mischa was leaning against the wall of the pool, her face flushed with the heat.

"What about your family?" Jan asked suddenly. "Won't you be leaving anyone?"

She did not answer for a moment. "No," she said finally. "I won't be leaving anyone."

Jan breast-stroked to the edge of the pool and levered himself out. Standing on the edge, dripping on the flagstones, he reached down to give Mischa a hand. "Come on out. You shouldn't stay in too long if you're not used to it."

She took his hand, put her foot on the side, and let him pull her out. As she leaned forward, Jan caught a quick glimpse of white scars across her back. He drew in his breath involuntarily. "Gods, Mischa . . . who did that to you?"

Wrapping herself in a towel, Mischa shrugged. "It was a chance I took."

"A chance at *what?*"

She smiled, but it was not a pleasant expression: it was sardonic and self-mocking. She told Jan what had happened, why Madame had been chasing her, though she left out the ice-eyed administrator and the deprivation cell. He could not keep his gaze from slipping to her scarred wrists.

"And after that," Jan said, when Mischa had finished, "even after that, you could still come here?"

"After that I had to come here," she said. "It was the last place. I haven't got anywhere else to try."

Jan wanted to put his arms around her and comfort her, but Mischa seemed to have no need of comfort. Jan realized it was he himself who needed reassurance, against the slow shattering of his basic assumptions of human rights and human dignity. He found Mischa watching him with something like understanding in her expression and her deep green eyes.

"It's over," she said softly. "Never mind. That's all over."

Wrapped in terrycloth, padding barefoot down the hall, Mischa felt deliciously sleepy. She was more content than she had been in a long time, though she recognized contentment and overconfidence to be dangerous. But she knew that with this one chance she could prove herself worth training. That was the hard step; compared to that, asking Subtwo to let Chris come with them would be easy.

Outside her room she started to say good night to Jan Hikaru, but hesitated. For the first time since she had met him, his seemingly impervious, glassy inner calm felt shimmery and penetrable. She could feel only quick refracted rays of his true emotions, and any flaws in his defenses had begun to fuse already, hiding him from her again. Still, Mischa had felt enough and seen enough to know that despite his apparent self-sufficiency and invulnerability, he was troubled.

He glanced over at her. "Do you want some tea?"

She did not, very much; the steaming pool had relaxed and even enervated her, but she accepted and followed him inside. He sat cross-legged on the rug and prepared the tea in silence, not speaking again until he had handed Mischa the fragile cup.

"When people die in Center, what happens?"

His question was not completely clear, but Mischa put together things he had said with his sorrow. "Their friends put them in the river."

"Is there a ritual, or someone to perform one?"

"No. Nothing like that."

"Are coffins used?"

"People use shrouds, if they can afford them."

Jan put his fingertips together and stared between his hands. "I promised my friend I would put her body back into the earth. Will you show me what I should do?"

"Of course."

In the blockhouse, near the rack where the suits were kept folded inside their helmets, Mischa watched Jan dress for outside. She could hear the sand skittering against the walls of the blockhouse above. "I'd like to come too," she said, trying to temper her eagerness.

Jan seemed ready to make some formal protest about necessity and discomfort, but he said nothing, stood, and picked over the suits until he found a small one. Mischa put it on, mimicking actions she had carefully watched Jan make. The suit was cut for a body fuller than hers, but it was not uncomfortable.

Jan glanced over the controls and pressed a button. The squeal of the door in its tracks was wiped out by the unbaffled scream of the storm, and the air around them filled with sand. Jan plunged into it; Mischa hesitated in the doorway and stared out into the swirling blackness. She had never seen the storms before. The air seemed hidden by a glittering black curtain shot with unordered streaks of color.

"Come on."

She started at Jan's voice, so close to her ear, saw the tiny microphone near her mouth, and laughed at herself. She moved from the sparse shelter of the blockhouse into the full force of the wind. She staggered, but caught herself. Jan placed a contact key against the entry panel, and the door closed slowly.

A writhing rope led away into the gloom. Mischa recognized the material as an extremely durable plastic, but in the wind, the strands had begun to fray. Holding the rope, pushed against it, Mischa followed Jan into the desert. When she looked back she could see nothing but the black sand and the rope, which struggled like an eel in her hand. She could hear the individual grains of sharp sand pecking against the sheltered side of her helmet.

She understood, now, why the contours of the land around Center changed so drastically every year, and why the caravannaires never lingered near the city into the fall, but began their trek across the desert before summer seemed nearly over.

"Are you all right?"

"Yes." They seemed to have been walking for a long time. The rope slid past Mischa's side as she pulled herself along. Their path was perpendicular to the wind. Jan walked on ahead of her, bent forward, shoulders hunched.

Then Mischa saw a darker spot in the blackness ahead, a dull darkness behind the sparkling obsidian. The sand thinned and they entered the lee of a great ship. Mischa stood looking up at it, unable to make out its lines. She knew what it looked like, low and wide and sharp-edged. She had seen others skimming into view, but had never realized they were so large. This one balanced on spraddled stilts and a central shaft, against which sand piled high on the leeward side.

Jan opened the hatch, and they entered the ship in a cloud of sand that settled to the floor around them. The hatch slid closed, and the small room drew them into the ship.

Jan threw back his helmet. Small drops of perspiration slid down his temples. Mischa took off her own helmet, and when the cool air touched her face she realized she was sweating too.

Jan opened the other side of the airlock. Mischa peered beyond, into the ship, at walls of pale, self-luminous plastic. She was mildly and indefinably disappointed, though she could not have said what she had expected. Her shoulders ached and her hands were sore from gripping the rope.

She followed Jan into the ship. Touching the walls, she could feel only smoothness through her gloves: no heat, no vibration, nothing.

Jan finally stopped outside a closed door. He reached for it, and hesitated, eyes half-closed, somber. Mischa wanted to prevent his opening that door, for a little while at least, long enough for her to see the ship, but she felt that to do so would be cruel and selfish. Mischa could be either or both, but she did not want to hurt Jan Hikaru.

Jan opened the door.

Cold air seeped out of the room and surrounded him. It was tinged with the unpleasant smell of death. Beside him, Mischa shivered.

Jan approached the figure that lay on a narrow bench inside. It was covered with an embroidered satin cloth. He stroked the black silk gently. "She liked to touch it, because she could feel the designs," Jan said, "so I gave it to her. She was blind." He lifted the cloth and looked down at the lined, relaxed face, still both frail and strong. His friend's expression was peaceful. The cloth sank slowly down, falling across her features, blurring them.

Jan enfolded his friend's body, and wrapped a metallic sheet around the satin tapestry.

"If you had a stretcher, I could—"

"Never mind," he said. "I can carry her."

A long tunnel led from the Circle to the burial cave. Jan followed Mischa inside until the reflected light faded to darkness and he could no longer make out her form.

"Is there any light?"

"Sorry."

He supposed that, with practice, her eyes had learned to accustom themselves to darkness more quickly than his. She touched his arm and led him forward, around a corner, to a chamber suffused by a blue glow that rippled with the sound of water. "Thanks." Jan carried his burden to the bank of the wide, flat river. The water was black, reflecting him in silhouette. The body in his arms seemed even lighter in death than it had been in life. He kept hoping, irrationally, for some feeling of warmth or movement beneath his fingers. Mischa stopped beside him.

"Is there an outlet?"

"Outside," she said. "After a while. A lot of little springs break through the ground every year after the storms, and plants grow around them."

"And the bodies?"

"I don't know. I don't think anyone knows. The water's clean when it comes through the sand."

It was clear that the river could not be easily followed, for it bubbled against the roof of its outlet canal, leaving no air space. Only there did the surface ripple and break. Jan stared into the water, at reflections that seemed to multiply.

"I'll wait for you," Mischa said, and left him alone.

He knelt on the sandy bank. The embroidery on the cloth caught the blue light, and the figures seemed to come alive like the creatures in the stories Jan's friend had told.

Is this what you want, my friend? Do you want to be drowned and dismembered in this cold river? I would have sent you to a bright and glorious destruction in any sun in the galaxy, if you had asked. You deserve a funeral pyre heaped with sandalwood and silk, or a blazing ship and a dog at your feet. Is this all I can give you, a return to the earth?

But the words themselves touched a resonance, and peace slipped up to caress him. He leaned down and touched the old navigator's body to the river's surface. The water immersed his hands, then his arms, and pulled at him. Slowly, reluctantly, Jan let go of the satin-shrouded body. The current caught it and dragged it away, very fast. The silken figures spun before him, and then the currents pulled them beneath the surface, and Jan saw them no more.

He knelt there for a long time, with his hands hanging in the water and gradually growing numb. He felt very calm, but slowly he realized that the flaws in the glassy surface of the water, the small marks swept away and obliterated as though the river could not bear the imperfection, were made by his own tears.

9

Mischa had never had a teacher before, nor access to a library, nor time and means to investigate anything that interested her. During the following weeks in Stone Palace, she had all those resources, and they gave her the planet, the solar system, the universe; a past, a present, a future. The Sphere worlds she read about did not disappoint her imagination. It was not long before she understood why Jan Hikaru had smiled when she told him she wanted to learn everything.

At first she was afraid that her ignorance would bore Jan, even disgust him. He could easily have told Subtwo that she was stupid and worthless, and thus relieved himself of responsibility and work. But as she got to know him better, she realized he would not have done any such thing even if she had been stupid, even if he had been bored. In fact he seemed fascinated, and sometimes even excited, by her progress, though he was by nature undemonstrative.

As they worked together, she watched him grow beyond his grief, neither forgetting nor dully resigning himself to it, but accepting the reason for it and cherishing his memories. Mischa began to trust him, though not quite enough to tell him everything about herself, until she knew how he felt about people not quite normal. Reading alone, she searched for explanations of her differences, and found only theories and new words that all had the same uncertain meanings.

Every subject she studied came easily. She seldom forgot anything she read. She was happiest with mathematics and theoretical physics: each level of study pulled more facets of reality into an elegant and intricate and consistent system of natural laws. The new knowledge pleased her in a way few things ever had, speaking to a sense of beauty and order that she had perceived, yet never had a means of expressing, as Chris had, in his work, before he changed.

Mischa had neither forgotten nor abandoned her brother, but she could not ask another concession from Subtwo so recently after winning the first. She knew she must prove herself here; she could not fail as she had failed before. If she did, Chris would have no chance at all. She put her concern into a separate part of her mind.

She discovered in herself a talent for making valid connections between diverse and apparently unrelated bits of information. She had no idea how she did it, and the ability sometimes startled her a little, inexplicable as it was. As her studies continued and the subjects became more complicated, more esoteric, she occasionally found herself pointing out the way to Jan. The reversal troubled her, but she could not say why.

And then one day, looking pleased but a little bemused that Mischa had explained a mathematical proof to him, Jan said, "I read that over last night, and I didn't really understand it. But you're right—what's the matter?"

Stricken, she stared at him. She suddenly realized why some of her intellectual jumps came so easily, so quickly, with intuitive understanding of the intervening steps. It only seemed that the information had always been there, locked up without framework or terminology. It had never really been there at all. Somehow, despite not being able to sense Jan's feelings through his self-control, Mischa decided that she must be transferring his knowledge to herself, stealing insights on the edge of his subconscious and claiming them as her own. She was no better than Gemmi, a relay for words meaningless to herself. She was worse than Gemmi: she pretended to understand, even to herself, which Gemmi did not and could not do.

Mischa dropped the library extension on the carpet and fled to her room.

She flung herself face down on the bed and pillowed her forehead on her arms. Perhaps every insight she had ever had was drawn from another person. Utterly empty, she could think only that she would have to keep up the deception, even in front of Jan, whom she had begun to think of as a friend. She would have to continue draining him, as Gemmi drained her, long enough to get Chris away from Center.

Just that long. Though practiced in deception, she had never betrayed a friend.

As she lay in cool darkness, a slow and just perceptible change occurred around her, as though a soft sound, the flow of a quiet stream, the whisper of air, had stopped. She finally noticed it, turned over, and sat up.

It took her a few minutes to recognize what was wrong. She jumped up and ran across the hallway and flung aside the curtain to Jan's room. "Jan—" She approached him, silent. He was sitting cross-legged on the floor, his eyes closed, his hands palms up, resting on his knees, in a relaxed but deliberate position.

Finally he opened his eyes.

"Are you all right?"

"Yes," he said. "Of course. What's the matter?"

"I couldn't . . ." He had closed in on himself so far that she could no longer sense him, even as his usual deep and quiet presence. She had grown used to his stability; he was very different from other people, with their changing moods and feelings. It was the changes that disturbed her.

"I thought—there was something wrong." It was a crippled excuse.

"There is something wrong," Jan said, "but I don't know what. I was . . . thinking . . . trying to understand what I said that upset you so."

She sat down in front of him. "It isn't you, it's me."

"You're doing fine," he said. "Beautifully."

"No . . ."

"Do you want to do something else?"

"It isn't that at all—" She cut herself off, hesitated, took a deep breath, and plunged ahead. "It's too easy. It's because of this . . . this trick I can do. I didn't mean to, I didn't know I could use it this way. I didn't know that must be what was happening until something you said a couple minutes ago." She tried to explain what she thought she was doing, and Jan's frown deepened.

"No," he said. "No, that's not what's going on at all."

"But I really do know when people are near, I can feel them. I—"

"Wait, I believe you about that." He smiled. "I can accept it—that's easier than trying to pretend you're nothing but a data-processing machine."

"What other explanation is there?"

"Tell me what you like most."

98

"Mathematics. You know that."

"I always hated it. Well—I didn't really hate it, but I never had any ability at it. You're farther along than I ever was before. I've been keeping half a step ahead of you for a week and I really can't do it any longer."

"So?"

"It seems to me, if you were lifting anything out of my mind, it would be something I'm passably good at."

She rested her chin on her fist, thinking. What he said made sense, and she wanted to believe it. "Then how do I do what I do? I get from one idea to another and sometimes I don't even know how."

"With a very few subjects—and math is one of them—a few people can do that. It's a rare ability, and a valuable one. No one has ever quite figured out how it happens. Gods, don't worry about it—accept it and use it."

"Maybe I don't get it from you. Maybe I get it from somebody else."

"Such as?"

"Subtwo?"

Jan laughed. "He has talents, but intuitive mathematics isn't one of them. He's intelligent and he has an encyclopedic memory, but he's essentially methodical. He takes one step at a time—very fast, but it's still plodding."

"You're sure? Whatever I'm doing, I'm doing myself?"

"Yes. You're much too consistent to be dragging this gift out of other people's minds. As consistent as intuition ever is, anyway."

Mischa chewed on her thumbnail, distractedly, feeling her self-confidence renew itself from Jan's assurance. "There's one thing . . . what I told you—"

"That you can sense what people feel? I'd like to talk about it sometime."

"All right. But only with you. Don't tell anyone else, will you? Please?"

"If you'd rather I didn't."

"Maybe it wouldn't matter in the Sphere, but it does in Center."

"Okay."

"Thanks."

Jan Hikaru's Journal:
 Mischa's one of those rare, strange prodigies, who know music or mathematics without being taught, and need only tools—an in-

strument, or an introduction to notation—with which to express
their talent. Because there are concepts that can't be expressed
otherwise. Once we were talking about rotation—lines around
points, planes around lines. n dimensions as a pivot for n+1.
"And a solid around a plane," she said. I agreed, and said that of
course that situation couldn't be visualized.

"But it can—!"

She tried to explain to me what she could see in her mind, but
finally shrugged and spread her hands. "There aren't any words."
I think she really can visualize a situation in four dimensions. I've
heard of people who could, but never met anyone before.

I used to wonder what it was about music and math, why
they're so integral to the human system that a few people know
them instinctively. I'm no closer to understanding.

I can still help her with other subjects, and the teaching is a
delight. But though she can continue beyond me by herself, I
think it would be better for her to have some direction. Even
more now, I wish my friend were still alive, because I think she
would have gotten great joy from working with Mischa. She
would have been able to help, but the navigator of the pseudosibs'
ship knows barely more than I do. I think Subtwo gives out titles
to make people happy and does all the real work himself. He's the
only one left to ask.

Subtwo made an error, stopped, and reached toward the pressure-
sensitive display screen. Placing the side of his palm hard against the
plastic, until he could feel the material give against the force, he
dragged his hand from one edge to the other, very slowly, obliterating
delicate lines and numerals in a bright green glow. Ashamed of his outburst, he touched a control and cleared the screen more conven-
tionally.

This was the second time he had erred in as many hours, and he was
disturbed by his lack of concentration. He sat back in his chair and
allowed the reactions of his body to impinge upon his consciousness.
Fatigue (lactic acid excess). Hunger (hypoglycemia). Tension, muscle
strain, impeded circulation. And a deep feeling of unease that he could
neither analyze nor dispel. He looked at the chronometer, and would
have thought it faulty had he not known better. There was no excuse

for mistreating his body; he had not rested nor fed it for two days, and for days before that he had acted in a similar irresponsible manner. He had not left his suite nor spoken to another human being for ten days, fifteen days. The isolation did not disturb him, but its effect on his attempts to live like other people did. He doubted he would ever succeed completely, but such withdrawals would make his differences all the more obvious, preventing even the appearance of normalcy. Now he should get up, leave his comfortable quarters, go to gym or common room or cafeteria, and play or work or eat with his people, instead of by himself as he pleased.

He did not want to do any of those things. He wanted to stay all alone, unreminded of his loneliness. Never before had he been jealous of anything, of anyone, especially of his outcast followers. They had always seemed pitiful to him; they were running from what would find them eventually, or toward what they would never find. They could not adjust, they could not adapt, they could not survive anywhere but in the exile-world they made for themselves. They would not try, because of some flaw of intellect or character, Subtwo did not know which. Yet they were content. He resented their trivial happinesses.

Though recognizing his body's need for food, if only concentrates here in his suite, he remained before his console. There was a great frustration inside him—that for all his own intellect, for all his dedication, he had found no path to contentment or happiness.

He keyed the records of the entrance hallway and watched Madame, the last time she had come to his rooms. He took comfort in her grace and poise, but felt distress that her image of perfection remained flawless even when she was alone. Of course she knew of the cameras. But Subtwo wondered if she ever allowed herself to relax, if she had any place where she knew she would not be watched.

In the spring, when they left again—perhaps a little before, if he could convince Subone to make the early departure—he could ask Madame to go with him. He would steal her away and give her her freedom. Steal her . . . he did not like to think of human beings as stealable, and therefore property; he did not like to think of Madame subject to the whims of Blaisse's cruelty, her fate, even her survival, in his hands, a saleable commodity.

A saleable commodity . . .

Saleable . . .

He left his machines and walked into the corridor. No longer did it please him, for Subone had changed it, strewing trash and artifacts on its floor, painting the clean, smooth walls with indelicate designs.

The alice tube took Subtwo to Blaisse's section of the Palace. He ignored the slaves who bowed to him as he passed. He could have ordered them to stay out of his sight, but he preferred to avoid any behavior patterns common to his pseudosib and Blaisse.

The guard at Blaisse's door announced Subtwo with questionable civility, a reaction he could not comprehend until he recalled the other guard, the murdered woman. He wanted to say something to this cloudy-faced young man who glared so at him, but he could not think of anything that would not injure his own pride. He would not make excuses for Subone.

Blaisse lay in bed, Saita beside him. Subtwo's upbringing, alone in a controlled environment, had produced in him an unintended modesty, which continued to be disturbed by such sights. He must have revealed his distress, or Blaisse remembered the party, for the Lord laughed at him. "You *are* a prude. I didn't know there were any in these fine days."

"I simply value my privacy."

"Yes, I know."

"I meant no censure."

"Nor I."

Conversations with Blaisse never took the direction Subtwo planned. Without waiting to be invited, he sat down in a chair that faced the bed, and rubbed his fingers across the brocaded upholstery. He could feel that the stitching was done by hand: inefficient, inexact.

"I've been observing your customs."

"And—?"

"Some of them appear . . . quite agreeable." Subtwo despised himself for the lie.

"Which ones, in particular?" Blaisse was smiling that dreadful, incomprehensible smile.

"Machines are insufficient companionship. Other options interest me."

"Your brother—pardon me, your pseudosib—seems to find everything he needs in Center."

"His needs are not mine."

"What are your needs?"

"A relationship of longer duration than those contracted in Center."

"Something permanent, you mean."

"Yes."

"But to your convenience alone, of course."

"Yes," Subtwo said, perhaps too quickly. He wondered if Blaisse could detect the reluctance of his answers.

"Then we shall certainly have to satisfy your urges. What you want is advice in selecting a slave."

Subtwo thought it politic to agree.

"A young one," Blaisse said. "To train yourself. That's always the most satisfactory arrangement. There's no worry about one's own sufficiency of knowledge. Of course you must be careful to train them, not teach them."

Subtwo felt that he must be purple with repressed fury, and he thought that his idea might fail simply because Blaisse would be offended by his manner. Saita watched, her usually gentle and unreacting expression troubled. Subtwo wanted to explain to her what he was doing, what he was trying to do, though he knew he should not care so much what people thought about him. Blaisse laid his hand on Saita's breast; she started and her color heightened, silver dulled and blue darkened, with embarrassment or fear for having let her attention drift from her master's pleasure. Blaisse looked down on her, but she did not meet his gaze; he glanced languidly back at Subtwo. "You see how well Saita and I get on?"

"I had in mind," Subtwo said carefully, "someone more mature."

"Indeed?" An ironic lift of eyebrow. "More mature. Older, you mean. And you so young. Well. No accounting for taste. So our problem will be finding a mature female who is not too badly used. Ah—excuse me—a female? Or a male? Or something more exotic? You've given me no chance to observe your preferences."

"A woman," Subtwo said, trying to resign himself to this humiliation of the spirit. He hoped Madame was not nearby, to hear herself discussed in such terms. It suddenly occurred to him, a dreadful thought, that she might misunderstand, just as Saita had, his aims. Even the knowledge that her misunderstanding would be for only a short time disturbed him.

"This is a difficulty," Blaisse said. "We may have to contact Clarissa's relatives and see if they have anything of the sort."

"I had someone under consideration, as it happens," Subtwo said.

He understood Blaisse well enough, he thought, to know that he must not seem too eager.

"Indeed?"

"Yes. One of your . . . one of your people. She seems about the right age. She's rather tall—I need someone tall. Dark hair. She wears black and silver—"

"You mean Madame? My slave steward?"

"Yes, I suppose so. I don't know her name—"

Blaisse did not use the opportunity to tell Subtwo Madame's name. Instead, he chuckled. "Madame? No, no, that's ridiculous."

"Ridiculous? I see nothing ridiculous about it."

"Whyever do you think her attractive?"

Subtwo had no answer for such a question; the question itself was ridiculous.

"Your tastes *are* unusual," Blaisse said.

"Then all that remains to discuss is the . . . price."

"Price? Oh—to buy her."

"That was what I came about." To buy her, to free her: to offer to take her anywhere, without obligation, somewhere he too could be free, he hoped, and then to start again, both of them, two free people, and see if they could love.

"It's out of the question."

I've been too eager, Subtwo thought. He felt ill, weightless. *He knows, and he plays with me.* "Why? You as much as said you did not find her attractive."

"Dear boy," Blaisse said. "That has nothing at all to do with it. She wasn't bought in the first place for beauty, just the opposite. How much work do you think she'd get done if my guests were always dragging her off to their beds? She was trained here. She's been steward almost as long as I've been Lord. We couldn't get along without her."

"It is not sensible to be so dependent on one person," Subtwo said woodenly. He had no idea of changing Blaisse's mind; that was simply his reaction to the statement.

"You're right. Of course you're right." Blaisse rubbed his middle finger across Saita's nipple, and his eyes went out of focus. Subtwo thought Blaisse was about to lapse into his characteristic boredom and order him away; Subtwo did not think he could tolerate an order. He stood up and turned toward the door.

"One moment."

Across Subtwo's shoulders, all the muscles tensed abruptly.

"We should work out an arrangement."

Reluctantly, Subtwo faced him, less than anxious to hear what Blaisse would say.

"She should have an assistant. Someone to train, someone who could take over."

"And—?"

"Bring me someone." Blaisse's blank look had changed to one of lupine watchfulness. "Raid it or buy it, I don't care, a young child, six or eight years old, young enough to tame, I don't want to have to flog it for obedience. Intelligent, not pretty, be sure of that. And if it works out, in a few years, we can repeat this conversation."

"A few years . . ."

"A few years, yes. My palace is not simple to run."

Subtwo gazed at the floor and slowly shook his head.

"Why so downcast?" Blaisse was truly mystified, or he was acting and laughing; Subtwo could not tell which. "If you're so infatuated with her, take her—you don't need her consent or mine for that. But don't keep her from her duties, unless you don't care that she'd be punished for neglect."

Without responding, Subtwo turned and stumbled toward the door. He felt totally exhausted.

Blaisse's voice, hard and victorious, followed him. "If you want her that much, steal me a child."

Hearing the music of the alarms, Subtwo jumped up from his bed as though he had not been asleep. He had lain down only to think. He looked around, recalling the familiarity of his rooms, and collapsed back. No law said he should feel guilty about sleeping during what others considered daytime. Who could tell, in this forsaken place? And there was no law that said he must speak with anyone who approached. He had more important things to do, plans to implement. He climbed to his feet, and reached for the front door's locking control.

"Subtwo?"

He spun at the voice. Jan Hikaru stood in the dimness of the next room, his hands in his pockets.

"What do you want? How did you get in here?"

"I thought you saw me—the door opened."

Subtwo glanced toward the intercom screen, expecting to see Subone's laughing face, but the communicator remained blank. He scowled; Subone was having a joke of his own. Subtwo decided then and there to sever the connections between the two suites. What had seemed a sensible safety precaution had proved a nuisance.

"What do you want?"

"To talk to you about Mischa."

Subtwo frowned. He had wondered if she might have trouble adjusting to a new situation, but he had expected her apparent determination to keep her out of trouble longer than this. "What has happened?"

"Nothing bad," Jan Hikaru said quickly.

Subtwo assumed, then, that he was being given a simple progress report, and that annoyed him. He wanted to plan how quickly the ship could be made ready—he should have done that without even needing to think, certainly before sleeping, despite his weariness. "I'm very busy. As it isn't important, come back another time."

"It is important."

"I didn't ask for status checks. Follow your own judgment with her education."

"I'm trying to do that." The tone of Jan Hikaru's voice was moving into exasperation, which Subtwo noticed and found interesting in such an even-tempered young man. He could not remember ever having seen him angry or as much as annoyed.

"What is it?" More patiently.

"I'd like you to help her with her math."

"Help her—what? If you're not competent to teach simple arithmetic—"

Jan did not appear offended by the outburst. Subtwo cut himself off and waited.

"She already knew arithmetic," Jan said calmly. "She's working beyond what I know right now."

"Then you knew less than I thought."

"No, I knew more than you asked me about."

Subtwo realized that was quite possible; he had not, in fact, pressed Jan's knowledge, merely ascertained that he knew enough to work with. "You are saying?"

"With the right help, there's no telling how far she could go. She's a mathematical genius—she just never had any reason or chance to develop the ability."

"You tested her neural responses?"

"I don't need to test her neural responses," Jan said with irritation. "I've worked with her for weeks."

"Send her along, then, and I'll test her. We'll see." He was already considering ways one could feign genius: Mischa would have to be quite clever if this were a trick.

Jan Hikaru looked hardly satisfied with the response, but Subtwo had no patience to commend a discovery he had not certified himself; his enthusiasm focused in other directions. "Will that do?" he asked sardonically.

"All she needs is a chance," Jan said. "There's no way for her to get one in Center." He turned and left the suite.

Relieved to be alone again, Subtwo bent over his intercom. He started to call Madame, but he wanted to be certain he could offer her a concrete plan, not possibilities, after his first failure. He contacted the common room, and, after a few minutes' delay, Draco.

"What is the status of the ship?"

"It's coming along."

"How much work needs to be finished?"

"Couple weeks' worth."

"How quickly could it be completed in an emergency?"

"Something wrong? There's nothing that couldn't be jury-rigged in a day or so."

"Approximations are not required, but I would like to be able to leave should that seem advantageous."

Draco laughed, a quick short bark that annoyed Subtwo and amused Subone; Draco pretended anti-intellectualism and put on a face of contempt if anyone spoke to him multisyllabically.

"Okay," he said. "Five days, then?"

"Thank you." Subtwo tolerated being annoyed because of Draco's competence. He shut off the intercom and walked through his clean, pale, soothing rooms, anxious now to speak with his pseudosib and get that ordeal over with; Subone was fully as capable of taunting him as was Blaisse.

He opened the door as Mischa was about to knock. "Oh—you."

"Jan said you wanted to see me," she said.

"He does not delay, does he?"

She shrugged. "I'll come back some other time." She did not look like a genius of any sort, she looked like a maltreated stubborn child, wearing the same clothes she had arrived in, not exactly grubby, but far from spotless. Though self-assured, she was not arrogant, nor did her bright green eyes hold the superiority or surprise Subtwo might have expected in a newly confirmed genius.

"What did Jan Hikaru tell you when he sent you up here?"

"A minute ago he only said you wanted to see me. This morning he said he wasn't very good in math and he thought he'd ask you to help."

"I see."

"I think he's good," she said defensively.

So he had not told her all that he believed, or had not let her know how much it might mean. Subtwo wondered why he had kept his silence, and admitted, though the fact was not flattering, that Jan might not have wanted to raise Mischa's expectations without knowing that Subtwo would be of assistance. He was honest enough with himself to acknowledge that he had been very close to sending Jan and his time-consuming ideas away.

"Come in," he said. "I want you to do something."

He called up the biomedical programs and uncoiled the electrode wires. "Sit there."

"What's that?"

"Electrodes—instruments to sense your brain waves."

"I know that—what for?" She looked very wary, almost afraid of the simple devices.

"Just to test the responses of your brain. It takes only a moment. It doesn't hurt."

"What's on the other end?"

"A sensor," he said, wondering why she was asking such questions. "A recording device, for the computer."

"No patterns?"

"Like a lock? No, of course not. That would be pointless. This does not compare, it only examines."

"Okay," she said, and after that seemed quite relaxed. He fixed the electrodes at her temples with adhesive, for he did not approve of the self-attaching kind. He dimmed the lights.

"Look at that screen."

She shook her hair back from her eyes and complied, gazing at the console. The design changed, and changed again. He turned it off and raised the light level. "Very good."

"Is that all?"

"Yes. You may take off the electrodes." Subtwo glanced down at the results, and froze.

"Wait . . ."

And then he remembered what Jan Hikaru had said: "I don't need to test her neural responses. I've worked with her for weeks."

He knew his instruments were not malfunctioning. They measured the time it took a mind to respond to the change in a pattern, an interval measured in milliseconds. It did not depend on learning, culture, motivation, any of the factors that could cause achievement above or below the average for ability. It measured only potential, and Mischa's potential was tremendous.

"Never mind," he said, half in a daze. "It's all right. Tell Jan Hikaru that he was correct to speak with me. Are you free tomorrow morning?"

"I can be, I guess."

"I will see you then."

"All right." She was looking at him curiously; he had the strange sensation that she had felt his astonishment, but she left without saying anything else, and Subtwo leaned over the console, staring at the amazing parameter, feeling a great, deep sorrow that Mischa had not been born somewhere else, anywhere else, where she would not have wasted all the best years for learning, her childhood.

Madame walked slowly down the pale plastic corridor. She did not want to reach its end, for she had no way of knowing what awaited her there, in Subtwo's suite. She was prepared for anything; in her years at Stone Palace she had silently witnessed cruelties beyond anything she thought Subtwo could even imagine. Pain did not frighten her; she had endured and survived it when she was a child. At least, when Subtwo caused pain, it did not gratify him; nor did he intentionally cause humiliation. Madame had been prepared to endure either for many years. In Stone Palace both were, sooner or later, inevitable.

She scratched at the door, heard Subtwo's deep voice, and slipped inside as the door swung open. Before she could speak, Subtwo took a single step toward her, holding out his hands as though in supplication. "Were you there? Did you hear? Did you understand?"

"I know you met with the Lord," Madame said, without expression. All her experience warned her to be suspicious, to guard herself, to find some way to stop the progress of Subtwo's desire for her, and her own, gods help her, for him. Free people and slaves had only one kind of relationship, that dictated by their status. The free person ordered, the slave obeyed. And eventually the former would grow bored, or the latter would err. There was no happiness, only satiation for one, destruction for the other.

"Do you know what we talked about?"

"It is my duty to know—"

"Stop it!" he cried. "How can you speak to me this way? I could bear it if you hated me, but you don't feel anything!"

"I feel," she said. He was so beautiful, now assured, now vulnerable, trying to speak with his deep, deep eyes. "I feel. I was born human." She was saying too much: after so many years of protecting herself, she could say one unwise word and throw her life away.

"Do you understand why I tried to . . . to buy you?"

"It was not necessary." Somehow, this was worse, that Subtwo would place Blaisse between them, that the Lord's permission and urging would erase her degradation from Subtwo's conscience. She was a fool to have hoped someone already possessing freedom might refuse to take advantage of another's slavery.

"No," Subtwo said. "Not necessary, but safer. If he thought I owned you he couldn't hurt you—you'd be safe until we could leave. Now, we'll have to be more careful."

". . . Careful?"

"I might have been foolish. He might know I . . . I . . ." Subtwo stopped, shook his head, and started again. "He might try to avenge himself on me by hurting you. We mustn't give him a chance. But it would be dangerous to antagonize him until the ship is ready, so we must act as though everything were normal. When you go back, be careful."

Madame had trained herself to respond as though nothing surprised or confused her; she had no nervous habits. She stood utterly still. "What are you saying?" she whispered.

"Blaisse won't let me give you your freedom, so we must take it from him."

She stared at him. By the rules of Stone Palace, his power over her was total. She wondered if he were trying to make her feel grateful so she would come to him willingly, though he could simply command the appearance of willingness, false or true. But his temperament was at times so ingenuous that Madame could almost believe he was sincere.

"The ship will be ready soon, and we can leave. Then you'll be free—free to . . . to accept me or reject me of your own will."

"Leave earth?"

The new lines in his face were deep, strained. "You will come? I promise, I give my word. I know captivity. I would not ask demonstrations of gratitude."

"I must not speak of this," Madame said, quenching her wonder in apprehension.

"You . . . prefer to stay here?"

"No!" She took a deep breath, calming herself, relaxing her hands from clenched fists. "No. But I must not speak of the future with you. If I did, I would hope, and if I hoped, Blaisse would know."

Subtwo's face relaxed; his expression was almost a natural smile. "Then we've said nothing. We'll say nothing until my ship is ready. Soon."

They parted, neither making a move to touch the other. Madame left knowing that of all the difficult days of her bondage, the next few would be hardest.

10

Gemmi expanded through Mischa's consciousness, laughing with delight despite having been forced to seek her out. Mischa cringed. "No," she said softly. "Not now. Go away." But she was speaking to herself, not to Gemmi. Gemmi could not understand.

Mischa stilled her mind, stilled her body, hoping Gemmi would lose her, and waited. Gemmi could be reliving old memories; they came sometimes, unbidden, and the child had no way of stopping them. But this was real: screaming, she found Mischa again and whimpered, telling her to come, afraid of being hurt.

Mischa had been expecting the summons, knowing at least one was inevitable before Subtwo was likely to leave Center. She had not worried about it too much; as long as she continued to keep her plans secret, everything should proceed as usual. But the command had come at the worst possible time.

"I can't come now," Mischa yelled into her lonely room. "I'll come later. Tomorrow. Go away." Her voice echoing back and forth in Mischa's mind, Gemmi cried, and screamed again. Mischa knew that no reassurance but her own approach could calm her sister. She got up and pulled her cache from its hiding place, a fissure in the rock wall behind a tapestry. Under her jacket, the leather surface of the box of eyes was smooth against her skin. With the bag of lesser gems nestled in an inside pocket, she left her room.

Going down the hall, she met Jan. Greeting her, he smiled, but sobered when he noticed her grim expression. "What's wrong?"

"I have to leave."

"What about tomorrow morning?"

"I'll try to be back," she said. She would, but she knew there was no way of getting to the edge of the city and back by the time she was supposed to meet Subtwo. "I can't help it, there's something I have to do." Gemmi felt that she had stopped, and began to scream again. Mischa closed her eyes to concentrate on calming her. "I'm coming," she whispered.

Jan took her arm to steady her. "Are you all right?"

She looked up at him. His pale eyebrows were drawn together with concern; Mischa realized dully around the screaming in her head that she wanted to ask his help. "Yes," she said, in a resigned exhalation of her breath. There was nothing she could ask him for. She started away.

"Mischa?"

She turned back quickly, impatient now.

"If I can help—"

She shook her head. "No. Thanks. There isn't any way."

After the regular tunnels of Center, the caves began to twist downward. Mischa's family, when it had been a family, had lived in the roots of the system, almost in the deep underground. As Mischa walked, Gemmi pecked at her, urging her on faster. Mischa neither sped up nor tried to push her sister away. Gemmi was not being beaten now. Their uncle had stopped that since the time he had made her sick.

Mischa sometimes hoped he would kill her.

Gemmi screamed at the thought of death. The fear swept Mischa like the taste of molten copper. The intensity of emotion shook her, but she recovered herself and soothed her sister until Gemmi only whimpered. Mischa leaned against the rough stone wall. Gemmi did not know what death was, but it frightened her; anyone in her range who died, she felt. Her perception of dying was so unfocused and colored by fear that Mischa could not tell what made her so afraid.

When Mischa stopped shaking, she continued, passing through the wellcell and the cool sound of running water, through a familiar tunnel in which fewer light-tubes burned every time Mischa returned. They wore out, and no one bothered to replace them. Now, at night, they barely glowed.

Mischa knew everyone who lived down here: as many different types as individuals. A few had had a life and lost it. Some had never had a chance, and many simply did not care. She spoke to those who noticed her. They grew angry at pity, so she never let it show; there was no point in hating them; and she could not feel superior. They were much too close to her.

Gemmi had forgotten her fear almost as soon as Mischa turned her thoughts away from death. The child gurgled with excitement and pleasure as Mischa came nearer, until the voice of her mind mingled with audible, garbled words. Mischa pushed at the clinging sour fog of her, but Gemmi just bounced back and laughed. Their uncle knew the signs of Mischa's approach.

"Hurry up."

The door was left ajar for her to enter; she pushed aside the new, plush curtain beyond it. In a cave that always before had been dim, the light was dazzling. Her parents had not cared much about light, for they had been content in their own separate mind-worlds, growing more and more remote as the years passed, until one day Gemmi had begun to cry, so loudly and so desperately that both Mischa and Chris were drawn to her, to comfort her, to quiet her, somehow to make her stop screaming directly into their brains. She had reason enough: her parents were dead, and that must have terrified her, though the two dead faces wore expressions of peace. Mischa sometimes thought they had not so much died as pressed their existence to its logical extreme. She had seen so little of them in their life: she did not know what caused either's near-oblivion to reality. It could have been madness, withdrawal, apathy, or some capacity like Gemmi's for living in the minds of others. They had wandered about, seldom speaking, satisfying their biological urges, eating, sleeping, coming together for sex, neither bothering to suppress fertility. They and their children were cared for indifferently by the children's crippled uncle, supported first by Chris, then by Mischa.

Mischa's uncle: son of her father's father, of her mother's mother, half-brother to both Mischa's parents, who had not been related at all. A double half-uncle. He had never been happy, never been satisfied with subsistence rations. Since learning of Gemmi's power, his demands had increased, and lately accelerated. Now Mischa knew what he wanted the extra money for.

Bedecked in the style of Stone Palace, the old cave held soft cushions, tapestries, many lights. Delicacies, fruit grown outside, imported and expensive, filled a bowl on a low table. A companion lounged near the back of the single chamber, dozing or watching: one of the smooth, beautiful, sexless ones her uncle favored, but this one was classes higher than Mischa was accustomed to seeing down here. Classes higher, classes more expensive. Mischa knew the value of what she had stolen: not this much.

Her uncle lay on a wide couch, dressed in a long, full robe that hid his crippled legs. In bizarre semblance of happy paternity, he held Gemmi cuddled in his lap. She nestled against him, content with any scrap of human contact. She was younger than Mischa but bigger, and beginning to mature. She wore only a shirt; no one liked the job of keeping her clean. The shirt had lost all its buttons, and its gaping revealed her breasts. The heavy chain on her ankle still secured her to the stone wall.

Mischa stood frowning, overwhelmed by the aura of *wrongness*. Only Gemmi, with her murmurs, broke the silence. The other children, the younger ones, were gone.

"Say hello to Mischa, Gemmi." He smiled. His teeth showed, in the very center of his mouth, as though he were sneering.

Gemmi tumbled over Mischa like a sandfall, but Mischa took the assault without flinching. "Where are the kids?"

"Gone."

"Where?"

"Where do you think?"

The blood drained from her face. She had expected him to send them out to steal for him when they were old enough, but she had never believed, never even considered, that he would use them worse than that. Her voice was calm and low with rage. "You sold them."

"They're mine."

"They're not. You had no right."

He laughed, and the harsh sound echoed around them. "Did *you* want them?" Gemmi cringed against his warmth, not realizing it was he whom she feared.

"But *why?*"

He gestured around him, and she could feel his pent-up envy and hatred. "For this. For this, instead of crying brats and boredom and stink and pain."

"You could have—"

"Depended on their gratitude?" He laughed, bitter and ugly. "They didn't have your talent." He was enjoying his hold on her. "Gemmi couldn't touch them. I'd never have got a thing."

Mischa's eyes burned with tears of anger and guilt that she willed back. "Where did you send them?"

"Where you're going."

"You try and make me."

"You got caught."

"So what?" Her voice broke, high, angry.

"You can't do anything for me when you're in trouble."

"I wasn't flogged for stealing."

He laughed again. "Sure." A long drawl of disbelief. "That's a lot of scars for nothing." He held Gemmi closer, fondling her absently, in a parody of love. "Take off your shirt."

"No."

He started, flushing, then relaxed and smiled. Contentment did not fit easily on his face. "You might not be worth much. They like to start you clean."

Mischa caught her breath involuntarily, for he had just told her, by implication, that her two small brothers and her baby sister had been sold as beggars, to be mutilated at some owner's whim and made into performing animals.

"When?" She backed toward the door, ready to turn and run, do something, anything.

"Long enough," he said. "They wouldn't even recognize you now. All they know is that they have to beg."

Mischa touched her knife.

"Oh, stop it," he said. "They didn't mean anything to you. Stop pretending they did."

"That's a lie." But it was true she had never tried to take them and raise them as Chris had taken her. None had really been a person to her: though more aware than Gemmi, they had all been of severely limited intelligence. Mischa and Chris had kept them adequately fed, adequately clothed, but now Mischa knew she had had one more responsibility that would never be discharged, because it was too late. They had deserved a chance to have their own lives.

Her uncle thought of pain, and of delight in her humiliation. Gemmi broadcast it. Mischa forced the intrusion away, but her resistance only hurt the little girl, and Gemmi cried through the incomprehensible war. "Leave her alone," Mischa said. Her mind crawled and spun. "I won't do it."

"I have an investment in you," he said. "And I think I should get it back."

Mischa pulled the bag and the small flat box from inside her jacket. She threw the bag at his feet. "That's from Chris." The box followed. "And that's from me. See if you still think we can do better kinking with some chuckie or crawling in the dirt."

He picked up the bag first, hefting it. "Maybe I don't need to call him back after all," he said. "But I heard he's sick."

"He's all right," Mischa lied.

He tossed the jewels aside. "He's harder to call than you are. But I will call him if he doesn't do better next time." Leaning forward, reaching around Gemmi, he picked up the box, slid his fingers across the smoothly pebbled top, and loosed the delicate clasp. Open, the box caught the light in its interior and flung it, even brighter, against the new tapestries. The companion sat languidly up, but even such a small reaction was a serious breach of pose, revealing covetousness. Through her tears, Gemmi saw the reflections and reached for them. The eyes scattered in the sand. Her uncle shoved her off his lap and slapped her. Mischa felt the wrench of muscles and the clacking pain of teeth hitting together; she tasted the salt of blood. She caught herself against the wall. Gemmi lay on the ground, writhing feebly with half-formed crawling motions. Beside her, similarly, their uncle scrabbled in the sand, picking up the shiny bits, and his companion, swaying, moved to help. Mischa stumbled away from the cave. She had not gotten very far when he realized she was gone. Gemmi began to scream. Her insane and stupid mind swirled down around Mischa, suffocating her. She could feel Gemmi being beaten. "Mischa!" The only name she knew. Mischa turned back. One final blow smashed against her temple, and darkness followed the pain.

Suddenly everything was quiet, everything around her and in her mind. The stone wall was cool against her cheek. She pushed herself away from it and shakily stood without support. Gemmi was gone.

Mischa knew that if she went back to Center now she might be forced to return as soon as her sister was able to call, but she would not stay and wait to be summoned like a slave. For a short time, at least, while her sister was unconscious, no one in the world had any hold over her.

Jan Hikaru's Journal:

Ah, I don't understand. Mischa came, and now she's gone, but I don't know where or why, or even if she's coming back. When she did not return for her lesson, Subtwo called me in, asking where she was, and I gave him some kind of incomprehensible babble about emergencies. I'm worried about her, but I don't even know where to look for her. How can I help if I don't know what's wrong? I thought we had built up some trust . . . maybe her troubles require more than trust to solve.

I had to get out of Stone Palace, beyond the arc, the bars, the beggars. Only on top of the hills can one get even a spurious feeling of spaciousness; otherwise, anywhere in Center is like being in a cell.

Late in the morning, Mischa reached the floor of Center and started along the Circle. Gemmi had not called her again.

The cries of hawkers and drunks and parties and beggars closed in around her as she entered the arc. It was like walking through an invisible morass. A twisted child crawled toward her and caught at the back of her jacket. She walked faster. It clutched at her ankle. It mewled at her, and she broke into a run. She could not look at it, even with the sneer with which her peer group usually regarded beggars. Especially with the sneer. She was afraid to look at it, afraid of new mutilations on familiar bodies, afraid of blanked-out memories, afraid of the dull resignation in all the eyes.

She had always forced herself to do the things she thought she feared, but she did not force herself to look at the beggar. She fled it, running faster through the arc until her breath exploded in her throat with every inhalation. She pushed herself between people who grew angry and would have beaten her if they could have caught her. Tears spilled down her cheeks and half-blinded her, but still she ran. The deep sand seemed put there purposely to slow her down. Then, in front of the Palace, ranks on ranks of the beggars confronted her. She stumbled to a stop, and they turned to stare at her. She looked back and forth quickly, almost frantically searching for an alternate route that did not exist. A hand with only the first joints of fingers pawed at her; she shied like one of the caravannaires' ponies. "Get away—" They came closer, smiling when she looked away. They had two weapons in their trade: guilt and fear. Either was effective. The hunched, ancient children advanced on her; they knew her: the aloof young thief with never a coin nor a sympathetic word, only arrogance. They saw her scared; they smiled, baring rotten teeth. One of them laughed. Its voice was a high stringed instrument, badly bowed. Mischa backed away, until a rough wall barred her, the ramp above just too high to reach. She pressed her hands against the stone. The beggars moved closer to her, seething like a tide of rats. Mischa was frightened, but not of the physical danger they represented. She tried not to look at their faces. One moved toward her from the edge of the semicircle. She slammed him on the chin with the heel of her hand. Her hand sank into boneless flesh. Next to the wall, she leaped over him; she pushed past another and jumped for the edge of the helix-ramp. She pulled herself by her fingernails and began to climb, headlong.

Mischa left the door ajar behind her. The curtain of Chris's niche was torn a third of the way across the top and no lights showed beyond the gap. But Chris was there, she knew he was there: she stood very still and finally heard his shallow breathing, and felt him, almost silent in his mind. She pushed the curtain aside and saw him lying in his bed. She moved, and light from the doorway touched his hair. His eyes, half-closed, glinted beneath his long eyelashes.

"Chris?"

Some time later, he answered. "Yeah?"

"Can I stay here for a little while?"

Again a pause. Chris pushed himself up on his elbow, barely raising his shoulders and head. His bones were prominent. "Mischa?"

"Yes."

"Sure."

She slipped past the curtains. He squinted against the brief, bright illumination, gone before his translucent hand could cut the glare. Mischa glanced at the drab cloths hiding the far wall, relieved that anything on it was obscured.

"Hey," Chris said. "What's wrong?"

She sat on the floor next to him. "I just went home."

He touched her hand with fingers like a bat's wing, narrow and frail. "Can I help?"

She shook her head. He was helping just by being there and being alive; he was helping because though his eyes were bloodshot and the pale skin below them shadowed with exhaustion, his gaze did not wander.

"What else?"

Mischa had somehow almost forgotten how calming and pleasant Chris's voice was when he was not whining. He sounded concerned, and very tired.

"He sold the kids."

Chris tightened his hand on hers, slowly. "Ah . . ."

"We—" She stopped. She could not put any of the blame for this on him. "I never did anything for them. I should have taken them—"

"He would have made Gemmi make you bring them back."

"I could have *tried*. I couldn't with Gemmi, I couldn't stand her so close all the time, but maybe with them . . . like you did with me."

Chris looked away. "That was different, between you and me . . . it wasn't the same at all."

"Why not?" She said it dully, not for an answer, because she did not think there was an answer.

Chris shrugged without speaking, still staring at the covered wall. After a while he turned his head and looked at her and pushed himself half up. "Misch . . . Misch, you know if he really wanted to do it, there's nothing either of us could have done." His voice was gentle.

"Nothing . . ."

He reached up, lifting a great burden, and touched the drying tears on her cheek. She wiped them on her sleeve, quickly, ashamed. Chris moved over. "Come and sleep."

Gratefully, she slid under the thin blanket beside him. Chris did not tell her that everything would be all right, and for that she was grateful too. He took her in his arms and held her; in her exhaustion she could imagine him to be the dependable and defiant person he had been when both of them were younger. Huddled against him, she felt him smooth the tangled hair back from her forehead with a gentle hand that trembled.

Chris seemed not to have moved at all when Mischa woke up, nor, she thought, had he slept. But he had felt her waking; he was not shutting out the world.

"How are you?"

"Better," Mischa said. "Okay." She stretched, hands over her head, fists clenched. She sat up and looked around Chris's dim room. It was almost empty. The drab cloths hung across his work-wall like a shroud. She got up and wandered through the room; she was hungry, but there was no food.

"Chris, I'm leaving."

He raised his eyebrows in a question; they did not ordinarily explain themselves to each other.

"I'm leaving Center, I mean. The Palace has new people in it. I'm leaving with them in the spring."

"That's good, Mischa." She could hear nothing in his voice, no envy, no regret, no joy.

"Will you come?"

His green eyes appeared black in the dimness; then, for a moment, they caught light and reflected it like an animal's. He looked away. "No . . . hell, no."

"They could help you out there."

"Just go ahead and go."

"I don't want to leave without you."

"Yes you do."

"You know what I mean."

He closed his eyes and said nothing.

"Don't go sullen on me, Chris. Please."

"It wouldn't work."

"If you keep saying that maybe you'll believe it."

With his eyes still closed, he nodded very faintly.

"It'd be interesting," she said.

He shrugged and turned his head away.

Mischa began to get angry at him, and her voice rose. "It isn't working here, so what difference does it make?"

Shallow lines of annoyance crossed his smooth forehead, but he did not open his eyes when he spoke. "You were never like this before."

"Neither were you!"

The tension rose between them in the silence.

Chris let his breath out in a long sigh. "You don't owe me this."

She knelt beside his bed, leaning forward. "I owe you."

"Then leave me alone. Just leave me alone for a change."

Mischa sat back on her heels. The air felt cold. She stood up, crossed the room, and stood beside the shrouded wall with her fists clenched.

"Have you been working?"

He shoved himself up, abruptly, startled, attentive. His dirty hair fell across his eyes and he flung it back. "Get away from there." Chris never raised his voice. When he was most angry, his voice was this grating whisper.

Mischa grabbed the gray cloth. "Is this all that's left of you?" she cried.

He crawled toward her, out of the bed, across the floor, trying to get to his feet. He stumbled and fell forward. Mischa tried to catch him, but his hands and elbows slammed into the floor. He lay in the dirt, panting; he hid his face in his hands.

Mischa touched his grimy hair and took his thin hand, gently pulling it away from his face. Tears streaked the dirt. "Just come stay with me," Mischa said. "For a little while."

"All right," he said, without looking at her.

As Mischa approached the tall double doors of the pseudosibs' quarters, she could feel the emotionless passion of Subone flowing slowly around her, obscuring all but a tendril of intellectual involvement from Subtwo. She hesitated before knocking on the door, thinking that she could put this off, that she perhaps should not disturb him. She was already a day late. She knocked.

The door slid open. The geometric symmetry of Subtwo's quarters had not been disarranged by time. No echo or limestone odor hinted that the rooms were built inside a cave; no smell or sound indicated that a person lived within. Mischa went into the next room and found Subtwo sitting with his back to her, playing his computer as a composer might an organ. He did not turn; it occurred to her that with his automatic responses to external stimuli, he might have let her in almost without noticing. She waited behind him, but he did not slow his work, or turn, or speak.

"I'm back."

If he had not known she was there, he showed no surprise. He shifted slightly and Mischa could see the screen that had held an image of the corridor the first time she had come. Now her own face looked out, moving left when she moved right, and vice versa. She glanced at where the camera must be, for the angle, but could not find it.

"It's a new one," Subtwo said without looking at her. "It's very small." Continuing his work at the console, he watched Mischa via the screen.

"Where have you been?"

"In Center."

"Jan Hikaru said you had an emergency. I hope everything is all right."

"Not really."

"Fine."

She thought he was being sarcastic, but realized he had simply responded with one of his inappropriate automatic phrases, without listening to what she had said. "I need to talk to you," she said, rather louder than necessary. Now was not the best time to speak to Subtwo about Chris, but she was afraid to put it off any longer, now that he was here.

He glanced up at the screen, then over his shoulder at her, as though he had no image of a proper response and had to look for a signal in reality. "You missed your lesson."

"I know, I couldn't help it, that's—"

"It's all right," he said instantly, interrupting her. He stood up and wandered around the room as Mischa watched with astonishment. His wandering had a posed quality to it; he seemed to be trying it for the first time to see how it fit on him. Mischa had expected anger, sarcasm, or insult. Subtwo stopped before a shelf on which stood a sculpture with planes of symmetry in two dimensions. He turned it so the vertical symmetry faced obliquely and was much less obvious, put his hands behind his back, and regarded it. "I'll see you in the morning."

"In the morning?"

"We'll start your lessons then," he said impatiently. He left the shelf and moved to a desk, where he began systematically to disarrange the papers. Mischa both saw and felt the tension rising in him as he continued.

"What are you doing?"

He looked at her sharply, then slowly returned his gaze to the desk. "I have noticed," he said, "that . . . other people . . . do not live as I do." He moved the chair, and then the desk.

"People live the way they like to. If they can."

His face remained impassive, but the tension continued to increase. "I make people uncomfortable." He moved a table, and a couch.

"Other people make you uncomfortable."

The smooth skin of his forehead furrowed into two small vertical lines. Mischa realized that, in the short time since she had come, his face had begun to develop permanent lines of feeling and reaction.

"That is true." He turned his head, and the black hair fell across his cheek. "But I should, perhaps, make some concession."

"Why?" He seemed to her totally free to do as he pleased; though his tastes were bizarre, he forced them on no one, as others, considered normal, often did.

He raised his eyebrows, looked at his desk, and pushed a stack of papers back into place. He regarded the result, and smiled. "Well . . . perhaps not." He moved more papers. "Until tomorrow," he said, sounding eager. "Your lesson." The eagerness began to slide into excitement.

"I'd like to talk to you about something," Mischa said.

"Tomorrow, tomorrow." He finished straightening the papers, and concentrated on placing them in an even more symmetrical pattern. "Please, not now."

"It's important."

"Tomorrow!" His agitation engulfed her. He pushed the desk violently back against the wall and thrust the chair beneath it. Mischa clenched her fists. Working himself into a frenzy of delight, Subtwo rushed past her to replace the table.

Mischa turned on her heel and left.

Chris lay on Mischa's bed exactly as she had left him, flat on his back, eyes open, his thin body almost hidden in the soft mattress and thick comforters. Mischa stood beside him, watching, waiting, but he did not notice her until she touched him.

"Chris," she whispered. He blinked his eyes, but did not respond. Mischa swallowed and spoke more steadily. "Chris, do you want anything? Can you eat something?"

He licked his cracked lips. "I just want to sleep. Did you bring it?"

"There wasn't any more."

"Oh, yes," he said. "That's right. I finished it." He smiled, unpleasantly, vindicating himself. "You should have left me alone."

"Shut up."

He raised his head and Mischa could see some of his old spirit struggling up to strike out at her. "Did you think bringing me here would change anything?"

"I'll get you some," she said. "I'll get you something. Will you stay here?"

His cracked lower lip split; a thin drop of blood trickled down his chin. "I'll do what I want," he said.

Again, Mischa looked for Jan, but could not find him, nor could she wait. She supposed he had gone on another of his excursions into Center, which lasted sometimes as long as two days. He liked people more than she did, she thought; he liked to watch them and talk with them. She had accompanied him outside twice, taking him beyond the bars and brothels of the arc, telling him place names and landmarks, explaining the structure of the city and its society. The first time outside, people had reacted to him as they would to anyone from the Palace, with deference, suspicion, and fear. The second time, without Jan's having changed overtly, they talked to him, chatted, laughed, complained, and as Mischa listened, Jan's unaccented speech softened to match hers and theirs. He did not look like anyone Mischa had ever seen in Center, but now, somehow, he blended with her people.

She wished he were here now. She could not decide if coming to the Palace had weakened or strengthened her, whether she had a new resource or was losing her self-reliance, but she wished Jan were here now.

11

That evening, after search and argument and even pleading, Mischa headed toward the Palace with a capsule of sleep held firmly in her pocket. She hurried, thinking of Chris left alone the whole day. Few people used sleep, and it was difficult to find. The lights flickered in preparation for night.

"Mischa!"

Behind her, Jan Hikaru stepped from a hill path into the Circle. He was dressed in the same kind of clothes he always wore, but his boots were scuffed, his dark pants were dusty, and his jacket looked much older than it was. With his pale hair uncombed and his red-blond mustache bracketing his mouth, he had about him something of a brigandish air. Mischa thought Jan one of the gentlest people she had ever met, but had she just met him, she would choose to avoid crossing him. Waiting for him, stopping even for a moment, increased her concern for her brother.

Jan nodded a greeting and glanced up at the ceiling lights that alternately shadowed and illuminated his face. "That could induce epilepsy."

"How long have you been gone?"

"Since yesterday afternoon. Why?"

"You didn't get my message."

"No—have you been back?"

"Yes." Her worry increased, and a feeling more definitely crept into her mind. "Let's hurry."

"What's wrong?"

A threat of excitement drifted against her, bringing a tenuous link with Chris. "Subtwo wouldn't let me tell him—"

Startled, Jan said, "He didn't throw you out, did he?"

"No. Nothing like that." Above them, from the edge of the cavern to the center in a rapid spiral, the lights dimmed to half their intensity. "Oh, damn. Damn." She began to run.

She could hear Jan behind her, but her attention focused on Chris; when she reached the arc she realized he was not even in the Palace. She stopped and stood with her head down, eyes closed, listening, reaching out through a cacaphonous blend of music.

Just ahead, light-curtains filled the open front of a bar. Mischa slipped between and through their insubstantial forms, following Chris's faint aura. Among purple and green lights she saw him, standing against the wall, facing Subone who slapped him like a child playing snatch, with motions too quick to ward off. Mischa pushed the capsule of sleep far down in her pocket and buttoned the flap over it. Laughing, Subone spoke to Draco, who laughed in turn. His face set in anger, Chris pushed himself upright and moved away from the wall. He pulled his knife and snapped out the blade. Mischa hesitated, to watch him, feeling pride in the person he had been and might be again.

He said something to Subone. Mischa could not hear him, but she saw and felt Subone's rage. He reached for Chris's throat. Chris brought his knife up and slashed the pseudosib's bare forearm. Taunted by blood, the blade flashed ruby-red. Subone shrieked. Mischa could see from where she stood that the wound was minor.

, She knew what was going to happen before Subone reached inside his tunic. Chris could have fought on even terms. He was good; he had been good.

Mischa cried out and sprang toward them, but they did not hear her. Subone's weapon was a laser lance. Her reflexes took over. She threw her knife.

Fire seared her from shoulder to hip. She heard Subone, still screaming, as she collapsed.

Through the obscuring mists of soft color, Jan saw the flash of Subone's weapon beyond Mischa, and when she fell he cried out, believing she had been hit. He was vaguely aware that Subone had fallen as well, but the odor of seared flesh overwhelmed his senses. Clenching his teeth, he knelt beside Mischa and turned her over, afraid of what he would see. But somehow, aside from an abrasion on her cheek where she had fallen, she was unharmed. Her eyelids flickered; he felt her muscles tense as she collected herself. She stared up blankly, then intelligence leaked back into her green eyes. "Jan . . ." She struggled up, searching; she froze, and made an inarticulate, involuntary, keening sound of despair. Jan followed her gaze. He saw the young man lying sprawled in a scarlet and purple shroud of flowing lights. Jan could see the edge of a terrible burn rimmed by the charred and melted fabric of his shirt. Mischa stumbled to her feet, using Jan as a support. He helped her. "You're not hurt?"

"Not . . . burned," she said. "Get out of here, Jan. I don't know what's going to happen."

But he followed her toward Subone, who lay bleeding on the floor, groaning in pain and rage. Draco knelt over him, applying pressure to the wound high in Subone's chest. Mischa fell to her knees beside the young man. Subone lunged for his weapon. Jan kicked Subone's hand, hard enough to hurt and bruise, not hard enough to crack bones, and picked the lance up himself. He ripped out the power pack and crushed it under the heel of his boot.

"You are a fool," Subone said.

"And you?" Jan calmed a slow surge of anger and adrenalin.

"You jeopardize your position."

Jan said nothing.

"He's alive, Jan," Mischa whispered. "Gods, he's alive."

On one knee beside them, Jan took the young man's wrist and felt for a pulse among narrow frail-feeling bones. It was light, rapid, irregular. A crystal knife, held loosely, slid from limp fingers. The fight had not been between Mischa and Subone but between Subone and this boy. The smell of burned flesh and vaporized plastic hung heavy around him. Jan saw he could do nothing himself. Blankly, Mischa reached out and picked up the knife.

"I'll go for help," Jan said.

Suddenly, harshly, Mischa laughed. "Subtwo won't let you."

"When he finds out, I'll worry." He wondered briefly if Subone's actions might complete the pseudosibs' estrangement.

Mischa stood up. "He already knows." She gazed into the multicolored mists, the set of her shoulders, her face, her eyes showing no spirit, no hope, only defeat.

Agitated, the curtains swirled, and Subtwo burst through them, trailing wisps of their substance. He ignored all but his pseudosib. "What have they done?" Kneeling, he shouldered Draco away, and supported Subone in his arms. His eyes glistened with unshed tears of sympathy or actual pain. Subone sagged back, his expression set in suffering, weakened by loss of blood, or, Jan thought bitterly, arranged in a pose.

"I told you she'd do you no good."

With pure human hatred, Subtwo glanced at Mischa. "Everything will be all right," he said to Subone. His voice was a parody. His face became a mask of tender concern, the unfelt reaction of a man insufficiently experienced in tragedy or life. "I had hopes for you," he said to Mischa. "You could have gone anywhere and done anything."

"It's finished, then," Mischa said. "Because he's committed murder, and he wronged us—but you can't split yourself off from him."

"Yes."

Mischa looked down at the body by her feet. "I can't split myself off from Chris, either. Let me take him out of here."

Subone revived, grasping at Subtwo's shoulder. "Don't let them go."

"How much more do you want to hurt him?" Mischa cried.

"He's dead," Subone growled. "I want you."

The scene froze, like a dream going wrong and shading into nightmare. But dreams . . . dreams could be changed; Jan had stepped from the edges of his dreams to their centers, from the part of onlooker to that of director, and ordered the characters here and there, even characters like Subone, pure distillations of the self-centered unconscious. But he could not do that in reality; Jan understood that his own adventure was reality, or must become so. He could only direct himself, and he must: he must act rather than observe, make the decisions of his life rather than allow life to flow around him.

Jan spoke to Subtwo. "He's not like you any longer. You don't have to match him and he doesn't deserve your loyalty."

Subtwo said nothing, though the tiny lines in his forehead deepened. Subone, as if bored, said to Draco, "Take him out."

Jan allowed Draco to shove him, once. Then he braced himself, and when Draco, encouraged, rushed him, Jan turned, grabbed his arm and the front of his shirt, bent into his path, and threw him over his shoulder to the floor. Not knowing how to land, Draco fell hard and lay stunned. Jan had not helped him land, as it was possible to do when performing the *ippon sei o nagi*. Now he waited, in case Draco revived and reached for a weapon.

Subtwo faced Mischa warily, for the knife glittered in her hand. "You understand, don't you?" he said to her, as though asking forgiveness.

"I think so." Her voice held equal regret. "I should have killed him."

"No!" He cut his protest short. "No. That would have sealed our enmity." He gestured to Chris. "Take him, and leave." He looked sadly to Jan. "You align yourself against me. I can no longer keep my promise to your friend."

Subtwo appeared sincerely regretful, but Jan did not believe he had progressed that far; Jan believed that this was another of Subtwo's careful acts. Perhaps someday his feelings would match his words. "She would have understood what has happened," Jan said coldly, and saw that Subtwo missed the implication: that understanding did not equal approval.

Mischa appeared drained, precariously balanced on her endurance, yet angry and despairing and grateful, all at the same time. "You're crazy," she said. "You're just crazy." Beyond them, Subone said, "Don't let them go. Kill them now."

"We've got to get out of here," Mischa said. "Before they change their mind."

Subtwo spoke to Subone in a soothing tone almost inaudible to Jan. "I am not armed."

"Against a youth and a child?"

Jan knelt beside Chris, steadying himself against the sight of the terrible burn. It was as bad as anything he had feared. Its presence shut him off from the surroundings, the arguing voices, the world. Ancient words spun uselessly at the back of Jan's mind. He caught them and held on, closed his eyes for a moment, concentrated, set the phrases solidly; the nausea receded from the back of his throat. He touched the large vein at the corner of Chris's jaw. "I can't find a pulse."

"He's alive," Mischa said.

"All right." He picked Chris up. The mists flowed from the body, from Jan's arms, and swirled around Jan's feet.

"Will you let them go after what they've done to me?" Subone dug his fingers into his pseudosib's arm, as though to transmit his hatred.

"Come on, Jan." The urgency in Mischa's voice startled him.

Subtwo spoke, purring like a cat, in a tone of hunger and expectation. "When you are recovered, we will hunt."

The light-curtains slipped together and fused as Jan passed through them, following Mischa, and the voices became indecipherable.

Mischa led Jan to her niche as fast as Jan, burdened as he was, could go. Mischa was afraid Subtwo would be convinced by Subone's anger, and begin to hunt them now. They were somewhat concealed by the darkness, and by the reluctance of Center people to talk to offworlders, but Mischa had no doubt that Subtwo could have the lights turned on, and that he could frighten or bribe information out of almost anyone.

"In here," she said, and helped Jan bring Chris through the narrow fissure, a clumsy job. She was glad Chris had not regained consciousness. A flicker of life still glowed in him, deep down.

Her cave was exactly as she had left it; no one had tried to take it over. Jan stumbled and she remembered he could not see; she pulled the cover from the lightcells, which glowed faintly, their activity suspended by starvation.

Mischa straightened her rumpled blanket quickly; Jan laid Chris on the bed, stood back, and massaged the strain from his arms and shoulders. He could not quite stand upright, even in the middle of the chamber. Mischa opened her wooden chest and found cloth to use for bandages, and a mildly anesthetic salve that she did not think would help.

She knelt beside Chris and gently pulled the charred and melted edges of his scarlet shirt away from the burn. Skin and flesh came with it, and the wound began to weep. She choked. Jan knelt near her, moved her hands away, and sealed the air from the burn himself. The muscles along the side of his face were tight and strained; Mischa did not think he had seen much death or violence. She reached for him, to touch his arm, to thank him, somehow. He finished, wrapped the blanket around Chris, pushed himself back on his heels, remained head down and motionless. He tried to speak, cleared his throat, and tried again. "Sometimes the nerves are cauterized, and there isn't any pain." He looked up blankly. "I read that somewhere." Mischa could see that he too knew Chris was going to die, and that he did not know anything to say to her.

"I'm sorry," Mischa said. "I'm sorry I got you into this."

He grasped her hand, half-lowered from its hesitant gesture. "You didn't," he said. "Whatever happens, believe one thing: people are responsible for their own decisions, and no one else's."

"I wish I could believe that."

"It's true."

Perhaps it was, in the utopia she thought the Sphere to be, but not in Center. "It's my fault he's here like this," she said. "It's my fault you're stranded."

"Who is he?"

"My brother."

Jan nodded slowly. "But you told me once that you weren't leaving anyone."

"That's why I brought him to the Palace . . . I thought they might be able to help him."

Jan asked the question with his silence, with his expression.

She reached into her pocket and closed her hand around the yielding capsule, drew it out, and showed it to him. His pale eyebrow arched; he recognized the writhing white filaments of the drug.

"I had to leave him alone to get it. And . . ." Mischa doubted she would ever know if Chris had left the Palace in one last show of defiance, or if he simply had not known what he was doing.

Jan ran his hand across his tangled hair, a nervous gesture. "There isn't any way . . ." But he did not finish. "Then . . . what now?"

Her hands clenched like crabs. "I don't want him to die," she said. Broken glass, the words hurt, but they were said. "If he dies . . ." She felt the shape of the phrase.

"What about you?"

Mischa shrugged. The question had to be asked, and answered, but she could not make herself think about it now. "I don't know how close we are."

"Is there anything to do?"

"Only wait."

Kirillin hobbled through the sand, feeling clumsy and conspicuous, grateful for the night. *There's no grace,* she thought, *for a cripple.* The sand fell away from the path as she climbed a hill, searching. She could only look, and wait. Her leg hurt; she had no cane and saw nothing to pick up as a support. Her lower right eyelid began its tic, revealing her agitation despite her ruined and half-paralyzed face. Accelerating, time flowed past her. She had forced her angers to burn silently for so long that they were covered by an ashy gray layer of time. She limped onto a rooftop to stand among the dim voices of Center's lights. She did not understand people who left their windows unblocked and uncurtained; there was nothing to see beyond them, and the openings allowed others to peer in. She wished she had a cloak.

"Where are you, damn you?" She received no answer. Ashes flaked away. "I need your help." Her voice carried. Someone below shouted for her to shut up. She imagined vandalism to his house, but did nothing. Leaning down, she massaged her leg above the knee, feeling ridges of scar tissue move across muscle. She left the rooftop, and climbed.

The summits of the hills were not coveted locations, for they were difficult to reach and the view was a panorama of monotony. Alleys lay deep between buildings. Kiri's knee began to flash messages of pain that included ankle and hip. "Please," she whispered more calmly. "It isn't the time to punish me."

"My friend, the young skeptic."

Kiri spun, wrenching her leg; it collapsed and she fell forward. On her knees, she raised her head. Perspiration slid from her forehead down her cheek, from her armpits down her sides. Above her, gazing down with careless amusement, sat the person for whom Kiri had been searching. The healer was very old, stately, distinguished; she always seemed quite mysterious, and often quite mad. "Get off your knees," she said. "You look ridiculous. You could have been whole, and your weaknesses offend me."

Flushing, Kiri pushed herself to her feet and stood awkwardly with most of her weight on her good leg. The old woman's expression softened. "At least take something for the pain. I can give you something that would make you believe in me."

"I earned these scars," Kiri said. "I deserve them all. If I didn't believe in you, would I be here now?"

"Perhaps not. You're prouder than most of the rest of them. Despair does not give you faith. You should have lived when I was young. People were prouder and steadier then."

"I think you're badly needed now," Kiri said. "Will you come with me?"

The old woman shook her head very slowly, so for a moment Kiri thought she was observing the tremors of old age; then she realized her request was being denied. "Don't punish me through them!" Kiri cried. "You'll destroy Chris, and Mischa with him. They've done nothing to deserve it."

"I'm hardly that petty," the healer said archly.

"Then come!"

"No."

"But he may be dying."

"The boy has been dying for a long time. I would be helpless."

"How can you be sure?"

"My dear," the healer said, "my dear, do you really suppose my sources of information are no better than yours?"

Kiri glared sullenly at the path, and shifted her weight painfully. "Then you won't help them."

"I will not come with you."

"That's your final decision?"

"That is my only decision."

Kiri thought of things to say, and knew they would change nothing. She turned, head down, shoulder sagging, to make her way to the Circle again.

"Come back, you foolish child."

Kiri swung around like a challenged animal. "Don't play with me."

The healer stood on the ledge overhead, her dark robe shimmering about her. "Children never listen. Did you listen? I said I would not come, but I did not say I would not help." She flung a glittering bauble; Kiri snatched and caught it clumsily. "Take that and go."

The sphere was so black it appeared empty, a hole. It warmed Kiri's palm. "This is all you can offer them?"

"That is a life," the old woman said. "And a painless death."

"I know," Kiri said softly. "One life. I had hoped for two." She looked up, but the healer was gone.

Chris had no middle ground of drowsiness or sleep; Mischa felt him awaken abruptly from complete unconsciousness. His eyelids flickered; he peered out as from a tunnel, frightened. Mischa felt his confusion, his disorientation, and touched his uninjured shoulder to give him some contact with reality. "You're in my niche, Chris."

He opened his mouth to speak, but began to cough, and then could not stop. The foam on his lips turned pink, and pain shot through him in uncontrollable spasms. Mischa hunched her shoulders against it, and felt Jan's hands on her shoulders, steady. The coughing eased, slowed, stopped. Chris lay exhausted, his green eyes wide open. "I might have known," he said. His voice had become harsh and ugly. He began to laugh, but cut himself off abruptly. "Your niche. I might have known."

"Chris—"

"Do you think you're my owner?" He shoved himself up on his elbow, and fell back with a shriek of agony. Mischa caught her breath at his reflections. "Let me help," she said. "Please . . . let me help." Her voice shook.

"Leave me alone." He turned away, moving only his head, very slowly.

"Mischa—"

She shook her head, breathing hard, not looking at Jan.

"This is going to tear you to pieces." He touched the sweat already filming her forehead.

"I can't leave him. I owe him too much."

Jan gripped her arm, as though to convey to her some of his own strength.

"Mischa . . . ?" Chris flickered back to awareness, clear and innocent and forgetful, and Mischa's hurt dissolved.

"I'm here."

"Have you got any sleep?"

She brought it out of her pocket. His anxiety and his need increased, and Mischa could feel his disappointment that she had only one capsule. "It was all I could get," she said. "They didn't want to give it to me." She put it in his mouth. He sucked it greedily, and as the capsule dissolved the feel of writhing filaments against Chris's tongue nauseated her. As they dissolved, he changed again. Becoming more aware, he looked at Mischa with her own eyes. "Thanks."

"Yeah."

He retreated. So little of the drug could not let him sleep; it pushed him slowly back through stages of exhaustion. The pain crept toward him from another direction.

"When are we leaving, Mischa?"

For a moment, she could not even think what he meant. She clamped her hands against her temples. The pulse throbbed beneath her palms. She concentrated on the patterns of scratches on the stone floor. "Soon," she said, and hoped he would not hear the lie.

"When?"

"In the spring. As soon as the storms are over. Maybe even before."

"That's good," he said. "That's good . . ."

The silence stretched out like a taut wire. Once they had talked, when the balance between their giving and taking was almost even, after Mischa was old enough to take care of herself and steal for both of them, before Chris had forced himself, or felt himself forced, down this endless path.

Mischa heard him move, and braced herself, but that did not help. She looked up, and he was lying with his head thrown back, the tendons in his neck quivering. Beneath the blanket that covered him, his hand clutched the bedding; he seemed to be searching for any sensation but the pain. "Oh, gods, Mischa, it hurts . . ." A tear squeezed out, beneath his long, fine eyelashes, slid down, back, into his hair.

Mischa choked on a sob but could not stop it.

"Mischa . . ."

When she realized Jan had spoken to her, she turned. He sat against the wall, looking down at his hands, flexing his strong fingers very carefully. Watching him, she shuddered.

"It wasn't enough," he said.

". . . No. I couldn't get any more."

"What do you want to do?"

"I don't know." Her mind felt dulled and slow, distracted by Chris's visions, and though she realized she must begin thinking again in terms of Center rather than in terms of escaping it, the backward transition was very difficult.

"I'm offering my help, Mischa, for gods' sake, will you accept it? There must be someone or something in this city that will ease him."

"Will you go?"

He hesitated. Mischa hunched in on herself, preparing for an argument.

"All right," Jan said sadly. "I'll go."

Jan left the cave, disturbed that Mischa would be linked to Chris, yet alone. But she was so little afraid of what might happen to her that he could do nothing more than she asked. He could have argued, but he would have lost.

The lights had not yet begun to brighten. Jan had no idea what time it was, but he thought at least half the darkness must remain. He had never seen anyone claiming medical knowledge in Center, and he wondered if Mischa, in her remaining unsophistication, had sent him hunting a faith healer, a fraud, a charlatan.

He stopped at the junction of radius and helix where the main cave opened out before him. The dim canyon of the Circle below held no movement, but in front of Stone Palace, along the arc, a crowd of people was gathered.

Jan started down the helix, running, letting gravity pull him along, beside the precipice. Below and before him, a figure toiled up the slope, head down with the effort of movement. In the dark, Jan could tell nothing about the person, past the lameness. He slowed as he approached so they could pass safely on the narrow path. The figure was a young woman dressed in black, who raised her head as he approached. He nodded to her and looked away, not because the birthmark and scars revolted him; they did not, but he thought she might be sensitized to stares.

As he tried to pass, she grabbed him, clamping her fingers around his arm with great strength. Startled, he stopped, and this time did not avert his gaze when she looked at him. Her face was grim and strong beneath the scars.

"You're Mischa's friend," she said. "From the Palace." She spoke with an undercurrent of urgency.

Jan did not feel a need for evasion. "Yes."

"Is Chris still alive?" Her voice was steady, but her hand tightened on his arm.

"I'm going for help for him."

She released him and extended her other hand, in which lay a small opaque black bauble. "This is what you're looking for."

"Mischa asked me to find someone—"

"I've seen her. She won't come. She sent this."

Jan glanced out at the hills, where he had been sent. The woman took his arm again, shaking him. "You won't find her."

"But—"

She pointed at the crowd. "Do you see them? When they come this way, they'll be looking for you."

Jan still hesitated, seeking the truth in her face, finding that, and desperation.

"If I could run," she said, "I'd gladly let you go on and get caught. But there isn't time to waste. Mischa needs this."

"All right," Jan said. She tipped the dark sphere into his hand. It was vaguely soft, warm, reflective, spreading shapes across its surface.

"She'll know what it is."

"Thank you," he said. Holding the bauble as gently as he would a winged insect, Jan began to climb the hill again, leaving the crippled woman behind. He glanced back once. Half-obscured in dim light, she followed slowly.

Mischa sat with her face buried against her knees, as though shielding her eyes from the claws of dark demons. In the dull blue light, they could easily be fluttering unseen above her. Jan laid his hand on her shoulder and was surprised when she started.

"I'm sorry," he said. "I thought you'd heard me."

"Chris was hallucinating. It—I hoped you'd get back, but—where is she? How did you get back so soon?"

Jan held out the black bauble. "She gave this to a woman with a birthmark and scars on her face. It's for you."

Mischa stared at it silently. The hope ran out of her face with the blood, leaving pallor.

"She's not coming?" Her voice was totally emotionless.

"This seemed important. To get it to you. But I can—"

Mischa was shaking her head, staring at the black sphere as though she and it were alone and Jan was speaking to them from a great distance. Worried, he closed his fingers around it. Mischa grabbed for it, but Jan drew back. "What is it, Mischa? What will it do?"

"Give it to me, Jan."

He simply looked at her.

"It will help him die," Mischa finally said.

Shaken, he let her take it from his hand.

Mischa pulled back the blankets. Chris murmured a quiet, unconscious imprecation. She was glad he was not awake and could not see what she was doing. She did not want him to know he was dying. She could feel his dreams fading and dissolving as he weakened; the drug had pushed him back to the state he had sought, but still would not let him rest. She pulled the charred and fused edge of his shirt away from the bandage, cutting the material with Chris's knife until his chest was bare. The black sphere she placed in the hollow of his breastbone, next to the edge of the wound. It shivered as it touched him, and suddenly shattered with a sharp high sound. Even expecting it, Mischa flinched, throwing up her hand, but nothing touched her; whatever the sphere had done, it had not exploded. The black fluid spread slowly across Chris's chest, flowing first over the wound and then beneath the bandages, which curled away and disintegrated.

"Good gods," Jan whispered. The spreading shell reached Chris's throat and paused, crept across his stomach, beneath his pants to his groin. The material flaked away into ashes, and finally his shirt crumbled.

"What is it?"

"It . . . drains away the pain," Mischa said. "I've never seen it before, I've only heard about it."

"I've never seen anything like it before."

Mischa reached out and touched the slowly expanding layer of shiny plastic. It was very cold, and her fingers came away damp with condensation. The black shell closed around Chris's chest, and rippled slowly with his breathing. "In the Sphere," she said, "in the Sphere, could they have saved him?"

She could not tell why he hesitated. He might not know if they could have helped her brother; he might not want to tell her that anywhere else, he need not have died.

"I don't know," he said. "Maybe, if someone had been right there."

"I can feel him getting numb. It hurt him before, but he doesn't feel it now . . ." Her voice trailed off as she felt Chris begin a slow searching-out of consciousness, and she became resonant to his echoes, as though she were hollow. She put her hand to his face, to shield his eyes, to comfort him.

"Mischa?"

"Yes, Chris."

He started to reach for her with his right hand, but the muscles were deadened. He relaxed and lay still, spending all his energy for breath. Then he reached up left-handed and drew Mischa's hand away, holding her gently, not letting go. Raising his head, he looked down at himself and saw the blackness. The pinpoint pupils of his brilliant eyes dilated slightly, then closed back down. "Oh, gods." Pink foam was collecting on his lips. "What's going to happen?"

"I don't know," Mischa said. "I was never close enough before."

"It scares Gemmi."

". . . Yes."

Chris did not respond, and Mischa searched for some way to reassure him. "Everything different scares her. She can't tell good from bad."

Chris tried to smile, but his smile was gone; Mischa saw both their fronts of bravery crumbling. "That's right," Chris said. "I . . . I know that . . ."

"Try to sleep," Mischa said, a rote line to dam up the thousand things she would rather have said.

"Mischa—" His hand clenched around hers with some of his old strength. "I wanted to go with you." He closed his eyes, exhausted again. "Nothing worked the way it was supposed to." He looked at her again. "I'm sor—"

"Don't." They had had arguments, but never recriminations; disagreements, but never blame. That was the honor between them, that they were, finally, responsible only for themselves.

Chris nodded, lay back, and let himself rest.

Mischa felt tears slipping down her cheeks and realized Jan was still there, still quiet, still watching. "Damn," she said. "I never cry."

He put his hands on her soulders. She stiffened.

"No one can use it to hurt you."

She did not believe that. She had kept herself to herself for so long, in self-defense, that she could not believe it. And she had thought that she trusted Jan, but the trust was not quite strong enough. She felt her control slipping away as Chris's visions whirled around her. His exhaustion wrapped her; she wanted to sleep for him, to enter his dreams. His mind opened to her more deeply than it ever had before; she glimpsed his torments and his pride, his hopes, his weaknesses, his shames, his love, slipping through the synapses of his brain, slowing with the cold and the cessation of his pain. The black shell grew, sucking warmth from him, from the air, from Mischa. She shuddered, and Jan pressed her shoulders, looking down at her, frowning.

"He took me when I was born," she said. "He raised me. He even named me. He used to be beautiful."

She had never before lost anything, so irrevocably, that she cared about. Whatever she had lost before, she had told herself it never really mattered. Now that was impossible.

She put her fists against Jan's chest, and cried.

12

Kiri climbed awkwardly into Mischa's niche, but this time she did not wish for a place easier to find and enter.

"Kiri," Mischa said, relief obvious in her voice.

Kiri struggled to her feet. She glanced beyond them, to Chris. She had not wanted to see him like this. She had not really thought she would ever see him again. "Mischa, I'm sorry—" Her voice caught and she fell silent. Mischa nodded.

"You've got to get out of here."

"Not yet."

"Everyone's after you. The news travels faster than I do—there was a mob in the Circle before I started inside."

"They don't know where to find me."

"A few of them are offworld people. They have ways we don't even know about."

"She's right," Jan said.

"Go ahead, then." She turned her back on them, self-controlled again. The black plastic helmeted Chris's hair. Urgency warred with Mischa's stubbornness; Kiri was almost beyond patience.

"They're after you too," Kiri said to Jan.

"So you said."

"You seem very calm about it."

Jan shrugged.

"Have you had a price on your head before?"

Despite himself, despite the situation, Jan laughed. "A price? No."

"Do you think they're hunting you for love of the pseudosibs? You're worth a good deal of money, so be careful around strangers."

"I appreciate the advice."

Mischa backed away from Chris, bumping into Jan. Chris's face was immobile and waxlike; in the blue illumination, Mischa seemed as pale.

"Mischa?"

She did not answer. Her expression was blank, her pupils contracted.

"Get her out of here," Kiri said to Jan. "Go as far as you can, stay as long as you can. When you *have* to come back, come at night and I'll try to help, at least I'll know if you're still being hunted."

His expression changed. Kiri believed this was the first time he had really understood how serious a situation he was in. He nodded, and urged Mischa toward the fissure. Mischa moved like an automaton.

"Wait," Kiri said. "Have you got a light?"

Mischa seemed not to hear her, but Jan turned back. "No."

"Here." She held out her flash. She wondered how he would survive in the darkness, in the underground. But for now, this was the only option.

"Kiri . . . ?" Mischa's voice sounded lost, childish.

"It's all right, Mischa, go ahead."

"Not much longer . . ."

"Hurry up," she snapped. "Get her away from here."

Jan nodded a quick thanks, accepted the flashlight, and took Mischa into the corridor.

In the blue bioluminescence, alone with Chris, Kiri missed her light immediately. Like others, she had been more careful of carrying it since the main lights' failure those few terrifying minutes. She drew the bowl closer.

Only Chris's face remained free of the plastic. Bending down awkwardly, Kiri touched his smooth, cold cheek. In all the years she had known him, his life had been strong and his living a celebration. Now, emaciated, drained, he was no more recognizable than she was to herself; in her mind she was not the pitiful creature who hobbled instead of running, who stared out at her from reflective surfaces she could not avoid. She moved her fingertips to Chris's temple, feeling for a pulse. The only sensation was of cold, as the shroud pulled the last bits of energy from his body. The plastic pushed her fingers slowly, almost imperceptibly, across his forehead. Kiri realized that Mischa had not left before her brother died. And Mischa was alive: that was some relief. But she had been affected. When Kiri was powerless, she worried more.

She pushed back the light and did not look at Chris again. She had watched such an engulfment years before, and every moment of it had repeated itself in her dreams, in her daydreams, in brief moments of inattention, again and again. Now, in order to take her memories back to more pleasant times, she had to see it once more. Though she expected and waited for the sudden liquid clicking, it startled her. The plastic sealed itself over Chris's eyes. The echoes of the end faded; Kiri's duty was finished. Chris lay shrouded in the dark, and she could do nothing more.

She left without looking back. In the tunnel, limping slowly, tiredly, back toward Center, she watched as the mob passed. Most of the people carried lights, a few carried weapons, none had supplies. Driven only by their greed, they would falter at the deep underground. Kiri did not think Mischa and Jan had too much to fear from them; she doubted that even the few offworld people would go far. But soon, the pseudosibs would come, and then the danger would be real.

The light-tubes stopped; the rough, natural tunnels continued downward, branching and narrowing as Jan's flash sought out the straightest course.

Sometimes Mischa negotiated dangerous ledges automatically; sometimes Jan had to help her along precarious distances. She did not speak, she did not react. Sometimes they were surrounded by echoes, the distorted sounds of running water, air currents . . . their pursuers.

But finally, they had to rest.

Jan held Mischa, urging her gently back to awareness. She looked up into his black eyes, that seemed so strange paired with his bright blond hair. His golden skin was smudged with dust and his jacket, open, was sweat-stained in large patches.

"Are you all right?"

She felt the heaviness in her limbs, and glanced past him; recognizing the place, she noticed listlessly how far into the deep underground they had come. Her eyes would not track properly. She mumbled something that even she did not understand.

"Never mind," Jan said. "Go back to sleep."

Mischa sat bolt upright, crying out, caught in the midst of fragmentation. She grew aware of Jan, steady, calming, flawlessly whole.

"Dust," she whispered.

"What?"

"Dust. It was like he turned to dust. He had nowhere to go. There's nothing left of him. . . ." Unfamiliar tensions built up, closing her throat, blurring her vision, and she had no strength to stop them. Her face was wet.

"It hurts for a long time," Jan said finally. "But the pain fades."

She held him tightly and slept.

Mischa felt herself being shaken from a deep and dreamless sleep. She did not feel tired, but lethargic, lost, and stupid.

"I think we'd better go on."

She looked at Jan for a long time. His cheek was flushed and imprinted where he had pillowed it against his arm. The light cast shadows about him and glinted from the fine gold hairs on his chest. She blinked slowly, but the meaning of his words eluded her. He took her hand and helped her up. She did not resist.

Always, they continued downward.

Jan led Mischa on, following the insubstantial beam of Kiri's flashlight. He became more and more aware of his debt to her; blind, he would long have been lost.

Mischa was paying no attention to him or to their surroundings. He progressed from being glad she had survived her brother's death to worrying whether she had survived intact.

The caverns were beautiful in their changes, but so many subtle variations slid by, obscured by the dimness, that Jan felt effects of sensory deprivation. He had to force himself to listen for sounds of pursuit; then, with the concentration, his mind began to play games with the echoes of their footsteps and their breathing, until they might have been walking with an army. He had no count of hours. He searched for anything he might have done to change what had happened, and found nothing, until his self-inspection arrived at the immediate past, and memories he tried to avoid.

The religious rituals kept in his father's house had been re-created or invented to uphold the old man's delusions. The rituals had never meant anything to Jan, nor had he ever found a faith that suited him. Though he had never made a conscious decision not to believe in anything at all, disbelief was easier, now, after Mischa's mumbled words. Whole philosophies had been built on less. He had to keep telling himself not to take too seriously what she had said in the midst of exhaustion, nightmare, and grief, but he could not stop thinking about what they might mean. *He had nowhere to go. . . .* But perhaps she had not been able to follow Chris far enough to *know* what happened.

Jan knew he was only trying to comfort himself in the face of eternity, infinity, entropy. It was not what he wanted: a destruction rather than a justification or confirmation. Yet, if he was not to begin ignoring unpleasant information, perhaps all philosophies were wrong: no afterlife, no vengeful and malevolent hell, no meretriciously sentimental heaven, not even the unself-conscious awareness of Nirvana. Simply, finally, nothing. He glanced at Mischa, moving expressionless and uncomprehending, and wondered if anyone who understood what she had seen would be destroyed.

The passage jogged and ended in a steep and narrow tube. Above it, painted on the stone, a spidery symbol flashed back the light, then phosphoresced, pale silver-green. The delicate design was the only evidence Jan had seen of human beings in the deep underground. Jan held the light at the tube's mouth, but saw only shadows below. He grasped Mischa's shoulders. "Mischa, try to understand, do you know where we are? Do you know what's down there?"

Mischa looked into it blankly and shook her head. Jan could not tell if she were answering, or refusing to answer.

"We'd better try another way."

She suddenly put her hands in her tangled hair and clenched them into fists. "No . . ."

Just the fact that she had spoken gave Jan great relief. "Are you all right? Can I do anything?"

"Just . . . be calm." Her words were slow and carefully formed. "Be quiet, the way you were," and he understood she did not mean word-silence.

"I'll try."

Jan crawled into the narrow shaft. It was barely wide enough for his shoulders; he did not want to think about getting out should it narrow any farther. He heard Mischa following. He hoped she would keep on; he wished they could move abreast instead of in single file. Following her, he might drive her into a danger neither of them saw; leading her, he might not know if she stopped.

In places the tube widened slightly and he could see her. She did not speak again, but seemed to have retreated from even partial awareness.

Several times the passage narrowed almost beyond Jan's ability to slide through. It twisted and turned, always leading downward, now dry and solid rock, now damp, terrifying, and muddy. It continued for hours, like some topological freak that led onward forever. Jan's knees and elbows began to ache with bruises; his hands were rubbed raw. His shoulder muscles screamed from the constant downslope. Before him the tunnel stretched out or closed in as the angle of the light changed. It was awkward to carry the flash and crawl.

He thought he could feel a slight air current; then he thought he glimpsed an open space beyond the confining walls. Incautiously, impatiently, he plunged forward. The light glinted from the floor and ceiling, but he could hear the hollow echoes of a cave. He pushed on.

His hands came down in knives. He gasped and pulled himself back reflexively, away from the pain. Above him, blades ripped through his jacket and into his flesh, breaking with the sound of wind-chimes. He cried out and fell forward again, over the rim of the tube and into the empty space beyond. The light rolled away, clattering, metal on stone. The point of his shoulder hit rock and he slid down an incline; he fell into sand and lay curled around his hands. Blood gushed from his palms and wrists, and down his back. He felt on fire. His hand brushed a shred of cloth and the nerves shrieked.

"Mischa—"

He could not see; fear that the light was broken or that he was blind were almost equal. He realized he had called Mischa into the same trap and tried to warn her, but heard only his own shaky, disembodied moan. He tried to get up, struggling to elbows and knees, trembling there, unable to raise his head. When he tried to move, shards of shattered crystal ground against each other, cutting deeper, working their way toward bone. Hearing seemed the only sense he had left, except pain, and every sound was thunder. He tried again to warn Mischa, and even his hearing dimmed. He lost consciousness.

Mischa heard the crystalline music, and felt Jan's cry of pain and warning. She knew that she should understand what had happened, but the effort was too much. Without Jan's calmness and unspoken encouragement, she stopped, confused and apathetic. The stone beneath her hands was cool and comfortable; she lay down and put her forehead against it. She felt battered and numb. Needing time to rest and sort her thoughts and feelings, she had let herself be pushed on, withdrawing to the interior of her mind, leaving free only an isolated bit of reason.

No echo of Chris remained. Always before, no matter how far apart they were, a resonance had existed between them. That contact was gone, leaving scattered bits of blankness, like a painting leached of a single color. Mischa did not believe anything could replace the loss: she might fill in around the spaces, close them off, but the spaces themselves would still remain. She found herself unconsciously reaching out for contact with her brother, and stumbling into his nonexistence. She did not yet accept his death, though she had slipped with him from half-sleep to unconsciousness to coma. She had been pulled into the dissolution of his personality, losing contact only at the last critical moment, when she realized how deeply immersed she was, how closely her own thought processes paralleled his disintegrating ones, how near her mind was to fragmentation.

After freeing herself, she had still had to watch and feel Chris die.

She had never thought very much about death, deflected, perhaps, by Gemmi's terror of it. That, at least she now understood. With no belief in any afterlife, nor any philosophy of a soul, she had still felt that beneath the intricacies of personality every person must possess some basic and immutable core. Yet she had seen that there was nothing left of Chris. Each facet of him had shattered, and the shards had collapsed into uniformity: complexity into homogeneity. An end product of entropy. Nothing.

That seemed very welcome now. She was so tired, and all her chances were gone, worth as much as a cat's tenth life. She had tried as long as she could, longer.

Yet she heard the crystals shatter again . . . with some satisfaction, that *she* would not have to face them. Then she felt a hesitant touch on her shoulder . . . and tried to ignore it, but the presence of a living being drew her back up.

"Leave me alone . . ."

A soft clicking sound echoed in the narrow tunnel, and the creature that made the noise reached out to her with its mind, resonating on familiar overtones, sharp, clear, unverbal. Human, yet ninety degrees skewed from any human mind she had ever encountered, the square root of minus one. It was not an infant, it was not unintelligent, but it had no words. It met her and pulled her back to life with the joy of its greeting. Its kinship was unmistakable. It latched onto her, urged her, dragged her, forced her to return.

Sighing, unwilling, Mischa opened her eyes, turning her head so her cheek lay against the stone. The creature bubbled and shifted, and the crystals sang again.

Mischa remembered Jan Hikaru.

Adrenalin pushed energy into her tired body. She got to her knees. The creature squatted before her, in the midst of the crystals, impervious to them. He was barely recognizable as human, his body wide and flat, hunched over short, bowed legs, his head hardly distinct from his shoulders. His eyes protruded. He raised his hands—his claws—and clicked horny digits together. Only his thumbs were distinct; all his other fingers were fused into one. His skin was thick and scaly.

"I have to get to Jan," Mischa said, projecting the image, hoping he would understand. He backed up to the mouth of the tunnel and slid out of sight.

Sliding her hands, Mischa crept forward. The tunnel was warm enough to see, and the crystal gardens above and beneath were cooler, darker, black-shattered waiting spears. The broken bits soaked up heat and blended into the floor, unshadowed. When her fingers brushed sharp edges, evoking the cruel and toneless music, she stopped, braced her feet against the stone, and jumped.

She cleared the treacherous crystal growths, twisted, landed awkwardly in deep sand. The underground person huddled beside Jan.

Blood glowed scarlet, and Jan's mind was very quiet. Mischa touched one of the bits of glass against her tongue. The taste was like acid, sour and sharp. She spat it out: no natural compound, mineral, insoluble, but one of the chemical wastes that leaked from Center's industrial processes.

Jan's jacket tore as she bared the long slashes down his shoulders. The blood flowed freely, prevented from clotting; in a less extensive wound that would have been good, but Mischa could already see the difference in Jan's body temperature. Probing carefully, she found an unyielding shape. As though Jan had been snakebitten, she leaned down and sucked until the crystal point emerged. She spat it out.

The creature hovered, projecting worry and regret that he could not help.

"Is there anyone else down here? Is there anyone you could bring?"

The creature scuttled a few steps into the exit tunnel, and back. Mischa bent down again. She could not take time to explain.

Jan's blood salty against her lips, Mischa could feel his hammering pulse as she worked, and she did not think she would get the poison out in time.

"Crab?"

Mischa looked up, startled by the voice. A blue glow of bioluminescence flowed around her. She made out two people beyond it. They stopped: a slight and fragile-looking red-haired woman, a taller, heavier, bearded man. They wore leather, spider-silk, and weapons. They stared at Mischa. She stared back.

The creature scuttled toward them, clicking his claws. The woman reached for him, but he evaded her. He returned to Mischa and touched her hand and Jan's hair.

"He fell through crystals," Mischa said, hoping they would understand. "I have to get them out."

They came toward her. She flinched when the shaggy, ferocious man reached toward her. He knelt down. The woman stood farther back, but moved slowly closer. Mischa saw her more clearly and reached instinctively for Chris's knife, then let her hand fall again, with no idea why she had, for an instant, been so afraid.

"We will help," the woman said.

Jan remained unconscious, but Mischa and the underground people could find no more of the sharp bits. Mischa sat back on her heels and lowered her head, nauseated by the poison she had not been able to avoid swallowing. She did not want to consider the dose Jan must be fighting.

Now, having done as much as they could to save her friend, the underground people watched her. In the blue light, they looked like ghouls, black with blood. Mischa wiped her own face; her sleeve came away smeared. She closed her eyes, shuddering. The misshapen little creature who had found her touched her hand. She grasped his claw and was comforted.

"Come," the red-haired woman said. "We'll take him to a better place."

The huge man picked Jan up easily and gently, and started out of the cave. Mischa stood, and stumbled.

"Wait, Simon." The red-haired woman steadied and helped her; Simon stopped for them.

"Thank you," Mischa said. "Who are you?"

"I am Val."

Mischa was lightheaded and sick; Val and Simon seemed more immune to the poison. She wanted to ask more questions, but had to lean on Val and use all her own energy for walking.

A dry, dimly illuminated chamber contained Val and Simon and Crab's possessions—few enough, Mischa thought, to carry away all at once. They had a blanket, which they wrapped around Jan. Mischa sat down, grateful to be able to stop, but frightened by Jan's pallor and the silence of his mind.

"Do you think he'll be all right?"

Val glanced at her quickly, lowered her gaze, looked to Simon; she seemed to withdraw.

"He still might die," Simon said.

Previously, he had not spoken. The relief and gratitude in Val's expression gave a reason for the breaking of his silence, but no clue to the keeping of it. His voice was low and pleasant; his teeth were sharp. His fingernails too, were sharp, by nature or by artifice, but they were also very thick, like claws, and he could extend them like an animal's. His hands seemed to Mischa an insufficient reason for banishment.

"We'll do all we can," Val said, easier now.

"He doesn't deserve this," Mischa said. "He's down here because of me." Before, Jan had had no terrors, but Mischa had hurt him now, thrice over. She had pulled him into isolation, and introduced him to pain, and taken away whatever beliefs he might have had about death. She never would have said a thing to him about the last minutes of Chris's life, not a thing, had she known what she was saying. She knew him too well to hope he might have dismissed her words as the meaningless product of nightmare.

Crab nestled in the sand near Mischa's knee, half-burying himself, waving one claw contentedly, taking her hand in the other, drawing her from guilt and depression with his welcome.

"Come here, Crab," Val said. "Leave her alone."

"He's all right," Mischa said. "I looked for people in the underground. I never saw anyone before."

"We stay very deep. We keep watch. We only come up for the children."

"I knew you were here. I could feel you were afraid."

Val frowned and looked away again; Mischa saw she was annoyed by the mention of their fear, though Mischa had not meant it as a criticism. "You're lucky Crab found you," Val said; a defense, a change of subject. "He never found anyone before."

"It wasn't luck."

"What do you mean?"

"He can hear me. Or sense me. My mind, I mean."

Simon had moved back into shadow against the wall, but Mischa could see his skeptical expression. Val leaned forward eagerly. "But how?"

"He must be just a couple years younger than I am. He was abandoned when he was born, and he doesn't remember it too well, but he must be my brother."

"I don't understand."

Mischa shrugged. "I don't know how we do it. I could sense one of my other brothers almost as well, and one of my sisters better. Most people are a lot dimmer . . . and sort of smeary, but they're there."

"Is that why you were driven out? Because this ability was discovered?"

"No . . . not exactly." Mischa told Val what had happened in Center, and as much as she remembered of their flight.

"I see," Val said. She looked disturbed, but not quite angry. "You are one of us, but you are not."

"I guess so."

"And people may be chasing you?"

"They were, I know that, but they stopped. They must have been afraid of the tube."

"What about him?" Val nodded toward Jan.

"He can't go back either. Not for a while."

"There isn't anything wrong with him. He isn't one of us."

"No," Mischa said, unwillingly. And then she tried to comprehend why she was afraid again, what there was about Val that made Mischa feel instantly antagonistic at a certain tone of voice, why a certain angle of the light across Val's features made her seem familiar, cruel, and cold. But Mischa's memory gave her nothing. Val turned, and the illusion disappeared. "He's a good person," Mischa said. "He's only here by accident. You can trust him."

"So you say."

"Yes, I say!" She folded her arms around her knees, hunching her shoulders, and continued more quietly. "I trust him. Crab trusts him."

Val's expression softened, then she laughed at Mischa's graceless scowl, a pleasant laugh, not one of ridicule. "Then your friend is safe, for now."

This time, Simon did not break the uncomfortable silence as Mischa tried to think how she could convince Val of Jan's honor.

"Tell me how you talk to Crab," Val said.

Mischa did not want to change the subject, even to avoid argument, but she realized an argument would be useless. Then she remembered that she herself had not trusted Jan either, for a long time, not because of him but because of herself. When he got better, he would overcome Val's deep fear, and her suspicion. When he got better. . . .

"It isn't exactly talk," Mischa said of Crab. "He can't talk, even in his mind. His brain grew wrong. It garbles things. He's not stupid, he just can't put words together."

Crab pinched Mischa's hand, gently, insistently. She looked down at him. His green eyes protruded. He made a request in swirls of blue and an amelodic cluster of sounds. "He wants you to know . . ." Mischa said, "he wants me to tell you he used to believe you were his mother. He knows better, but he still thinks of you that way sometimes. He hopes you don't mind."

"I am his mother," Val said. "Or might as well be."

"He's glad."

"So am I."

"He's tried to talk to you," Mischa said. "But the words come out wrong, and the harder he tries to understand, the more they get mixed up."

Val stroked Crab's thick gray skin. "Poor Crab. He must be lonely."

That was the first time Mischa saw what was different about Val: the back of her hand was covered with a soft pelt of short scarlet hair; the fur continued as far up her arm as Mischa could see. The light glowed across the glossy hairs as Val sadly patted Crab, and Mischa could feel Val's own isolation, her clear memories of brighter places and even of outside. Val had not been in the underground all her life. "He's better off here than back there," Mischa said. "However it was for you, he's happier here."

Mischa slept for a long time, fitfully. When she awakened, she had no idea how many days they had been in the deep underground, no idea how far they had fled, or even how long it had taken her system to rid itself completely of the crystal poison. They were deeper than she had ever been, except one of the times she had tried to run away, and her memories of that trek were battered to nonsense by the force of Gemmi's calling mind.

Jan still had not awakened. Sometimes he slept like a corpse, still and pale and cold; sometimes he thrashed and burned with fever. Mischa stayed near him, watching, waiting. There were no diurnal cycles. In the underground, people worked to their own rhythms. Still regaining equilibrium in a world where Chris was dead and Crab was discovered, Mischa found herself without orientation. She could not tell how long Jan remained unconscious, and Val did not know either. If Simon knew, he did not say. Crab had no conception of time at all.

At the end of the incalculable time, Jan awoke, and then Mischa was afraid. She did not want to see what she had done to the symmetry of his spirit.

He was dazed, at first, half-dreaming, half-awake, comfortable. She did not touch him until she felt that he was about to move.

"Lie still, Jan."

He obeyed. After a moment he opened his eyes, no longer so calm. "I remember part of it."

She began to feel the pain that showed only around his eyes: a readiness to flinch that had never been there before. But he steadied himself, and her perceptions of him disappeared. If she looked away she would barely know he was there. "I'm sorry," she said. "I wish you could forget all this, and everything that happens till you're well." It seemed wrong that she could not share his pain. "I wish you hadn't got mixed up—"

He reached toward her. His hand was bandaged.

"Don't—"

Dark lines crisscrossed the golden skin on the back of his shoulder; as he moved, Mischa could almost feel the wounds breaking. She grabbed his wrist and stopped him. He winced and closed his eyes.

"Val—"

Mischa felt sick with helplessness and memory. Val appeared from maroon shadow, carrying a skin bag. She knelt beside them. Mischa envied her tranquillity, and tried to copy it, molding her mind to ease and acceptance. Then she realized that Val did not care about Jan; she did not care if he lived or died, healed whole or crippled, brave or frightened. He was not one of Val's people. Touching that spot of coldness and suspicion, Mischa pulled away. She could understand, but she could not accept it.

Val put the spout of the bag to Jan's lips. A milky fluid dribbled into his mouth and down his chin; he choked on it, coughed, pulled his breath in sharply: the movement jarred him. "Drink it," Val said; her voice was hard. He gulped and swallowed without gagging, and turned his face toward the floor. The muscles from his temple to the corner of his jaw stood out in lines. He rested, with his forehead against stone. Incongruous thoughts flashed through Mischa's mind and out again. Val's hands, as she tied the sack, were like scarlet and white birds in this skyless space. The sack was like the body of a spider, soft and round and venom-filled.

"What did you give him?"

"A drug to ease the pain. Only that."

"It's better," Jan said, very slowly. Each word was separated by a distinct pause. "It's better . . . can I have some water?"

He ate a little, later on. Crab was very good at catching blind cave fish. Cleaned, they were no more than bite-size. Mischa carried some to Jan. "It's raw," she said. "It's okay this way, but I could cook it."

Jan lifted his head. His eyes seemed cloudy; he had to concentrate to focus them, but he moved without wincing, though not very far. "Raw is fine," he said. She did not understand his smile.

His hands were wrapped in bandages. The thumb and forefinger could not touch, so he had to pick up the pale-pink bits of fish between the first two fingers of his right hand. He ate slowly, still lying down, with his chin on his left forearm. Mischa would have fed him, but he seemed able to manage on his own.

"They didn't follow," he said.

"Not yet." Then she wished she had only said no.

Jan stopped before he had eaten all the fish. Even so little exertion exhausted him. He rested, cheek pillowed on his arm. Mischa thought he was asleep, but he opened his eyes again and looked toward the dim blue light, glanced into the deep shadows or rock crevices, away, and closed his eyes again. "It's dark down here," he said.

Mischa shuddered. Only what she had experienced in the deprivation cell allowed her to know what he must feel in real darkness, and that was terrifying. She switched on the flash, which Crab had found and retrieved from deep sand; she moved the light bowl closer, making sure nothing shadowed him. The only sound was Jan's slow breathing.

"Stay a while and talk to me," he said.

"You should sleep . . ."

He glanced up. "We have to talk sometime, Mischa. I have to know what happened."

She hunched down in her jacket. "I don't know what happened," she lied. "I was confused. He hurt so much—" She stopped, and Jan said nothing. The narrow vertical lines between his eyebrows deepened. She could lie to him; he would not chide her. But he would know.

"All right," she said. "He shattered like glass. When he died there was nothing left of him—he died because there was nothing left of him. There was no place for him to go." She was sitting cross-legged; she worried the fraying hem of her pants. "It's not a truth you want to hear."

Jan stared at his clenched fist.

"Damn," Mischa said. "Damn you, you're so crazy. Why do you let me hurt you? How can you—"

This time he stopped her; he reached out, slowly, and she fell silent. "How did he feel when he died? What did he think of?"

She tried to re-create the scene so she could answer. "He didn't think of anything. I thought he was afraid, but that was me. . . . He was tired, and he was calm. His mind started breaking. Or tearing. In pieces, again and again, until the pieces were too small to be part of him anymore." The memories were very strong.

"Maybe it's true . . ."

"What?"

"Oblivion after death. Nirvana. I never understood exactly what it was. I always thought there must be some awareness of condition. Even if it wasn't self-awareness."

"There's supposed to be *something* after," Mischa said. "All the crazies say so, the ones who think about it. I never thought I wanted to believe any of that before."

"Neither did I." He unclenched his fingers. In the blue light, his palm looked black.

Mischa cupped his hand in hers, then untied the newly bloodied bandages. She wondered if she had solved anything by telling Jan what she thought had happened. He seemed to understand much better than she did herself; or he was making himself believe he did, in self-protection. She almost wished she had lied. "I'm sorry . . ."

"You don't have to be sorry, for anything. After . . . my friend died, I had to break with Subtwo. You speeded it up, or you slowed it down. This"—he lifted his hand, and Mischa knew he meant much more than his wounds—"all this was an accident."

Mischa rebandaged the deep cuts roughly. "You talk like nothing was ever anybody's fault."

"I don't think it is, the way you mean it. Not when another person can make decisions too."

Jan Hikaru's Journal:

Since I came to, my body has wanted little more than rest, though I find it difficult to sleep. Whatever incredible crystal garbage dump it was I fell through, the chemicals have affected me. First it was a fever that only I could feel, then a chill I did not notice until I regained consciousness, warmed on one side by Simon, on the other by Mischa, to overcome the hypothermia. When they took the glass out of my back, they could not get all the smallest pieces, the bits the size of grains of sand, or I would have bled to death. What's left is dissolving gradually, in quick flashes like showers of electric sparks. Unpredictably.

It might be only the interminable darkness that's so depressing; it might be that I tried to understand and accept what Mischa told me, and couldn't, except in the most superficial way. Is it "understanding" to realize that other people have used up their lives trying to explain what one philosophy or another said about death, and life?

And I'm homesick. I miss Koen. Green grass, sunlight, thunder, rain. I'd even be glad to see Ichiri, fraudulent old man that he is.

Once Mischa knew Jan would live, she did not stay with him so much. He slept most of the time, and watching him sleep made her want to cry. The peace in his face was interrupted by his wounds, by his dreams, so when he slept, she would go away; but she did not stay away long.

She explored the nearby tunnels with Crab, who knew most of them well. Though he was very strong and could move with great speed for a short time, he had little endurance. His deformities pained him under extended physical stress. So they did not go too far, and they rested often. After a while they communicated quite well. Beyond Mischa's gratitude for Crab's having saved her mind, and her life and Jan's as well, beyond Crab's joy at having someone who could understand him, they became good friends.

Once, dirty and tired, returning slowly from an unusually distant place, they came on Val sitting alone by the edge of a small rivulet. Crab scuttled stiffly toward her. Mischa had not seen her for several days. She was bloody and grim, and the body of a cave panther lay beside her on the bank.

"Val, what happened? Are you all right?"

"Yes."

Mischa sat on her heels and touched the panther's side, where the ribs showed sharp beneath dark, soft skin.

Val dipped her hand in the water and scrubbed at the dried blood clotting her short soft fur. "I hate to kill them. We have to, sometimes. They come in during the storms, and there isn't enough for them to eat. They get dangerous."

Mischa had never been so close to one before. "I always thought they lived in the underground."

"They hunt outside in summer."

"There's a way out? Without going through Center?"

"Several. But not now. Not until the storms are over."

Mischa pushed the new information here and there, trying to make it work for her, but it was as Val said: exits or not, there was no way outside until spring.

"I'll show you how to get to one, if you like, sometime."

"Thanks," Mischa said. "Do you ever use them?"

Mischa felt Val fold away from her. She always grew defensive when Mischa tried to turn a conversation to anything but survival in the lower caves. "We never go outside."

"Why not?"

"People live out there." It was obvious that she did not even feel the question deserved an answer.

"The traders come. But they live on the other side of the desert."

"They come to this side. That's enough."

"They're not like people in Center," Mischa said, remembering days and nights in their encampments, among the market booths and the storytellers. "They don't care much if somebody's different."

"Mischa, the desert's theirs, and the caves are ours. We accept that. It's no use trying to find us a better place."

"I don't see why you're scared of them, you're not scared of anything else in the world—"

"We won't speak of it anymore," Val said in the tone that always put Mischa on her guard.

"Who are you?" Mischa asked abruptly.

Val frowned.

"I mean—who were you? In Center?"

"You never saw me. You'd hardly have been born when I was driven out."

"I finally remembered who you look like."

Val remained silent.

"They hardly ever come out of their dome, but I've seen a couple of them. Your Family runs the reactor."

"Yes," Val said. "I was a great embarrassment to them."

Mischa had never heard of any of the Families' abandoning their children; she had assumed, like everyone else, that they were somehow immune to changes. "You don't act like them."

"I used to." She touched the bright, fine hair on the top of her shoulders; it grew down her arms, across her back, and tapered to a point at the base of her spine. "When this started to grow I was frightened, but I thought I could hide it. I pulled out the hair, but it always grew back. That's when I began to understand what it was like to be powerless."

"How did they find out?"

"My shoulders bled, and stained my clothes. They tied me down until the hair came in again, and they were sure . . . I suppose I was lucky."

"Lucky!" Mischa imagined days of being tied immobile, waiting, being cursed by people who had been friends.

"It was my cousins who noticed first. If my Family had discovered me, they could have arranged an accident. But all the cousins knew, so I couldn't be got rid of gracefully. My people would have lost face if they'd allowed one of their children to be murdered. Their firstborn, no less."

Val's voice was almost steady. She had gone from highest to lowest, and survived. It was not death she was afraid of when she drew back from discussing Center, but humiliation.

"Come on," Val said. "Help me get this beast home."

13

Mischa picked slabs of edible fungus from the bank of a stinking creek and tossed them to Crab. He caught them, holding them against his squat body, and popped one into his mouth. "Ugh," Mischa said as he chewed noisily. "Wait to wash them, at least."

The stream continued a little way and spilled viscously down a fissure in the side of a cliff Mischa had climbed a few hours before. As she explored, she planned escapes and ambushes. She kept expecting Subone and Subtwo to come, but one after another periods of time resembling days were passing, without feel of the pseudosibs, or sound, or general alert. Though no one from Center had come hunting in a long time, the people always watched. All Mischa could do for now was wait, hoping the pseudosibs would not come before Jan could travel, yet wishing they would come and get it over with.

She and Crab stuffed the lumps of fungus in a sack and started back toward Val and Simon's cave. They met no one. The other people in the underground were widely separated, to make the best use of the food. Shelf fungus and mushrooms grew near the polluted streams, fish swam in the cleaner ones. All life in the deep underground was, finally, the result of Center's discards. The outcasts knew it and resented it.

They were still leery of Mischa, whose strangenesses were invisible. When Crab was with her, they accepted her. Her ability to get around unfamiliar places without a light astonished them. Somehow, no one had ever noticed that Crab could do it too.

She stopped in the entrance of the cave. "Jan—"

Standing, bracing herself against the wall with one hand, he held off her objections with a gesture. "I'm all right."

"It's too soon."

He looked down at himself, his trembling legs, his chest already filmed with sweat. "This is ridiculous."

"You almost *died*."

He took his hand away from the stone. He closed his eyes, balancing without support, and his legs stopped shaking. Mischa expected him to collapse, but after a moment he stood quite steady. "That's better," he said. He opened his eyes and smiled. "I couldn't lie still anymore. I thought I was about to begin hallucinating."

Mischa wondered if he were reacting again to the crystals, if a layer of solubility remained to affect him, this time like a stimulant. But when she was near enough to distinguish his pupils from the near-black of his irises, she saw that his eyes were not dilated. Though the pulse beat rapidly in his throat, it was not frenzied. Jan held out his hands and flexed his fingers: he had taken off the bandages. Scars striped his palms from lifeline to wrist. Mischa saw relief and something close to joy in his face: now he was certain no nerve had been cut. She smiled too, for just a moment almost able to comprehend how he could be glad he was not permanently hurt. Her own reaction was fury that he had been hurt at all.

"Nothing of Subtwo yet?"

"Neither one of them," Mischa said.

"It's Subtwo who's dangerous."

"Subone's the one who did all this!"

Jan nodded. "And he did it for fun."

Mischa started to object, but he was right. She did not want to admit that Chris had died for a man's amusement, but it was true. "He's still dangerous," she said sullenly.

"Yes," Jan said, and hesitated, reached back to the wall, and lowered himself onto the tangled blanket before Mischa could help him. He rested his elbows on his knees. "As long as he's interested, or pleased, or waiting for something to happen. But his attention span isn't very long. He gets distracted. Subtwo—I've seen Subtwo force himself to finish something he didn't want to start in the first place. You've seen it yourself. He has a compulsion to finish any task he begins . . . sometimes he fights it, but I don't know if he'll ever beat it."

"If they don't come soon . . . I don't like so much waiting, either."

"We might have to go after them," Jan said. She had expected him to advise caution. "They wouldn't like it here. If we could lure them far enough down and make them feel lost enough, we might get them to concede."

"I don't want Subone to concede," Mischa said.

"Why not?"

She looked at him, frowning, for though she sometimes did not understand him, he almost always seemed to understand her. "I owe him."

"Not enough for you to kill." He stressed "you" only slightly less than "kill," but Mischa chose to misunderstand his point. "I can," she said. "I have to. I will."

"Whatever it does to you?"

"Life's not so important on earth," Mischa said.

Jan reached absently up to massage the top of his shoulder, the trapezius muscle. "Will you promise me one thing?"

"What?"

"Don't swear any unbreakable oaths."

She saw what he was doing and hoping, and she did not want to be kept from her decision, but she felt she owed him that much: to delay a little while. "All right. But I haven't changed my mind."

"Thanks." Suddenly he smiled, and began to chuckle. Then Mischa saw the humor of the situation: the two of them against the pseudosibs, against Center itself, deciding fates as they sat trapped in a cave. And she laughed too.

"Did you see when Crab left?"

"No," Jan said. "He came in with you, I think."

"I can't feel him . . ."

"He must know his way around."

"He does, but . . ." She had hardly been separated from Crab since he found her, and she missed not being able to touch his mind. The spaces he touched were not Chris's empty ones, but the contact was reassuring. She crossed her legs under her, and chewed on her thumbnail, and uncrossed her legs, and stood up. "Maybe I better look for him—" They both heard Val's rare laugh. "Maybe he's with Val," Jan said.

Simon and Val came in together, damp and laughing from a swim in the fishing stream. Simon held out his hand, offering something to Mischa: a small mushroom, one with intoxicating effects. "No, thanks," she said. "I can't find Crab."

"Don't worry," Val told her. "He goes off alone sometimes."

Even intoxicated, Val would be concerned if Crab could be in danger, so Mischa sat down again. Simon offered the mushroom to Jan, who looked at it doubtfully. "Is it like the medicine you gave me before?"

Simon did not answer.

"That was a distillation," Val said. "This is much milder, much slower." She had lost her suspicion of Jan, gradually, as she realized his honesty and his worth.

Jan accepted the gift and chewed it slowly. Mischa had not expected him to take it, but as she watched he relaxed, and the faint lines at the outside corners of his eyes, the lines pain had given him, disappeared. He leaned back and sighed.

A wind-chime voice floated to them, echoing gently. "Aura!" Val called. "Aura, come down, see what we have."

Aura drifted toward them, laughing, giggling, keeping herself well beyond the circle of Val's light, even when she slipped into the cave. Mischa could see her, but not her shape or her face, for the veils she wore blurred her outlines. "Tell me," she said, almost singing.

Simon opened his belt-pouch and picked out one of the mushrooms with his claws. "Ahh," Aura sighed. "A span of forgetfulness, however brief . . ." Her tears fell around them.

"Come down."

"No, no." Her veils drifted past, wafting cool breezes against their cheeks. She held herself against the fissured walls by incredible physical strength, and she moved as quickly as anyone could walk. Simon reached toward her, and she brushed his hand with a veil. The mushroom disappeared. "Thank you, my friends."

"Stay," Val said. "Even in the dark. Talk with us. Sing to us."

"All my songs are old," Aura said, her voice fading as she moved away from them. "When they are new, perhaps I will return."

"She never sings anything twice," Val said when she had gone. "Even when we ask her."

Jan, sitting very quietly on the blanket, leaning against the wall, opened his eyes, and closed them again; sadness formed in his expression, and left it, and he appeared content. Val lay down, her head in

Simon's lap, and stretched, as feline as he. Mischa had never seen her happy before. Simon stroked Val's silky hair; she reached up and drew him down and kissed him. When they parted again, Val stroked his forearm. "You are so beautiful," she said. "They were so stupid to put you down here."

His voice was so low, and Mischa was so unaccustomed to hearing it, that she did not realize he had spoken until he was silent again. "We are human beings."

"As human as—" But Val cut herself off. "Mischa, I told you Crab was all right."

Crab scuttled through the entrance. Mischa could feel his excitement: triumph and some fear; adrenalin. He was dragging something behind him.

"What have you got?" Val asked in her fond parental way. Crab placed his trophy before her and stood back, blinking his green eyes, waiting for approval.

"Val—" Mischa did not know exactly what the battered machine was, but she was certain where it had come from. Bits of it fell to the cave floor, clinking metallically. Mischa glanced toward Jan, and he met her gaze: he, too, knew who had sent it, and he knew its purpose as well. "Did Crab kill it?" He pushed himself to his feet and circled behind Val and Simon, approached the device, reached around it and unscrewed a lens. Rather abruptly, he sat down again. Val stared at the metal beetle as Jan picked it up and turned it over, and Mischa could feel her contentment dissolving.

Crab sidled up against Mischa, confused by Val's reaction. Mischa patted him, and he showed her the scuffle between himself and the looker; no other being entered the scenes he remembered: not Subone, nor anyone from Center, not even anyone else from the deep underground. Mischa had not known just how agile and strong Crab could be. The looker was not built for combat, but it was well defended. Crab had stopped it, crippled it, upended it, and smashed enough of its components so it could no longer move or see.

"It's from Center," Val said, and she was suddenly very sober.

"It's quite dead," Jan said, continuing his inspection. "Crab did a good job."

"But it *is* from Center. It—looks for people."

"It's Subone's," Mischa said. "He won't bother you, he only wants me."

"They'd kill or capture anyone they saw. It's always been that way."

By the entrance of the cave, Simon waited. Val glanced at him, and he nodded. She got up. "We'll have to go down."

Urgency and fear sparked soundless activity. Crab huddled against Mischa, upset by the change in routine, knowing that somehow he had caused it. Mischa patted him reassuringly, sitting on her heels to wait while Jan dressed. Only a small dim globe remained in the cave. It highlighted Jan faintly, but not enough to overpower the radiance of his body's warmth. He bent down to pick up his boot. His fingertips were black, his hands maroon, his arms and shoulders burgundy; just below his heart he was scarlet. He put on his mended jacket, and the ghostly glow disappeared.

"You should go with Val and Simon."

"All things considered, that might be best."

Mischa refused to let herself be surprised or disappointed. She knew he would stay if she asked him, but she would not ask, however much she might wish him to remain. He really was not ready.

"But if I do, they'll just hunt us down one at a time, and Val and Simon and the others with us."

"Can you—"

"If you don't think so, then you'll have to come too. That's the only way I'm going."

"You think I should, don't you?"

"I don't know, Mischa," he said. "If I have to fight, I'd prefer to do it under better conditions. But if the pseudosibs are going to follow us, they'll follow us here, or with the others. The only difference is a little time, and I'm not sure it's worth it."

"All right. I wish you were stronger, though."

"I'm strong enough."

Mischa picked up their sack of provisions, and she and Jan left Val's cave for the last time.

Light-globes radiated glimmering paths across the dark, still water. The outcasts launched rude rafts in spreading waves of ripples. The paths of light shuddered and grew indistinct.

Jan and Mischa stood with Val, watching the people climb gingerly onto unsteady floating platforms built of scavenged plastic bottles and cord. "Even our escape is made of Center garbage," Val said bitterly.

The hunted look had left her face; she was always more comfortable with plans made and implemented. "Well . . . I never thought about anything I threw away either, back then."

The outcasts seldom gathered all together; some of the people Mischa had never met or seen. There were three infants, carried close. Even the mental defectives were guarded and cherished, though now they were confused and terrified, and one, very old, was crying. "We choose not to bear children," Val had once said. "The chances against them are too great. And those of us who never grow, in their minds . . . they need our care and our love."

The first raft, full, was poled and paddled away from shore. It faded into the black water until it resembled a small cluster of fireflies.

"What's on the other side?" Jan was leaning against the stone wall behind them, his arms folded across his chest. He had come unaided, as though forcing himself to move once had overcome what remained of the effects of his injuries.

"The desert caves. The rivers flow from another source, so the water's clean, but nothing grows."

"You can't stay there long."

"As long as our supplies last."

Jan nodded.

The sobbing of the old man drifted across the water, recalling other lost sounds. "If Center ever really wanted to hunt you," Mischa said, "they could starve you out."

"They could . . ." Val's answer came slowly; she seemed to contemplate possibilities and disasters. "But they never have. I don't think they could stand being in here that long."

"They could do it. They could stay in shifts."

"They hunt us as animals—we never do anything to frighten them, so they don't come to kill us, and I don't think they'd take that much trouble to catch us for a zoo." That was the real bitterness in her, and the real fear: the memory of being exposed and displayed as an animal, less-than-human; the determination to keep that from happening to any of her people. "But you *should* fight," Mischa said. "You shouldn't let them chase you. They think they're better than we are, Val, but they're *not*."

"It's time for us to leave." Val started down the beach toward Simon.

Crab followed her, then turned to Mischa, then scuttled back and forth on a middle ground between them. Val looked at him, sadly. Mischa went to him and knelt down.

"He doesn't know what to do. He hasn't got any way to decide." She could feel that his mind did not and could not choose between strong loyalties. He moved faster, back and forth, back and forth, growing more frustrated, more frantic. Mischa tried to calm him. "Crab, you've got to go with Val." She said it in words and symbols, several times over. He slowly understood, but responded incoherently, as Gemmi might. Mischa pulled away from the entanglement, but made herself approach again. "It's important. You'll know when it's safe to come back." He huddled against her. She urged him toward Val, but he would not go. She took his hand and led him down the shore.

Val waited. Mischa reached her and stopped.

"Mischa, you do understand? Why we have to leave?"

Mischa wanted to deny that she did, but she could see what a small and powerless group they were: their resources were directed inward, to keeping themselves and each other alive. If they stood and defended themselves, they might be scattered and tracked down and destroyed. Still, Mischa could sense the strength of their cohesion. She wondered if they underestimated themselves. "I understand," she said. "I understand . . . why you think so."

Val took Crab's hand, and he moved closer to her than to Mischa.

"Good-bye," Val said. She boarded the last raft, with Simon and Crab. They poled away, and disappeared into the darkness with the other fireflies.

Within a few minutes, Mischa knew the pseudosibs were near, and soon after that both she and Jan heard the approach of the machines.

Hours later, the temperature was rising as Mischa and Jan climbed downward, leading the hunting party on, luring them away from the outcasts. Like multiple river outlets in a three-dimensional river delta, tunnels spread around them, separating and rejoining, rising, falling, flowing. The humidity rose with the temperature, and soon they were walking among myriad tiny streams that broke from the floors and pattered down the walls and fell in splashing fans of spray across the entrances of passages. Soaked and hot, Mischa took off her jacket and tied it around her waist. The echoing roar of water was distracting, but if she stretched her perceptions hard, she could just sense people behind her. They were too far away to distinguish as individuals. She touched them as infrequently as she dared.

She was worried about Jan. He was not ready for a chase, though he did not yet admit to fatigue. She wished they were farther ahead of the pseudosibs, but they had had too little warning; and they had needed to be sure the lookers would follow them and not the underground people.

Over eons, the heat and the water had slowly eaten away at the limestone, speeding reactions, leaching out the soluble minerals, weakening the structural material until the entire section had the consistency of cheese. They moved carefully among stone curtains that resembled delicate slices of honeycomb or sponge, along narrow pathways facing spectacular chasms.

Mischa spun at the rumbling of breaking rock. She grabbed for Jan as he slipped, his light swinging wildly from his belt. The seemingly solid bank collapsed beneath him; he threw himself forward and she managed to hold him. He fell hard on the crumbling, muddy rock, and lay still for a moment, until the pebbles stopped clattering, far below.

It was a treacherous fairyland.

The terrain became increasingly difficult. Steaming rivulets flowed into the channel below them, to increase the water's flow almost imperceptibly, but inexorably, until the bank was no more than a narrow ledge above a roiling pool. They slid sideways, balanced precariously. Mischa could hardly see Jan for the steam. She stopped until he caught up with her. Condensed mist sparkled on his eyelashes. He flashed his light around them, seeking out currents in the fog.

"This is incredible."

"Yes," Mischa said. She leaned against the stone, savoring the damp, slightly cooler surface, gazing into the grayness. "I've never been this far down before." Pressing her hands to the wall, she let her eyes go out of focus, and reached back toward their pursuers. Their aura seemed diffuse, as though they were beginning to separate, but she could not be sure, they were still too far away. Yet a major part of the group seemed stationary.

"I think they've stopped."

"Stopped—?" For a moment he looked hopeful, then laughed once, drily. "They've stopped for the night," he said. "That would be just like Subtwo."

Adhering rigidly to a schedule would be almost a necessity for Subtwo, Mischa saw that. "Subone would just keep pushing his people until he caught us."

"Probably. Or get bored and go home."

"Then where is he?"

"*I* don't know." He sat down on the ledge and closed his eyes. "Can we stop for just a minute?"

The fatigue he had held off for so long lay almost visible over him, and Mischa felt sorry for directing her anger and petulance at him. Balanced on the precarious ledge, she knelt down. "On the other side, okay? This is a bad place."

Adhering to his schedule, Subtwo called a halt in a dome-shaped cavern. This time no one bothered to argue or offer to continue, as they had the nights before. He ignored the shrugs and snickers: if his people failed to see the sense of conserving themselves, he could not help it. They would see his reasoning when slow and steady and inexorable progress brought them success. He supervised the arrangement of the camp and the setting up of his own tent.

His head ached and spun from the irregularities of the underground and the darkness. He wanted to be home, he wanted never to leave his rooms again, he wanted light, he wanted to get far, far away from Subone and his threats and desires. Yet, now, he felt uneasy: in a deranged maze of tunnels, Subone had insisted on splitting the hunting party to search more efficiently. He said the lookers were too slow and too undependable; he said there were too many scent-trails and fluorescences for them to work well, and too few antenna leads for them to report in time to be useful. He said he could get in front of Mischa and Jan and trap them; and taking his contradictory reasoning with him he had tramped away at the head of his party down another tunnel, with every indication of eagerness and even pleasure.

At moments of greatest stress, when Subtwo most needed serenity, Subone's emotions insinuated themselves into his mind. He forced them angrily back and plunged on cold and emotionless. He had decided to perform this last duty, then cut the connection between himself and Subone, no matter what the cost.

Yet his thoughts kept slipping back to Mischa, that sparkling naive child, to be killed at his hands or trapped in the underground forever, and he wanted to nullify all the time since the fight.

The portable shower had sprung a leak during the previous rest period, and nothing had been brought with which to repair it. Subtwo had not bathed in nearly twenty-four hours, and he felt filthy and sticky. Though the miasma was not so bad since Subone had taken half their followers with him, Subtwo could smell the odors of perspiration and bacteria and human secretions from the people still around him, male and female, and anger, excitement. The machines were little better, for they were hastily put together for the hunt and exuded smells of lubricants and ozone. He was not satisfied with them; he hated a job badly done. Silent now, they were when running very noisy, and the lights they carried flashed brilliantly and erratically across the tunnel walls. Subtwo felt that he might as well be in a rowboat during a hurricane.

When his tent was inflated, he walked around the camp and stopped next to Galiana, who watched the display screens: eleven dim and static-marked pictures of caves and streams and lifeless stone, jolting fantastically in quadruple-time playback, and the one blank square whose machine had been destroyed. Subtwo wished they could watch the scenes in real-time, but the dense rock made direct communication impossible. They could only watch for antenna leads, hook into the network when they found one, and hope a looker was in broadcasting range of a pickup. He watched the instant-feed recordings.

"Is there any more sign of the creature?"

"No. Nor of anything else. I'll tell you if there is."

Subtwo realized he had probably offended her: by asking the question he had implied that she might not have the intelligence to tell him of a change. He was too used to dealing with machines that required questions to respond with information. Sometimes he wished he himself were a machine, with an easily erasable memory; he could not forget the quick glimpse they had had of the deformed, asymmetric beast, one look at the end of a fastfeed, a few seconds of real-time as the looker trundled away, still in range of the antenna lead. Then the beast set upon it, and it sent no more signals.

They had passed the place of attack, finding nothing but a few broken parts. And since then, nothing definite, nothing concrete, nothing but questionable trails and a vast, lightless labyrinth.

Subtwo slept badly, and woke abruptly, trembling with exhaustion.

168

Someone was vibrating the balloon walls of his shelter. "What is it? What do you want?"

Draco flung open the tent flap in his overtheatrical way and stood poised in the entrance, his mahogany face sweat-varnished, a streak of yellow clay bright on his high cheekbone, below the smudged fluorescent-paint flames. "We've been attacked."

Harried and haggard, a few of Subone's people approached the camp, carrying two stretchers, one covered completely, one bearing Subone, his tunic bloody. Meeting them, Subtwo shouldered his way through the small group. His pseudosib lay pale, breathing shallowly.

"What happened? What happened?"

Subone moaned, and groped for his hand. Subtwo wanted to pull away from the grimy touch, but he remained motionless. "They attacked us," Subone whispered. "The freaks . . . they killed Nicola. . . ." He shook his head, closing his eyes. "They were dreadful, they were inhuman."

"Where are the rest of your people? Dead?"

"Perhaps . . . we could not wait to find them all."

The medic from Subtwo's camp arrived, panting, with Draco close behind. He uncovered the wound, and began to clean it. Subtwo looked away.

"They tried to cut me off . . . and Hikaru and the Center girl were leading them—be careful!" He flinched as the cold spray of a mist anesthetic touched raw flesh.

"You should have stayed with me," Subtwo said. "This never would have happened."

"I was afraid you wouldn't help, I was afraid you would stop me." He gripped Subtwo's hand and pulled him back. "Perhaps you were right, perhaps the link has dissolved . . . I can't tell what you think anymore."

"I never felt this happen," Subtwo said, wondering. Hope overcame his doubt. "Are we finally separate?"

"Can you understand now why we have to finish this? This is what they can do, with leaders who know us."

"It's all right now, you're back, you're safe."

"They'll come again. I drove them off, but they'll come. They want us, brother."

Subtwo drew back and could not answer.

"We *are* brothers," Subone said. "In this."

Subtwo gazed down at him, at the long diagonal wound beside his collarbone and the scar of the stab Mischa had inflicted, at his elegant, dissipated face. "Yes," he said. "We are brothers in this."

His anger like acid, Subtwo took Draco aside. "I would appreciate your impressions of the incident."

"You could have them," Draco said, "except I wasn't there."

Subtwo had not imagined Draco in any place but the forefront of a disturbance; he wondered if he had misjudged him. "Then where?"

"We didn't have enough lookers for all the tunnel branches. Subone didn't want to wait. We split up at the junctions. He and Nicola were alone."

"That was very unwise."

Draco shrugged elaborately and expressively.

"I am surprised . . ." But Subtwo did not finish; it was not his and Subone's habit to disparage each other publicly.

"So were we."

Subtwo sent for the rest of Subone's people; the main camp gathered itself to hunt again.

14

Metallic grinding, clanking, the clatter of pebbles, the whirr of bearings against solid lubricant: Jan opened his eyes to blindness and reached instinctively for the light.

"Wait—" Mischa spoke in a whisper that would not carry.

"Is it that close?"

"Maybe. Stay here. I'll be right back." He heard her get up; he heard the looker stop, as though to sniff the air.

"If you kill it," he said, "if it doesn't communicate again, they'll know where we are."

The pattern of his own blood vessels flashed against his retinas as his mind searched for something to look at. He turned his head like a blind man, listening for Mischa, afraid she had gone on.

"You're right," she said finally. "Damn you anyway."

He reached out to get his balance, until his fingers brushed the wall behind him. Then he felt the cool, dry touch of Mischa's hand; he rose and she led him away. Walking hesitantly, free hand outstretched before his face, he followed her. They moved slowly for the sake of silence. The tunnels, which before wound interminably, now stretched straight and dark forever. The sounds of the looker diminished almost imperceptibly. Jan began to feel the walls moving in and the ceiling coming down around him. *This is no time,* he thought, *this is no time*—he felt the cool delicate prickle across his shoulders, warning—*no time to indulge*—but a wind seemed to blow against him, bringing terror—*to indulge your psychological*—crystals leaped into flame across his back. His balance disappeared. He flung out his hands, Mischa pulling at him. "Jan—" But he stumbled and fell.

The impact of his palms on stone, with all his weight behind them, brought him back. He was panting. The sound of his fall echoed around them, and the pain fled in one bright flash as Mischa flicked on the light, kneeling beside him, shielding her eyes. Jan blinked. "I'm sorry . . . I—"

"I know," Mischa said. "Never mind. Can you walk?"

"I think . . ." He pushed himself up. "Yes, okay." With the light on, the floor returned to its proper position beneath his feet, and the ceiling stayed above him, though they were so alike that he wondered briefly, really, why they should.

Behind him, the looker whirred smoothly toward them, steadily, following the light or sound or both.

They ran.

Jan realized they were trapped.

Twice he and Mischa had turned back to avoid lookers, trying to regain some uncertainty of position, and now it was too late to kill one of the machines and break through to clear tunnels. The lookers no longer moved singly, for the caves had come together like tributaries, and with them the machines. Even the antenna mice seemed to have nested here, for the walls were studded frequently with leads; Jan thought it quite possible that the pseudosibs were now able to watch for them in real-time.

He could hear the lookers behind him, moving down the single unbranched tunnel. He was no longer leading on a merry chase, but being driven. Both he and Mischa were too tired to run any more.

"Faster!"

Jan swung around, and Mischa with him: the voice was Subtwo's, clear, close. But the tunnel was empty to the end of Jan's light-beam, and the voice did not come again, only a mechanical gibber and buzz.

"Subtwo's close," Mischa said, "but he's not that close. The caves do that sometimes." She strove to keep her voice steady, but Jan heard the beginning of fear. He had seen her angry, elated, grieving: but he had not seen her afraid.

They kept going.

"It might branch out again," Jan said. "Mightn't it?"

"Maybe. Probably. But who knows when? I wish I'd let Crab stay. He's probably been here."

"You can't reach him."

"No. Maybe he can sense me this far but I have to touch him, almost, to get anything clear."

"What's that up there?"

The beam of Jan's light touched an abrupt ledge, and speared empty darkness.

The ledge was the end of the tunnel. Standing in the opening, Mischa whistled shrilly: the major echo took full seconds in return. Jan's light would not reach the other side. On the floor of the wide cavern, stalagmites glittered damp gray, dull yellow, gray-blue. The shadows of the nearest rock formations were short and round, of those farther away long and attenuated as the angle of the illumination changed.

Mischa took Jan's hand. "Turn out the light for just a minute."

Reluctantly, he complied, and waited uneasily for Mischa's eyes to reaccustom themselves to darkness. He did not wonder that the underground people had little conception of time. Time in the light and time in darkness were different things, not even comparable.

"I think we can get down," Mischa said. "There's a kind of crevice . . ."

He turned the light back on and picked out the fault; it led steeply downward. Mischa lowered herself over the edge, clutching the bare handhold of the crack, digging her toes in for better purchase. Jan hooked the flash to his belt, pulled off his boots and tossed them to the floor, counting: fifteen meters. He followed Mischa.

"It's narrow right below you," she said.

"It's narrow now." The crevice was damp and grimy, allowing only a difficult purchase. He wished his fingernails were not already broken to the quick, for he needed every bit of help he could get. Three meters above the floor, the rock sheared away beneath his weight, and he landed in a shower of bits of stone.

"You okay?"

"Nothing broken." He put his boots back on, calming himself, straightened, flashed the light around.

They were in a stone forest, a lunar mountain range. The stalagmites were old and huge, towering above their heads, some standing alone, many so close together they formed double or triple peaks or free-standing stone curtains, flying buttresses without buildings, a labyrinth of pillars and screens.

"In a cave this big there's got to be another way out."

"I hope so," Mischa said.

The wall of the cavern continued in a smooth curve, unbroken by any route of escape. The hunters behind him did not blind Jan to the beauty. The stalagmites seemed to move around him, animated, disembodied fingers, whole webbed hands, gesturing and reaching as the light glanced from their tips and left their bases in darkness. They recalled to him a mountain near his father's estate, a solitary, ancient volcanic peak that disappeared sometimes in the clouds, "Gone visiting," people always said; or seemed to hover on a bank of mist.

Jan and Mischa stopped before a shield of fluted rock. "Think we can get over it?"

"Want to try?"

He gave Mischa a hand up, but she could not reach the edge, even standing on his shoulders. When she jumped down, she looked into Jan's face. He could see her searching out the lines of strain. "Let's not do that again," she said, and he did not argue.

The shield forced them toward the center of the labyrinth. Trying to round the barricade, they came upon another, and another: they were pushed gradually into a maze of baffles that cut them off from any sense of direction; they moved through chutes and canyons too high to climb or see over. The little sounds they made themselves, Jan's boots on the stone, the rub of fabric, their breathing, came back to them as echo from strange directions. Then they heard, overlaid, direct noises: voices, machines. Mischa looked up and around them. Jan followed her gaze and saw his light glinting from the petrified banners above, stabbing in shafts like flares that matched his abrupt shock of apprehension. He looked down again, into Mischa's bright green eyes. "Jan," she said, approaching tentatively, unwillingly, with her voice, "Jan . . ." He knew what she was going to ask him.

He reached down and turned off the light. The darkness snapped down like a box. Mischa took his hand, tightly, reassuringly.

"I wish I had your genes," he said.

"No, you don't, you'd have to take my family too." She led him forward. "Maybe we can get to the edge this way."

Jan touched cool stone with outstretched fingertips as Mischa guided him in what seemed like circles, a serpentine route around the pinnacles. He was lost.

Brilliant lights flashed through the cavern above and around them, then the flare died to a glow too dim for sight. Jan turned toward its source; he could not see the hunting party, but the lights they carried reflected from ceiling and rock peaks in a multicolored aurora as the people gathered in the tunnel entrance and prepared to climb down.

"Come on," Mischa said. She pulled him forward. In the brief explosion of light, he had seen a forest of solitary stalagmites and the cavern wall beyond them. They had passed through the maze.

He did not yet dare turn on his own light. Reflections wavered above him like sunlight on water, tantalizing, but never bright enough to show him a path. Mischa's hand tightened on his.

"What is it?"

"Just there—"

Blackness against blackness: a narrow passage. Jan could make out its borders when he looked at it obliquely; straight-on, it was invisible, like anything in darkness to normal human sight. But above it, and to its left, and to its right, three identical spidery painted symbols glowed with phosphorescence, fading slowly as the excitation from the pseudosibs' flare radiated away. Jan had seen the symbol only once before.

"Mischa—that sign . . ."

"Yes," she said.

"It means 'danger,' doesn't it?"

"It means strange," she said fervently. "It means don't go near it, because normal humans made it."

"It was above the tube."

"I know, but it might not, it doesn't have to mean there's glass down there."

"There isn't . . . another passage?"

"I can't see one, there's another maze beyond this one, I think." She came forward: he could see her eyes, like a cat's, picking up the dim, dim light, glowing brightly back at him. She gripped his forearms.

"I don't want to go in there," he said, very softly.

"I know."

He looked down at her, surprised he had spoken aloud.

As he passed between and beneath the symbols, Jan felt as though they were climbing from the walls like luminous spiders, following him, crawling up his spine, driving him into hell. Remembering a story from his childhood, he wondered where the Lord of the Dead was, to take his place. He wanted sunlight and peace.

"I think the light would be okay now."

Her voice startled him again; he had been following like an automaton, focused totally inward to avoid the darkness and his fear. He turned on Kiri's flash. He might as well have left it off, for there was nothing to see. The featureless night almost seemed preferable to the endless passages stretching to far-off terminations in curves or perspective. He was becoming disgusted with himself for his fright and vacillations, but he was too exhausted to collect himself effectively, too close to the experiences of hurt and loneliness to put them aside for later reflection.

The passage tilted upward and grew cooler. They left footprints in the condensation, Jan's booted, Mischa's bare, a clear trail.

"I don't think they're scared yet," Mischa said abruptly, "but they don't like this much."

Jan laughed, and for a little while it was easier. He could imagine Subtwo's unease in the caves, infinitely greater than Jan's own; and he could imagine a growing impatience among Subtwo's people. While competent, they were misfits; they were misfits because they were immature in certain special ways: unable to sustain enthusiasm or interest in any goal repeatedly delayed, needing instant satisfaction in their endeavors. Though Subtwo was tenacious, doubts would assail him; though his people were fearless, they had no persistence. But whether those qualities would create or destroy effectiveness in this hunt depended on how long he and Mischa could force its continuation.

Jan felt himself more and more on edge. Mischa seemed not to feel it: Jan was glad he still had that much control. But the symbols at the mouth of the tunnel must have had some meaning, and he wished the danger would come, so they could face it. All the unknowns of the underground combined against him.

He noticed, for the first time, a gentle current of air flowing past him from behind, almost too light to detect. "Mischa, do you feel that?"

"Yes."

"An exit?"

"I hope not. It isn't nearly time for the storms to be over."

As the tunnel narrowed, the breeze became stronger, and as they climbed, Jan could hear the whistle of wind in fissures of stone, the sigh of air, and behind it the faint, terrifying sound of wind chimes, singing in many keys.

The breeze blew cool on his back, and he shuddered.

Mischa scrambled up a giant-step, a petrified waterfall. Her shadow sprang ahead across a narrow rift. She slid into the fissure and out again. "We can get through. . . . But, Jan—"

He climbed up beside her, hardly able to understand her for the chiming. "Just go on."

In the narrow passage, the wind and the singing combined like the elements of a ghostly storm, pulling Jan's breath from his throat, confusing his hearing, dimming his sight. He slid sideways with his raw fingertips hard against stone, welcoming the solidity. The volume of the music increased.

The passage opened abruptly into a wide fan-shaped chamber. Mischa turned back; he knew what she had tried to tell him.

His light glanced from edge to point of a great multicolored glass blade, and beyond to a thousand more. They shivered; the wind, swirling from constricted passages to irregular cavern, stroked their tips and excited them, an alien lover.

Jan approached the hanging garden. The spikes were crystals within crystals: one shape, in one transparent color, overlaid by another geometric form, like the experiment of some gigantic child. They were a hundred times the size of the crystals he had fallen through, but he knew his blundering must have destroyed a place of nearly equal beauty. He took another step forward, lifting his hand, drawn to reach out for the brilliant spires.

"Jan—"

But he already knew that no natural deposition of mineral could have formed these constructs; their beauty was that of danger, their attraction that of disaster. Jan let his hand drop in a gesture of acceptance, denial.

"I'm all right now," he said. "Let's go."

In places they could move between the glittering blades, and their passing changed the melody of the crystal song, introducing discord, as though the inanimate growths were beings, resenting the intrusion.

Farther on, they had to crawl, and the wind sucked more strongly, for the crystals grew so close together that there was no room to pass between them. The tips of the glass shivered visibly, moving in rapid, minuscule vibrations. Then, just to Mischa's left, a delicate shaft shuddered and broke with a high, sharp note, and shattered on the stone. Jan saw Mischa fling up her arm to shield her eyes; his own reflexes pulled him around and away. When the bright music stopped, he looked back at her. Her face was unmarked, but she slid rapidly toward him through fragments of crystal so small they swirled in the air, sparkling. "Hurry up," she said. "It's bad to breathe the dust." As she spoke he smelled the acrid odor and felt the drifting chemicals dissolving in the back of his throat. He pushed himself on, hearing Mischa behind him. She started to cough.

The crystals they passed grew progressively shorter and thinner, until Mischa and Jan could stand, aching, and run beneath a glittering ceiling of natural semiprecious stones. Human laughter suddenly laced the music, and abruptly the wind-chimes changed from a song of solitude to one of destruction, directed by human voices. The blades broke and shattered, with a shriek nearly animate, of splendor and delicacy reduced to nothing. Entropy over all. Jan almost understood the strength of his own anger.

In the wide cone of his flash, Jan could see ahead to a cross-tunnel, where the mixing breezes spun wind-devils of dust. A scattering of black sand scratched against the soles of his boots. His throat burned. For a moment he thought that was the reason for a new smell that seemed to surround him, but it grew stronger as they continued. It was totally unlike the bitter chemical odor: it was the dreadful sick-sweet smell of decay.

It permeated the tunnel, even against the air currents, until, when Jan and Mischa reached the junction of passages, it was almost overwhelming. Jan saw Mischa clench her jaw tight, rigid, and he fought the same rising nausea.

The tunnel behind them they could not use again. To their right, the wind funneled upward to the surface, whirling through an unclimbable vertical shaft. Jan could not see its end, nor even a hint of daylight, but he could hear the whining of the storm.

From some other source to his left, the miasma emanated. There was no other choice. Jan said nothing, and Mischa did not break the silence.

The stench thickened, until Jan felt he should be able to put up his hands and push it away. He was breathing in tiny shallow gulps, his mouth slightly open, throat tight. His eyes watered.

The texture under his feet changed, softening. A gray mat of hyphae spread across the stone, up the walls, finally across the ceiling to join itself. At first it seemed dry and soft, but when it thickened, Jan's boots sank squishily into the growth, and rose as though from thick porridge. He looked over at Mischa, walking barefoot, and shuddered.

"It's—" Her voice was hoarse, half an octave lower than normal. She coughed and tried again. "It's just lightcells."

He turned out the flash; instead of darkness, he was surrounded by a blue-gray twilight. The flash had washed out the glow. Mischa was a shadow. Jan glanced over his shoulder: the two sets of footprints stretched away clear and black. His eyes began to adjust to the dim light.

"Are you all right?" The gravelly quality of her voice worried him.

"I will be."

They spoke no more; they needed what breath they could draw, and the air grew thicker, warmer, like the brightening growth of cells around them. The passage began to tilt downward again. Jan and Mischa moved more cautiously, for the footing became increasingly precarious as the pitch of the slope grew steeper. There was nothing to hold to, nothing to brace against. Jan's boots began to slide, with each step a little father, as the friction between him and the slimy floor became insufficient to hold him steady against gravity.

Mischa cried out. Sliding, she threw herself backward to counteract her forward momentum, landing hard on elbow and hip. Jan lunged for her, felt the rough material of her jacket beneath his fingertips, and lost her and his balance as well. He fell sideways down the slope; his palm slid through the mushy growth and he clawed for rock, but lightcells squished out between his fingers and he began to tumble and slide. He felt the mass piling up before him like snow, like surf; it washed over his head and he threw his arms across his face, sickened by the thought of its covering him, like grave rot. He abandoned any attempt to check his fall.

Jan felt the blow when he stopped: felt it but did not react to it; he was too dizzy, too sick, too confused. The atmosphere was so oppressive that he thought he could not open his eyes. A hollow breathlessness emptied him of strength. He thought he would faint: there could be no room for oxygen in the chemical soup he breathed.

He dragged himself up, using as support the rock that had stopped him. His ribs ached where he had struck.

The great vault into which they had fallen was suffused with the glow of life-surviving-on-death. Jan heard small sounds of animals, then, low at first, rising to a scream, the cry of something large and feline. He shivered.

The scar of Mischa's fall passed beyond the boulder. She lay a few meters farther on, face down, her hand submerged in murky, fetid water. She did not move. Past her, in the water, Jan saw other forms, some dark, shrouded, and new, some old and decomposing, overgrown with light. The shore of the pool was jagged and irregular with piles of bones: skulls; entire, articulated hands; shattered, fang-marked leg bones. This was the final resting place of Center's dead. The sour taste of bile rose in Jan's throat. He gagged and his reflexes overcame him; he retched drily, falling to his knees. Afterward, he knelt, breathing heavily, drawing the products of corruption into his lungs, accepting, knowing that he was their past, as they were his future.

He rose again and walked slowly to Mischa. She appeared so limp that he was afraid, imagining that she might have joined the luminous multitude. But as he knelt, she stirred. His relief was greater than any horror he had felt. He helped her up. Her hair clung in glowing strands to her cheek. She looked out over the water.

"Gods," she said. "So this is where they come."

"Yes." But for all Jan's acceptance, he did not look again. He was afraid he would see a shroud of black silk, embroidered with bright figures. "Let's get out of here."

Searching for an escape, they found a door. They almost passed it, but Mischa noticed the regular rectangular indentation and began to scrape away the lightcells. After a moment Jan helped her. They bared a featureless slab of gray plastic, the first evidence of construction Jan had seen since leaving Center. He recalled the three symbols of warning. They had survived the crystals, and the pool.

Mischa reached out and pushed the door. It swung open slowly. The musty air that flowed across them seemed incredibly, sweetly, blessedly fresh.

Subtwo fled, revolted, from the obscene pool. Even the respirator he wore could not keep out the stench. He was going to vomit: he could feel his body preparing to scorn him. He had never vomited in his life. The retching started and the facemask strangled him. He tore it away so he would not soil himself. He was forced to halt his flight. He tried to disassociate his mind from his body to spare himself humiliation and disgust, but failed.

He stumbled to his feet and ran again, headlong, hardly noticing that the fungal carpet no longer slowed him, that the tunnel was no longer a natural cave, that his people no longer followed him. It was only gradually, as the putrescent odor faded from his nostrils, that he realized he had escaped. The first thing he noticed consciously was that the air was clean: musty, but sterile. He slowed and stopped.

The hallway around him was white self-luminous plastic, perfectly smooth, perfectly regular: a golden rectangle in cross-section, a beautiful, elegant, naked place. Subtwo laid his hands against the cool wall and pressed his forehead to the surface. The exquisite smoothness calmed him slightly; lifting his head, he looked around.

He was alone. The open door at the end of the passage seemed very far away, and he would not return to it. His people . . .

They had broken the crystal stalactites, erupting in an orgy of destruction Subtwo was powerless to temper or control. Yet he had not been too displeased by their childish violence, despite the dreadful cacaphony. The sharp spires would be easier to walk over than between, and Subtwo was dedicated to expediency.

He noticed the bright dust and stepped back, as was his fastidious habit. The smell of it, the taste, burned the mucous membranes of his nose and throat just as Draco, at the head of the laughing group, doubled up and began to cough. The laughing stopped.

In a brief, shocked moment of silence between the end of the destruction of mineral and the beginning of the destruction of flesh, Subtwo flung open one of the carrying machines and found the respirators. He protected himself first, and called to his people to retreat.

Draco collapsed beyond the carpet of shattered jewels. Subtwo dragged him to a place where the air was clearer. The raiders who had been behind the dust were helping those who had been in it. Draco clawed at his throat, struggling for breath. Subtwo rammed a breathing tube past his swollen tongue and fumbled with antihistamines in the injector. The hunting party was well supplied, but the medic had stayed with Subone. Draco convulsed, and Subtwo held him still with sheer physical strength, no art about it, clumsily struggling to inject the medicine.

Three people choked to death before they could be helped. There were not enough breathing tubes, and more than half of Subtwo's people were crippled, needing aid that could not be given. He raged at the trap into which he had been lured, no longer needing to draw on Subone's anger: his own was by far more powerful. He had always been the more powerful, even in the early days of their lives when neither knew of the other's existence, but each controlled the other.

Those of his raiders who were still able readied themselves at his order. Draco rose and staggered about, searching for his weapons, respirator, another painkiller, a stimulant. Passing near Subtwo, he looked up, his pupils dilated wide. Subtwo understood that the young man was willing to kill himself, and this disturbed him vaguely, but he could not take the time to trace out why.

"I must leave someone in charge," he said abruptly. "There may be attacks on our casualties. We must be certain they are secure. Are you able?"

Draco started to protest, Subtwo thought, but words failed him; he had to suppress another spasm of coughing.

"I require someone I can trust."

Draco's voice, finally, was a hesitant rasp, burned out, resentful. "All right." He seemed shamed as much by his failure to protest as by his incapacity.

Jan Hikaru's Journal:

Mischa is sleeping. Her breathing is harsh, but it sounds better than it did earlier.

I'm very uncomfortable here. We're in a missile base, either for the defense of Center, or an offensive installation with Center as its backup—before the Last War. The third symbol: a place that humans made. It is indeed. But I can't feel any kinship with those humans.

But would we, in the Sphere, act any differently, given the same choices the people of earth had? We're very used to thinking of our home planet with contempt: they killed each other, they erupted in a tantrum of mass suicide and killed a whole world. There has never been another war.

We never mention that the same people drained their world dry to send us to new places.

Are we peaceful only because wars don't make economic sense anymore? Do we have a right to assume our superiority?

The myths are strong, though, and I feel oppressed. These are nuclear warheads all around us, I think—fission-triggered fusion bombs. The dirty kind, the kind that do more damage with their by-products than with their original explosions.

But the ones here were never fired. I wonder if that's because Center was never directly attacked, or because communications were destroyed and no one here ever received the orders, or, perhaps, because one person was unable, in the end, to push the buttons that would set them off.

I'd like to believe the last.

After resting, after making the injured as comfortable as possible, leaving them guarded and supplied, the remains of the hunting party had continued, breaking through the rest of the crystals while well protected in respirators and coveralls, and without laughter. Subtwo's people were frightened, and he had never seen them frightened before. Their unease affected him, for he had thought them beyond fear, or incapable of it.

They reached the fungal growth, which revolted him; he ordered it burned. The weapons cooked and sizzled it. But the task proceeded much too slowly, and frayed the nerves. The power of the laser lances made smoke and steam and heat billow up around the people, and the limestone began to crumble. Subtwo was disgusted at himself for failing to predict that particular danger: simple chemistry, which should be virtually instinctive. Exhorting his followers, he abandoned the burning and led them onward through the vile growths, pointing out the footprints of their quarry: See, there is no water collected in the indentations. See, how fresh the tracks must be. We have not much longer to wait now. But his people had abandoned their rages. They were exhausted, their throats were sore, their ears rang; they could not even sit down comfortably to rest.

When they came to the steep slick hill, they almost refused to continue. They saw that Mischa and Jan had fallen, and though rock formations prevented their seeing the bottom of the slope, they argued that their prey must have perished. Subtwo berated himself for preventing Draco from coming: he would not have faltered; he would have given the others courage.

Subtwo had stood before them, rage tightening his voice. But the mask muffled his words, and he sounded, even to himself, quite ineffectual. He broke off his speech and looked at his people in silence, seeing what a motley and pitiful group they were, outcasts . . . like himself. "Follow me or not, as you will," he said, turned and plunged down the slope.

It seemed to him as he leaped downward, trying to keep his balance, that the underground had tried to kill him thrice: by poison with the crystals, by disease and dissolution with the fungus, and now by falling. Irrationally he thought that if he could survive this time, he would succeed in all he sought under the earth, that if he faltered, he would fail in everything.

The pitch of the slope increased abruptly. He ran faster, trying desperately to remain upright. His feet squelched in the thick globs of mold. He was running down the wall like an impossible insect. He cried out before he even slipped, for all the factors came together in his mind, sliding into an equation of incredible complexity, and he understood that the unknowns had no acceptable solution.

He fell.

The water closed in over him, shocking him from insensible dizziness, closing over the facemask, dirty, bubbling. He struggled up, but his hands and knees sank into what had seemed like solid ground. He floundered toward the shore: the bank came away in his fingers, crumbling. One solid bar remained; he jabbed it down and pulled against it, and by sheer adrenalin-spiked terror he escaped the sticky morass behind him.

He stood shivering, his hand clenched around the only fragment of solidity in this place, whatever it was. But a ghastly stench reached him faintly through the respirator. Simultaneously, he saw the bodies in the water and on the bank, he realized how the mold could grow so lushly, and he recognized the thing in his hand as a human bone.

His breath rasped softly, then louder. He flung the bone away, and he felt the weight of water and organic matter impregnating his clothing, and blindly ran, clawing frantically at bits of damp matter that clung to him like leeches, crying faintly from deep in his chest.

The underground had won; this was to be his final resting place, the complete antithesis of all he had ever believed in.

Now, alone, totally alone, Subtwo stumbled down the corridor. His clothing seemed to crawl against his skin. He began to pluck it off, holding the material by corners and fastenings, in the tips of his fingers, even though he was wearing gloves. The gloves were last to go; he threw them down and they thudded wetly to the floor. He abandoned them gladly; naked, he proceeded, for he could not turn back, even to try to find his people. He retained only his laser lance, which he clenched tightly in his fist, as though it could stop the trembling of his hands. Unused to nudity, he felt uncomfortable and vulnerable, and wished for improvements in the male human body, or for Subone to take his place. Yet even the exposure was better than remaining in those stinking garments. The reek still clung to him, to his skin, to his hair. With vague gratitude he clung to the memory that he had not breathed the stuff, it had not flowed into his nose or mouth or lungs. If it had, he surely would have gone insane.

His body threatened to revolt again with nausea, so Subtwo dragged his attention completely back to the present.

The corridor ended abruptly with an elevator. Subtwo entered it, quite conscious of his peril. It looked very old: perhaps it would jam, and he would starve or suicide. But it was the only path. He did not even know if he was still following any kind of trail: he strained to remember if he had noticed footprints to this hallway, but he could not force himself to recall the scene. He touched the single button on the wall panel, a control without markings. The door slid shut, without a sound, but slowly like an ancient wraith.

Panic touched him again, when the cage fell. He did not want to go deeper into the earth.

As he moved downward, on and on, it seemed to him that Subone should be here; it seemed to him that his pseudosib had changed, since they had come to Center, in ways that would have permitted him to endure this trial much better.

Subtwo braced himself against the deceleration. The elevator door opened.

He was prepared for darkness, so the light startled and disturbed him. Much brighter than the dim illumination his eyes had become accustomed to, the glaring blue-white radiance dazzled him. He blinked into it, and gradually made out a long, wide, high chamber, as regular in design as the corridor and the elevator. Thick pillars rose in a pleasingly regular manner. Moving into the room, Subtwo felt a gentle whisper of air, which alerted him for the presence of other human beings. But the place had a calm and deserted feel about it, dustless, odorless; chromed machines clustered about the bases of the columns, metal shiny and unfingerprinted. He felt, he knew, no human beings lived here. The ventilation would be automatic, the machines self-sustaining. No organic matter soiled this vault.

Suddenly he stopped and spun around, staring up at the columns, straight-sided, sloping to a narrower radius at their centers and again near their tips, with round black holes above them; they circled him as though they were moving and he were standing still, as he recognized them for what they were.

15

Mischa drank sparingly from her flask. The water soothed her sore throat, which hurt less than before she had slept. Nearby, Jan returned his notebook to his pocket. He was covered all over, even his hair, with a dry gray dust of lightcells. Mischa brushed at her own sleeve, but the dust remained.

"Can you talk?"

"Oh . . . yeah."

"You sound better."

"What did you write?"

"That I didn't like this place."

"There's another on the other side of Center," Mischa said. "Not quite so far from the city. I used to go and look and wish the rockets were for people instead of bombs."

"That would have been better all around."

A soft sound whispered back and forth. Mischa moved to the entrance of the small alcove they had chosen as a hiding place for its view of the elevator. Jan had heard the sound too, and came to stand beside her. They watched in silence as the door slid open, and a single naked man stepped out.

"Is that—?"

Mischa could understand Jan's uncertainty, for Subone and Subtwo were very much alike in form. Their faces had both changed recently, but this man's face was smeared with dirt and filth. "It's Subtwo," Mischa said. She had no doubt of that.

He did have hair on his body, after all, but only around his genitals, not on his arms or legs or even under his arms. The small and insufficiently modest dark diamond made him seem faintly ridiculous.

"He must have fallen . . ." Jan's voice trailed off. "He's alone. His raiders broke."

Or they were hiding and waiting, but Mischa could catch no drift of deception in Subtwo, only barely repressed hysteria.

Subtwo moved slowly, gazing about. In the center of a square marked by missiles at its corners, he halted. His gaze moved slowly from the base to the tip of one of the graduated shafts, pausing at the symbols on its sides, hesitating at its summit. Then he spun, around and around, eyes wide open and head straight, with no attempt to avoid dizziness.

"He can't be thinking he could use them." Jan's voice was low and taut with disgust.

Subtwo stopped his solitary dance. It did not seem to have affected him, for he walked without a stumble to one of the missiles, and reached out hesitantly, gently, to touch its metal flank.

"Subtwo!"

Jan started, gasping, and grabbed her arm. Her hoarse voice reverberated, each echo more distorted than the last.

Subtwo jerked himself around, laser lance ready, but he could not find his quarry. "Who is it?"

"It's me and Jan Hikaru, of course," Mischa said. "Who did you think?"

"Ah," he sighed, and Mischa thought, but could not be certain, that the sound meant an instant's regret. If it did, the instant passed, and the regret with it, leaving only rigid anger. The muzzle of the lance wavered back and forth, searching.

"I don't want to kill you," Mischa said. "All I ever wanted was to get away from here. Before Subone—"

"There is only him and me," Subtwo said.

"But it's all one-way. It's always you doing what he wants."

Subtwo hesitated, and when he spoke was betrayed by the abrupt belligerence of his tone. "Come out! I refuse to speak to shadows."

"Throw away your weapon."

Subtwo laughed.

"It's useless," Jan said. "You can't take the chance of using it here."

Subtwo's good humor did not lessen. "Ah, generalists," he said. "You know a little about everything, but not enough about anything. Do you think I could trigger a fusion reaction with a pocket laser?"

"You could break the case of the fission trigger," Jan said. "These are bombs, not generators. Old ones. Dirty ones."

Subtwo lowered the lance and backed away from the nearest missile. Knowing approximately how the bombs worked, Mischa saw he was afraid of stray radiation, though the triggers might be too many half-lives old even to explode.

"I haven't got any quarrel with you," Mischa said again. "Why do you always have to fight for Subone? Where's he?"

"You should know. You attacked him."

"I hardly scratched him—that was weeks ago."

Subtwo's expression changed to a strange kind of uncertain pity. "Your mind is disarranged," he said. "You and your friends attacked and wounded him yesterday, the day before. And killed one of our people."

Mischa glanced at Jan, who looked as puzzled as she felt. "What's he talking about? He can't mean the looker Crab got."

"I doubt it," Jan said. "Subtwo may prefer machines to people, but he doesn't confuse them."

"Nobody ever attacked anybody down here," Mischa called.

"You lie."

But Mischa felt the uncertainty again. "Maybe it's somebody else who's lying," she said, to see what would happen.

"Stop this. Bring on your freaks. I am prepared to face them."

"Don't call them that!"

"What should I call them?" Subtwo asked, quite sincerely.

"They're people just like us. They're not here, Subtwo, they hide when anybody from Center comes around. They were gone before you even got close."

"They wounded Subone, and they have killed."

"Don't you ever doubt him? Are you so close you know everything he's thinking all the time?"

"I used to be . . ."

"He lied to you."

"If he lied . . . he mutilated himself. He murdered . . ."

"He's changed," Jan said. "He's changed, and so have you."

"I will not speak to shadows. . . ."

Mischa stepped out of the alcove. Jan tightened his hand on her arm, then let her go, hesitated, and followed her. She walked to Subtwo and looked up at him. "Then speak to my face. Tell me you know he's never lied. Tell me I ever lied to you."

Subtwo looked down. Mischa reached out and drew the pistol away from him. He tightened his grasp on it, lifted his head, meeting her gaze steadily, pleading. Mischa held on, thinking she had miscalculated Subtwo completely, but he did not try to pull back. "You must do one thing," he said. "If you do, I will cooperate in all things. My people will surrender to my order, and no one will oppose you."

She waited in silence.

"You must promise not to kill him."

Mischa scowled. "Why do you keep protecting him?"

"You came to me so you could leave earth. I will take you. No one else can fly you through the storms. Without our ship, Subone will be stranded here. That is . . . a considerable revenge."

Jan moved up behind her, putting his hand on her shoulder. "Give him that much," he said softly, with pity. "You've got his pride."

This serves his wishes well, she thought. "All right," she said finally. "I won't unless he makes me."

Subtwo released the pistol.

The pseudosib refused to return to Center the way they had come; even threats, Mischa could see, would not change his mind. Having explored the missile base on the other side of Center, she did not take long to find other exits. She thought the one she chose would allow them to pass behind Subtwo's people undetected. She was not very worried about meeting them: she believed they would surrender on Subtwo's order, or, at least, she believed he thought they would. Jan concerned her more, for he had held off his exhaustion much too long. As they reentered the caves and paused to let their eyes adjust to the dimmer light of Jan's flash, Mischa leaned against the clean gray tunnel wall beside him. "You want to stop and rest for a while?"

He smiled. "Sure. But if I stop now I won't move for two days. That's more time than we can take."

"Yeah."

"You're glowing."

"You, too," she said. The lightcells, in their dry form, were faintly luminous. Mischa glanced at Subtwo, who hunched down against the opposite wall, arms wrapped around naked legs, in a posture of abject misery. His skin gleamed softly in reflected light, as though he were oiled; only his hair retained the lightcells' glow.

"A halo on Subtwo just doesn't fit," Jan said. "Let's get going."

Mischa and Jan walked together, supporting each other; Subtwo walked mechanically, staring at the floor except when it was absolutely necessary to raise his head: for difficult trails, chasms, narrow ledges.

They stopped only when they could walk no farther, and then not for long, though when they found a clean stream they paused to bathe: even Subtwo immersed himself in the undistilled, unfiltered water with Mischa, Jan, and the fishes. All during the journey Mischa waited to hear or feel any hint of Subtwo's people, but she was too tired to reach out for them, and the time and distance passed slowly but steadily, until finally they reached the indeterminate region where the underground began to blend into the outer tunnels.

"Jan, look—"

He raised his head, reached up, pushed his hair off his forehead. "What?"

"There." She pointed.

He squinted, turned out the flash, blinked, and finally smiled. "Light-tubes?"

"Yeah." The tubes were blinking and dimming with approaching night, but they signaled the last lap of the journey.

"I wouldn't trade them for some sunlight, but they'll do for now."

They proceeded, but after a short way Mischa thought she could hear faint sounds behind them. She turned half-around. A few steps beyond, Jan halted.

"Listen." They heard, faintly, the echo of a tapping or clattering, very familiar. Then Mischa felt a faint exclamation of greeting and joy. "Crab?" She ran back into the darkness. The beam of Jan's flash lanced past her and picked out Crab's form in starker shadows as he galloped forward, blinking his protruding green eyes. Mischa fell on her knees and hugged him. "Crab, did you run away? What about Val?" But Crab was so excited that his mind was in complete turmoil; she could get no information from him at all. He grabbed her hand and pulled her the way he had come. "No, we can't go back—"

She saw a small group of lights at the other end of the tunnel, coming closer. Soon she could see their bearers: a forlorn group of Subtwo's raiders, some carried on stretchers, some helped along by their comrades, stripped of their machines and their equipment. And after them, the underground people.

Val walked at their head. In leather and silk, with her incredibly fine scarlet hair standing out around her head and a laser pistol held loose in one hand, she looked fierce and wild and beautiful. The other underground people, guarding the bedraggled raiders, looked uncomfortable, yet proud.

"Hello, Mischa."

The group behind her stopped; Subtwo's people put down their burdens and sank to the ground.

"Hi, Val. Hi, Simon."

Simon only nodded.

"Crab was worried about you," Val said defensively. "He wouldn't eat or sleep and he tried to come up after you, but he couldn't handle the raft."

"I'm glad you came," Mischa said.

"Why? You didn't need our help."

"Because now you know you don't have to run if anyone ever tries to drive you out again."

"But they prove nothing." Val gestured derisively at the raiders. "We didn't fight them, we just picked them up by ones and twos, like mushrooms. They panicked."

"But Center couldn't send anyone who would do any better."

Val frowned, shaking her head, and glanced toward Jan for support. "You're sensible. You explain to her."

Jan shrugged, not with indifference but with amusement. "I guess I'm not so sensible. I think she's right."

"Tell me," Val said, "tell me, and don't flatter us, if what you have just said is true."

Mischa wondered why Val was asking for reassurance, whether she needed justification for what she had led the others to do, whether she needed reinforcement for self-confidence or a strengthening of new reactions toward the people of Center. "It's true," Mischa said. She could not explain the differences between Center and the deep underground; it seemed to her that independence and initiative had disappeared from the city: that people ran in gangs or lived in families and used the ties to steal from or hurt each other; or that they lived all alone, in fear. "It's true," she said. "It's like Center is killing itself and eating itself, but you're still alive."

Subtwo passed Mischa, ignoring her, ignoring Val, dully approaching his people, looking from one tired face to another, holding himself stiffly so he would not sway and touch their filthy clothes. He paused at each stretcher, gazing briefly at the faces, until he came to the last, which was covered. Hesitating, he seemed to draw on some unfamiliar inner strength, even hope; he pulled aside the corner of the blanket.

Mischa recognized Draco, his chin smeared with dry blood. Subtwo, with anger and relief and disappointment in his expression, turned on them.

"Draco is dead. Have you killed Subone as well?"

Val faced him. A chill prickled across the back of Mischa's neck, along her spine: archaic reaction to Subtwo's tone and to the sight of the hair at the base of Val's neck standing straight up. "We killed no one," Val said, her tone low.

Wordlessly, Subtwo motioned toward the stretcher.

"He has no wound from us. He breathed glass dust, like these others he was guarding."

"So you killed him."

Val said, very quietly, "He was already dead."

Subtwo took a deep, audible breath. "And Subone?"

"If he was in the underground, he is still there."

Subtwo looked over his shoulder, back at the long, dark tunnel. "He was to wait for me to return. He will not know where to go."

"You wandered around down there for him," Mischa said, irritated. "Let him wander around for you. He'll probably even find his way back."

"He always . . . needed me."

"He doesn't need you anymore! How often are you going to let him make a fool of you?"

Subtwo did not answer and Mischa did not push him any more. "Val," she said, "Jan and I made a deal with Subtwo. We're leaving earth. Will you come with us?"

"No."

Crab gripped Mischa's hand, sad-feeling, understanding that she was going away. Mischa knelt beside him.

"You don't have to say good-bye quite yet," Val said to them. "It's dark in Center now. We'll come a little farther."

"Mischa, come!"

Mischa cringed, physically, at the shock of Gemmi's intrusion into her mind. *No,* Mischa thought, *no, not now, all I needed was a few more hours.* But Gemmi did not understand, she never understood; she pulled and called Mischa more vigorously, frightened by her resistance. Crab felt her too, and crouched down surprised, gripping Mischa's hand so tightly it hurt.

Subtwo was a double image before her. For an instant, Mischa thought that Subone had magically arrived and would convince Subtwo again that she and Jan had to be murdered. Her vision cleared. The group passed her and Mischa followed, nearly staggering, Crab creeping along beside her.

Jan dropped back. "What's wrong?"

She stared at him blankly.

"Mischa, come!" Gemmi bubbled through her mind, a brook, a stream, a flooded river. Mischa squeezed her eyes shut. When she opened them again Jan seemed to have moved away, two Jans staring at her, eight Jans reaching for her, and Mischa was looking at the world through a clear, faceted jewel that split and spread and altered light and images. Then, with every step she took toward him, the images clicked back to half their number, a quarter, an eighth, and Jan stood beside her all alone.

"It's Gemmi," Mischa whispered, "it's Gemmi, she's calling me, they'll never let me go. . . ."

"We're almost there," Jan said. "She won't be able to follow you off earth—"

"I don't know . . . she never gets any weaker."

"You've never been able to get very far away," Jan said. "Try, Mischa. Hold on just a little longer."

"All . . . right. . . ."

Jan put his arm around her shoulders, supporting her physically and with his deep, calm presence.

But she knew she would never get away; she had never really had a chance, not for all her dreams, for all her defiance. She saw Val and Simon and the others watching her curiously and with concern, but they were all very far off and could not reach or help her. Gemmi sensed that Mischa was not coming toward her, and she began to shriek and scream. Every step Mischa took seemed to be through quicksand, in which she would drown if she faltered or fell. She felt tears streaming down her face; she could hear nothing. The world blurred and spun. She pulled away from Jan; her knees and her palms hit stone. "I've tried to fight them before," she said. "Don't you think . . . I've tried . . . ?" She spread her hands flat on the hard rock. "I can't come," she whispered. "Not now . . ." She heard Jan's voice, and Val's, and even Simon's, explaining, arguing, discussing, and finally Subtwo said, "She must be let go, or she will go mad instead," and Mischa thought that he alone might understand how strongly she was being commanded.

She heard a loud crack, like something breaking or rocks falling a great distance, and everyone but Gemmi receded. She tried to get up; she thought they were leaving her.

She felt Crab's mind touch hers, and she fought even him. He pushed her identity to the edge of her brain. She could not spare the concentration to understand him. He was standing by her head, holding both her hands, sending little tendrils of thought toward her like bits of spiderweb. Gemmi felt Crab too, and drew back in fear of the never-before-encountered. But Crab lured her gently out again with the convolutions and precipices of his consciousness. For a long, long time, they stayed that way, Mischa watching half-insensible as Crab and Gemmi played. Mischa thought she heard a ship take off: she thought Jan had left and Val had gone back to the deep underground; Chris was dead, and she was all alone again, except for Crab and Gemmi, forever. "It isn't fair!" she cried to them, enraged. "Crab, I thought we were friends!" And suddenly he seemed to understand what all this meant to her, with an implosion of intuition that allowed him to untangle, for a split-second, the confused sensations of his mind. Mischa felt him draw on the power of her fury and reach out—as if his spirit were shaped like his body, with sharp claws—and pull her with him until she could see Gemmi more clearly than she ever had or wished to; in that split-second Mischa could see all that Gemmi could see: a mosaic of every consciousness in Center. But neither she nor Crab could stand it; they drew back, and the total melding was over. But Crab stayed near Gemmi; Mischa saw what he was searching for and pointed it out. He reached for it. "Wait, no," Mischa said. "That one first." He reached through a maze of connections and snapped a single thread.

Gemmi's pain vanished with the destroyed synapse. For the first time in her life, she did not hurt: her body could no longer hurt her, nor could the ugliness she could not shut away.

Crab cut the second synapse, and Gemmi disappeared.

Mischa sat up slowly, shaking her head. Expecting to see a bare corridor, and Crab, and no one else, she was astonished that everyone was still there, standing in a circle around her.

"How long . . . ?"

"Ten seconds, maybe," Jan said.

"I thought you had all gone. It seemed like days."

Jan knelt down beside her and brushed the hair from her forehead with his fingertips.

"She's gone," Mischa said.

"Crab wouldn't let us near you."

Crab clicked his claws together and Mischa remembered the loud snap: his sound of warning. "We did something to Gemmi's mind," Mischa said. "She can watch and see, but she can't call anymore. And she can't be hurt. . . ." She shuddered, and Crab squeezed close against her side. She could feel his amazement at what he had seen: so many people, all at once, each individual a different shade, a different hue, some whole, some shattered, some weak, some strong—

"Subtwo," Mischa said, "Subone's coming back. I could see him."

"Returning? No, he was wounded. He is resting, or he is dead."

"He's *coming.*" She knew that if she reached for him she could touch him again, coming closer, amused by his victory over his pseudosib, and always ready to slip back into a rage that would drag Subtwo into his battles.

"You say that to reassure me," Subtwo said. "So I will keep our bargain, whether he is dead or not."

Feeling light and dizzy, as though she had fasted for several days, Mischa let Jan help her up. "Believe what you want." She had no energy left with which to argue. Near her, his instant's flash of comprehension gone, Crab hardly remembered what they had done. He had thought only to help Mischa, and that he had achieved; but had they helped Gemmi? She was cut off from all experience but what she saw from others. She could no longer be hurt, but she could be crippled, maimed, killed. *She can't be hurt.* Mischa repeated that to herself, trying to convince herself that nothing more need be done. If the child were disfigured by beatings before their uncle realized Mischa would never return, if Gemmi were scarred and made ugly, she would not know it, any more than she knew now that she was beautiful. If she died, what guilt could there be? Mischa had willed her death a thousand times.

Mischa could have abandoned Gemmi when Gemmi could command her, but now it was impossible. The fine philosophical distinctions evaded her. Perhaps only the situation had changed; perhaps Mischa herself was different. She only knew for certain that she could not leave Gemmi where she was. She started down the tunnel.

"Mischa—where are you going?"

She turned back. She had not exactly forgotten that the other people were there; they simply had no connection with what she had to do now. Jan looked completely mystified, but she could not stop to explain. "I can't leave her," she said. "I can't just let her die." She turned and ran, away from Center, away from Stone Palace, away from the ship.

Her uncle's niche seemed much farther away than it actually was. Mischa was panting, her throat fatigue-raw, when she finally stopped before the new curtains and pulled them aside.

"Ah," her uncle said, putting down a delicate goblet. "Very good. Very fast. You'll have to do as well from now on." Gemmi lay on her pallet, smiling and cooing.

"There isn't any *from now on,*" Mischa said.

He raised his eyebrow and glanced at Gemmi, who began to cry. But

Mischa only sensed a dim distasteful aura, directly from her uncle. She ignored it, and nodded to the paid companion lounging in the back of the cave. "You can go back to Center now."

The companion pushed back a lock of heavy golden hair, stretched, moved to take advantage of highlights on smooth pale skin. "Are you paying?"

"I was. No more."

The companion shrugged, stood up, and moved languidly toward Mischa's uncle.

"Wait a minute!"

"Go on," Mischa said.

The companion kissed her uncle on the lips and left the cave.

"What do you think—"

"You can't do anything to me anymore." She went to Gemmi, who reached toward her, still sobbing. Suddenly their uncle sucked in his breath, a long, shuddering gasp of terror.

Mischa glanced around. "It's only Crab. Your nephew."

"Gods . . ."

Crab sidled up to Mischa, leery of new people but interested in Gemmi. He took her hands and the child quieted, wide-eyed. Mischa picked up the long chain that fastened Gemmi to the wall.

"Where's the key?"

"The key." He said the words with little inflection, still staring at Crab. "The key?" Recovering himself, he smiled, he laughed. "There is no key. When did *you* need a key? I poured acid on the lock."

Mischa bent over the heavy shackle. The acid had achieved its purpose, filling the lock with crusted metal salt, perhaps weakening the mechanism, but making it impervious to picks. "You think you're so smart," Mischa said. She had never been able to speak that way to him without the knowledge of certain punishment. The new knowledge, that he could not punish her anymore, gave Mischa no pleasure at all. She felt only pity.

She drew Subtwo's laser lance from beneath her jacket. She would have preferred to free Gemmi completely, but that would have to wait. The beam bit into the metal and stone, flinging out bits of molten material. With Crab hiding behind her, Mischa threw a blanket over Gemmi, shielded her own eyes, and fired again. The chain rattled, falling loose.

"Now what?" His voice was contemptuous. "What will you do with her? You still need me to take care of her—"

"I don't need you for anything. You needed me and Chris, but you couldn't admit it, so you had to try to make us both your slaves. And that's why he's dead." *Partly,* she thought. *Because you pushed us too hard, and I pushed him harder.* She looked down at Gemmi, who was as beautiful as Chris had been, but as empty as he was toward the last. The child was unhappy, reflecting the anger and hatred all around her. Mischa soothed her own thoughts and tried to make even ordinary things beautiful in her mind. With the hot end of the chain tied into the blanket, Mischa half-lifted and half-carried her sister toward the doorway. Gemmi was a large and healthy child, bigger than Mischa, unable to stand, awkward to move. Crab tried to help.

Their uncle tried to struggle up, but his legs failed him. "You can't just leave me!"

Mischa ignored the cry.

His voice rose in panic. "How do you expect me to live?"

Mischa glanced back, pitying him, until the pity dissolved in bitterness. "Beg," she said.

Jan followed Mischa away from Center. He was too tired to run. When Mischa turned a corner and went out of sight, he could still see Crab, but soon even Crab outdistanced him and he was alone in the corridor again, following blindly, hoping the tunnel would not branch.

He did not react when a hand grasped his shoulder. He was too tired even for surprise. He simply stopped, and after a moment turned, to see, with relief, that Simon had come after him. They continued together. Anything could happen now, with Val and the others guarding Subtwo and his raiders. The underground people were terribly vulnerable to public outcry, even in this sparsely populated section of the city's outskirts. If a mob were raised against them, they would be trapped between it on one side and Subone's group on the other; and Subtwo would be bound to his bargain with Mischa only by his word. Jan knew he should have stayed with the others, but he did not want to leave Mischa to a confrontation all alone.

The dimming lights at the far limit of Jan's vision sparkled in his fatigue, and he had an odd feeling of observing but not comprehending. Simon was a blur at his side. Jan stared down at the stone floor, watching his feet move one step, another.

Simon grasped his arm again; Jan stopped obediently and glanced around, blankly, until Simon shook him and pointed.

A hundred meters ahead, Crab stopped his headlong gallop toward them, lumbered a few steps back the way he had come, stopped again, and waited, moving a few steps this way, a few steps that.

He led them down the tunnel, and into a branch that Jan thought he himself would have passed, a narrower, dimmer place with a musty, fetid smell. A few minutes later they met Mischa, carrying and dragging a young girl with her. The child was half-naked and her movements were uncoordinated, reflexive, aimless. Seeing Jan and Simon, Mischa stopped. The stress of fatigue and frustration was plain.

"She never learned to walk," Mischa said. "She never could."

Simon bent down and picked up the dragging end of the melted chain.

"I can get that off," Mischa said. "I just need a little time."

"We haven't much time," Jan said.

"We will free her." Simon threw down the chain and picked Gemmi up easily. "She is one of us."

The Circle was very quiet, as though hibernating until its patrons came back from their quest. The few people who saw the raiders and their captors, and recognized what they saw, stopped, and backed into shadows, and crept quickly away. Gradually, the path before Mischa and the others became more and more deserted, as an electrified current of knowledge passed before them.

The underground people drew closer together, fearing what they had never seen. Crab held Mischa's hand, watching, interested in all the new places they passed. Jan continued doggedly forward with no resiliency left in his step at all, and Val walked with Simon, her nervousness increasing, but her pride and her confidence restored. She spoke occasionally in a voice too low for Mischa to hear, and once Simon answered. Subtwo led the group, still naked, for he would not touch the ill-assorted filthy garments his people had to spare.

Why Val and the rest had decided to enter the city was still a mystery. They were curious, but Mischa sensed more purpose in their actions, a purpose that overcame their fear.

Subtwo stopped before the closed door of the pseudosibs' section of the Palace. This was the first time Mischa had ever seen it shut, and she imagined that it might not open, that someone inside had been warned they were coming and closed them out. But Subtwo unlocked it with his voice and they entered. Mischa secured it again behind them, but there was no way to lock Subone out.

When she turned back, Subtwo was facing the small group, blocking the corridor. "How do I know our bargain has not already been broken? How do I know he is not dead?"

"He's alive! If we don't hurry, he'll be here."

Subtwo did not move except to lower his head, glaring; he would renege if he was not sure his pseudosib was alive.

"Call him, then," Mischa said. "He's near, he must be around antenna leads."

Subtwo scowled more deeply, suspicious, but unable to find deceit in her suggestion. He led the way to his quarters: through the long, carpeted halls, past a residence wing, in which the raiders were locked, disarmed but with access to food and medicine. They did not even protest. In the foyer, the light-fountain sparkled brilliant white. The underground people followed, into the paneled corridor that led directly to Subtwo's rooms, touching strange things gently; they seemed to have no need or desire to take or destroy. In Subtwo's workroom, they stood in a tight group, like small creatures who had blundered into the interior of a machine.

Subtwo sat down at the console, slowly, almost reluctantly. "If I cannot reach him, our agreement is void."

"I never lied to you," Mischa said.

He turned on his equipment. They heard static, scrambled Family chatter, channels of sensory input, as Subtwo scanned the frequencies for a clear calling band.

He called, paused, called, paused, and the response returned. "Is that you? Where are you?" Subone's voice: he sounded surprised.

"I am in our quarters."

"At the Palace! But—"

"Where are you?"

"Coming home. But you—"

"You were to wait for my return."

"I felt stronger—we decided—never mind me. Did you—?"

"I found them."

There was a hesitation, as of surprise. "Good!" Subone exclaimed.

"Excellent! I knew you would avenge me, brother." The tone was not one of satisfaction in revenge, but of gloating in power. Mischa heard it; everyone in the room heard it: even Subtwo. He raised his hand as though to smash it down on the controls, wavered, and slowly closed his fingers into a great fist.

"We are no longer brothers."

As Subone's voice, in confused protest, spilled from the receiver, Subtwo turned it off, very, very carefully. He faced the people in his quarters as though they all were honored guests. "He will return soon. We must hurry."

He seemed, to Mischa, as afraid as she was that Subone still could influence him, but now, at least, he was certain of the motives.

"Then let's go."

That infuriating, tolerant expression slipped over his face. "In a moment. Is there nothing you want?" He let his gaze wander over the room; he walked to his desk and touched bits of equipment.

"No, nothing. Nothing at all. Except to leave." She was becoming exasperated with him, and dreading that he would, in the end, delay until Subone arrived. Her fingertips brushed the sculpted handle of the lance. Jan turned her a little. "Give him a minute," he said. "I want to get a few things too, if they're still in my room."

She acceded, reluctantly, not really wanting to let him go alone, he looked so tired, but afraid to trust Subtwo, afraid everything would fall apart again. She sat on the floor and put her arms around Crab, telling him slowly, gently, that she was leaving, right now, not in his inde-terminate and unimaginable personal future. He had seen—and un-derstood, for an infinitesimal bit of time—what she was doing and why, and though the understanding had faded, he retained the memory of it. He did not try to convince her to stay.

Val padded over to them. "Is Crab going with you?"

"He's going wherever you and Simon go," Mischa said. "But I don't know what to tell him."

"We haven't changed our minds. We're staying here."

"Will you be all right without Subtwo as a hostage?"

"We'll be all right. Don't worry." Her eyes smiled; her aura sparkled with excitement.

Mischa leaned down to Crab again. He was, after all, very young, and preferred events to go as he pleased. In the end, she told him she would try, someday, to come and see him again. When she looked up, the underground people stood around her. "Now it's time to say good-bye," Val said.

Mischa stood up. "Good-bye, then." She hugged Val and Simon. "Good-bye, Simon."

"Good-bye, Mischa." He gripped her hands hard, claws retracted.

"Be careful." She embraced each of the others, wishing them well.

"When you get to the Sphere," Val said, "tell them we are still alive. Tell them not to send their renegades here anymore. Tell them our children should not have to be born crippled."

"I will. I promise."

Silent and strange, they left her alone with Subtwo.

Still naked, and of all his possessions only a microcomputer and two library input banks neatly stacked behind him, he was sitting at his console, moving his hands among the controls of his links to the Palace intercom, flipping the image from camera to camera.

"What are you doing?" Mischa cried it out; guiltily, startled, he pushed himself away the console. Mischa needed no more proof for her suspicions. She smashed her fist against the master power control and fused the panel with the laser lance.

"I was only trying to . . . contact someone."

"I'll bet."

"Not to call for help—"

"Come on. I want to get Jan."

"But I must—"

"No!"

He gazed down at the ruined console, at the blank, gray, depthless screens. "But she will think I did not care . . ."

"Hurry up!" Mischa did not listen to him; she had no patience for his petty intrigues and *affaires,* and the despair she felt from him would have to wait for any sympathy: she believed it to be because he was leaving Subone.

Shoulders slumped, Subtwo crossed the room, found one of his blue-gray coveralls, and put it on while Mischa fumed impatiently.

16

From her childhood, when Stone Palace had been a busier place, Val remembered the ways from one level to the next, and led her people through halls and alice tubes. She was glad she had left the children behind, safe, for they would be frightened and there was no time for reassurance or explanations. Simon stalked beside her, wary of the differences between this and what he was used to: light everywhere, passages more regular than any watercourse, the vast overuse of fabric, and finally the internal distortions of the alice tube as it drifted them slowly upward. Only Gemmi liked the feeling.

Val expected guards when they reached the main level, and her people were ready, but no one and nothing awaited them. She posted guards of her own, at the tube, at the silent barracks wing. The Palace had never used electronic surveillance fifteen years before, but that was during the old Lord's time; Blaisse, his son, had always been much more suspicious and frightened of threats from the city. But everyone behind her knew the danger; everyone had agreed to what they were doing. She led them deeper into ornate corridors.

The ancient, senile old Lord used to wander through these halls, never very far from his living suite, and the children would fall silent in their playing when he passed. Val could almost see his ghost, drifting among the jewels and metallic embroidery, where he had never seemed quite comfortable.

Val sent her people around the suites. Here, she knew, there would be guards, but perhaps not many, since it was winter. She had to drag all this information back from years of trying to forget it.

The first guard was dozing in a comfortable chair; Val remembered that it was night, though the dim illumination of Center's darkness had been, to her, like day.

She and Simon crept up on the young man. Simon held him by the throat, ignoring the fingernails clawing at his hands, until the man collapsed unconscious. They tied him with gold ropes.

The room beyond the small foyer was dark. Val pushed the curtain aside, letting in a shaft of light; the trim of baubles clinked and jangled.

"Who's there?"

Somehow, Val's biggest surprise of all was that she remembered her cousin's voice perfectly. She had to fumble a bit for the light control: it was no longer at shoulder height. Even with the inadequate diet of the underground, Val had grown taller. The lights came on slowly, automatically set so they would not dazzle any royal person's delicate eyes.

"Hello, cousin," Val said.

Clarissa sat up in the wide, low bed, sleepily. She was still beautiful and elegant, but now in a slovenly sort of way. She had changed, as much as Val or more; she had been sent to Stone Palace by bad luck of being firstborn of her Family. It was much too easy to do nothing here. When they were children, all of them knew what their work would be, except Blaisse and his younger brother, who knew they would have no work.

". . . Val?" Next to her, the pretty sleeping boy reacted to Clarissa's voice. Beginning to wake, he shifted, and Val could see the marks of Clarissa's fingernails and her whip on his back. Clarissa glanced at him and snatched a crop from her bedside. "Wake up!"

"Don't"—Val shouted as Clarissa raised her arm—"do that," she finished in a normal tone as her cousin jerked back the short whip. The boy cringed behind his arm.

"You never used to be so solicitous of slaves."

"I never used to know any better." Val was impressed by her cousin's composure, though she had not known what reaction to expect.

"So you're alive."

"That was the whole point, wasn't it?"

"Yes, I suppose it was, on the surface. But they really wanted you to die, you know. They just couldn't do it themselves."

"I know. Get up, Clarissa."

Blaisse's guard was awake, but could not oppose them without endangering the Lady. Val held her tightly by the arm, and it was not until the guard's laser lance hit the floor that Clarissa's taut muscles relaxed. Her laugh held an edge of fear. "Blaisse won't thank you for that." Leaving the guard well bound, they moved through the library, down the stairs. "I didn't know," Clarissa said, "what he might have told them to do if this ever happened." It seemed to Val quite characteristic of Blaisse that he would never have told them anything. The subject of an attempted coup was not one he would wish to contemplate.

They found him sleeping peacefully, like a child, his head pillowed on the breast of his slave.

"What do you intend to do with me?" Blaisse had tried to run away and Simon had caught and hit him; now the Lord nursed a bruised cheek and would look only at Val.

"Perhaps—exile you? Drive you to the deep underground?"

"I had nothing to do with what happened to you."

"No," Val said. "Of course not. You stood up and said, 'She's a human being like the rest of us, how can we do this to her?'"

He had the grace, at least, to flush. "Well, what could I do?"

"Never mind, Blaisse. You can make up for it now. You can go to the Families and tell them that the underground people hold the Palace, and that I am with them and of them."

"You want me . . . to go . . . out there?"

"You're mad!" Clarissa said. "They'll come and tear you all to bits."

"Cousin, you know better. They couldn't assassinate me even when I was a child. And if my Family could allow the others to kill me, would yours allow your death?"

"You expect me to stay here?"

"What do you care if you're my hostage, or Blaisse's?"

"They'll cut off the electricity—they'll turn out the lights—"

"You helped send me into darkness! Do you think we need their light to survive?"

"Val," Clarissa said more reasonably, "the Palace and the Families are balanced very carefully against each other. If you disturb the balance. . . ." She let her explanation trail off meaningfully.

"I remember all the plans our Families had. But they won't work against anyone who doesn't need all this." She glanced around Blaisse's bedroom. It no longer looked as grand as it had when she was a child, only overly ornate, and here and there a bit shabby.

"They'll fight you."

"At Blaisse's request? I think not, cousin."

Clarissa folded her arms and looked at the floor, sulking.

Val turned her attention to Blaisse. "Get ready, my Lord. You have a mission."

Blaisse stood up unwillingly and walked as though still asleep toward his dressing rooms. "Saita!" The strange young silver-blue girl moved quickly to hold the curtain aside for him.

"Wait," Val said. Blaisse turned back. "Are you still able to dress yourself, Blaisse?"

"Of course," he said bitterly.

"Then do it."

He glared at her, looked away, flung aside the curtain, and stormed out.

Val drew the two slaves aside. "You're free," she said. "You don't have to do what Blaisse and Clarissa tell you anymore. Do you understand?"

They both looked at her, not yet responding. She remembered how she had felt, when what she was used to had crumbled around her.

"They know nothing of freedom." Clarissa's tone was derisive. "None of them do. They're incapable of caring for themselves."

"So was I, cousin."

The young boy suddenly burst into despairing tears.

The settled order of Stone Palace had turned to chaos. Madame walked through it, untouched by it, still deferred to by those who passed: they stepped aside for her, but they did not wait for orders. She did not give any. She still would not dare to believe that she was free.

She remembered invaders, and she was afraid, but she heard no sounds of death or destruction. Clarissa's suite was deserted, so she went to Blaisse's.

Inside, strange wild people, underground people, outcasts, stared at her. Seeing them in the Palace allowed Madame to hope, at least, that the rumors might be true. The underground people returned to sampling bits of food and making faces not altogether disgusted. With the ease and intuition of long experience, Madame picked out their leader. The slender red-haired woman was sitting on one of Clarissa's velvet cushions. Saita sat near her, head down, as the slender woman spoke to her gently and gravely. Clarissa's attendant, the new boy, hunched in a corner and shuddered when anyone approached.

Madame spoke, hardly able to believe what she saw. "My Lady . . . Valdrienne?"

Madame remembered when Val had been driven out: a skinny little awkward child, bright, her arrogance shattered by the discovery that she was different from her siblings and cousins, different, and therefore less than human. She looked up, and their recognition was mutual.

"There aren't any masters anymore. Will you call me Val?"

"Are we free?"

"Yes."

Madame saw that Saita was crying, silently and stilly. "The child . . ." She did not know what to say about Saita, who had been forbidden knowledge of anything and everything but obedience, self-effacement, and the giving of sexual pleasure. "Her family had no future but poverty before they sold her. All her pride is based on that. . . . She *is* a child."

"I know," Val said. "But only because they forced her to be. She can still grow, with the rest of us."

"I do not wish to be discourteous . . ." Using titles was such an ingrained habit that she found it difficult to stop. "May I leave?"

"It isn't necessary to ask."

Madame stood another moment; for so many years she had asked, and asked if other services were necessary, and bowed, and feared those she served. She looked down at her hands: her own hands, now, the third finger of the left hand a little crooked from her twisting the slave ring off as she grew. But it slid off easily now, leaving a mark. She held the ring out. "Will you . . . give this to Blaisse?"

Val smiled. "Of course."

Madame threw down her whip. "I never used that."

"I know. I remember."

Madame lifted her head. "Good-bye." She turned and left Blaisse's palace. *I am not "Madame" anymore,* she thought, and the knowledge was the sunlight she had not seen since she was eight years old.

She entered Subtwo's quarters and found them empty. Suddenly she doubted what she had done: Subtwo had gone to the underground, but the underground people were here. She imagined him dead, bloody and broken at the foot of some cliff, lost, gone. She touched the arm of his chair, and knew no way to turn.

His suite was not as he had left it. A bit of furniture displaced, a closet door ajar, a few of his favorite things missing, not clumsily stolen by one of the invaders, but carefully chosen. He must have been here, and gone.

Why shouldn't he leave? she wondered. *I never responded to him . . . but he seemed to understand why I could not, though I wanted him. . . .*

She moved through the rooms until she reached the communications console and saw the destruction: the fused controls, the melted screen. She was afraid again, for a moment, but the only odor was of vaporized plastic: no seared-meat death-smell. Someone had wrecked the device as a precaution, or as a warning. Perhaps he had tried to contact her. . . .

She heard footsteps and raised her head, hoping.

"Where are you—?" Subone stopped just inside the doorway. "Where—?"

"He is not here."

Subone groaned. "Hikaru, that barbaric child, the freaks—they forced him!" he cried. "They— Has the ship taken off?"

"The ship . . . ?" She fell silent, clear in her understanding of what had happened. Subtwo was escaping from Subone, as much as Jan Hikaru and Mischa were escaping from earth. And if Subone caught them before they got away, he would be able to stop Subtwo, she had almost no doubt of that. If Subone caught them, he could return Subtwo to a kind of slavery as profound as her own had been. She faced Subone quietly, waiting for a minuscule vibration, a trembling of the city's matrix that would build and climb and quite abruptly cease, as a ship fought free of gravity. But no sound came, and no vibration: Subone's quarry still were earthbound, vulnerable.

He lunged forward and grabbed her wrist, hard enough to hurt her, crushing the velvet of her sleeve between his fingers. "Tell me!"

She remained silent, staring past him. She had never been flogged, but she had been prepared, every day, to endure it and survive it, knowing the people who owned her too well to think she could avoid it forever. She was as prepared to endure pain now that she was free.

Subone shook her, wrenching her shoulder. She was as unused to looking *up* at anyone as she was to meeting a free person's gaze, but she had to look up at Subone, and she met his fury, her face set and hard.

"I have no time!" he cried, and flung her across the room. She felt herself falling, a sharp blow, and that was all.

The blockhouse was silent. Subtwo carefully packed his belongings into a protective case. The outside winds must have died down since he came to Center, for the whining no longer penetrated the thick walls, but the sand could still drift and float and insinuate itself into delicate mechanical places. When he was finished Jan and Mischa had already put on suits, while he was still only in his coverall.

"Hurry up," Mischa said. Jan simply sat on the corner of one of the work-desks and crossed his arms. Even after the fight in which Jan had easily defeated Draco, Subtwo had thought of him as mild and peaceable; he had never seen the young man look so grim as now.

But Subtwo ignored the grimness and Mischa's impatience. He was elated, yet disconsolate. The satisfaction of having rid himself of Subone was incredible, but he had also lost Madame . . . he could only hope that she would remain in the Palace until he could return. He was afraid something would change by then: Madame could believe he had left without even thinking of her, or, worse, she could become the focus for one of Blaisse's incomprehensible rages. He could destroy her, and no one would ever know or care. Except Subtwo.

Revenge and grief, he realized, are for the benefit of the living only; the dead are beyond such actions and feelings. Revenge and grief were not what Subtwo sought.

"I must come back, you know," he said without turning.

Mischa hesitated, and then he heard her sigh. "Subone—"

"Not Subone!" He cut himself off. Mischa had no reason to be certain he had cut off the crippling relationship with his pseudosib. "No, not Subone."

"Mischa kept her part of the bargain," Jan said. "You might at least uphold yours with a little grace."

"You don't understand . . ." He felt himself blushing, fiery red from collar to hairline. He had never blushed before. It was impossible to say what he meant. "Because I'm free, and I might be able to give freedom as well. . . ."

"What are you talking about?"

He knew that his oblique conversations angered people, but in this instance he could not be more direct. "You made me leave." *She'll think I didn't care,* he thought.

Vonda N. McIntyre

"We haven't left yet," Mischa said angrily. "We never will if you don't hurry."

"But—"

"All right! I don't care, you can come back if you want, you're crazy. You have to take us where we tell you, first."

He nodded, and lifted his suit and helmet from their hook.

"Leaving without me, brother?"

Subone, filthy and tattered, half-naked, stood in the entrance of the blockhouse. Mischa had the lance out, aimed at him, but he ignored it. "How could you desert me, brother?"

Subtwo knew the regret was false: it overlaid triumph and amusement. He stared at his pseudosib for what seemed a long time. The similarities he had seen between them were gone, eradicated; had any remained, they would have been hidden by the filth and the uncombed hanging-down hair and the awful smile.

"You began the process," Subtwo said. "You pulled yourself away from me."

"No," Subone whispered. "We are still the same." He stepped toward Subtwo slowly, gazing quietly at him, his dark eyes deep, deep. "The link is there. I feel what you feel."

"Don't!" Subtwo cried as Mischa shifted. "We made a bargain. You aren't to kill him."

"I said if he didn't make me."

"She will," Subtwo said to Subone. "She is determined."

"What will happen to you, if I die?" Subone swayed before him like a snake. "Your blood will boil like mine, and your brains explode in your skull. . . ." He came closer, until Subtwo could smell his musky sweat and see the minute pale flecks of color in the black irises of his eyes. Subone's hypnotic voice droned on, until Subtwo could well believe they would die together.

"I gave my word . . ."

"What's your word, to thieves and murderers?"

Subone's dark gaze leached the meaning from Subtwo's unvoiced protest.

"We have no choice," Subtwo said finally. Sadness overwhelmed him, that he had almost deserted the person closest to him in the universe, almost abandoned him here on a forsaken dying world . . . what might have happened, had they parted? He could imagine space-time's collapse to a single dimension, to a dimensionless point.

"Yes, refuse them!" Subone said. "They can't kill you."

"I can," Mischa said. "If you won't keep your promise, I have nothing to lose."

Subone laughed: a real laugh, not the acceptable response the pseudosibs had learned by rote. But it was ugly. "You still have your life," Subone snarled. "Go back where you came from, and I'll let you keep it."

Subtwo wanted to turn to Mischa and apologize to her, explain what he must do, make clear that some obligations stretched beyond mere promises. But he continued to stare at Subone, rediscovering beauty.

"He's buying you too cheaply," Jan Hikaru said in his quiet way, as a statement of fact, not as an argument or persuasion.

Subone glared, his teeth glinting bright as a beast's. "I haven't given you your life."

But Jan's words caught in Subtwo's thoughts. "I'm not a slave. I own myself," he said.

"He owns you more than he could own any slave. He owns your soul."

Subtwo stepped back involuntarily and grasped the edge of a counter that pressed against his thighs. "No, I want—" But he did *not* want what Subone wanted. He squeezed his eyelids shut, searching for a moment of peace in which to disentangle his confusion.

He heard footsteps and opened his eyes again. Subone grinned triumphantly. "Our raiders are coming," he said. "Free and rearmed." He turned, smiling, toward the entranceway, but suddenly, paling, faced Subtwo again.

"They'll have to find the slave-ways first," Madame said.

Subtwo pushed past his pseudosib, ignoring his stricken expression. Madame walked slowly out of the dimness, moving carefully as though on an unsteady deck. Running from a terrible gash just below her temple, blood marked the line of her jaw and stained the silver embroidery of her bodice. Subtwo reached to steady her, but abruptly hesitated.

Madame took his hand and clasped it tightly. "I'm free." Her fingers were smooth and strong.

Subtwo gently touched her blood-matted hair. "How did this—"

"Never mind." But she glanced past him and saw Subone again; her pain-contracted pupils shrank to pinpoints.

"She—she tried to kill me! I had to defend myself!"

Subtwo felt a great wrench of betrayal, for this time he knew without question or doubt that his pseudosib lied, gratuitously, selfishly, viciously. He spun in a fury and struck out.

"No!" Subone cried, and crumpled with the blow, for it was totally unexpected and unprepared for. When his pseudosib lay moaning at his feet, Subtwo cradled his aching hand, thinking that he had done an impossible, perhaps unforgiveable, but necessary thing.

"We must hurry," Madame said slowly, rational but vague. "I broke the alice tube, and the slave-ways are concealed, but the raiders will find them." As destroying a mechanism in order to slow pursuit was an idea Subtwo would never have conceived, he was overcome with admiration.

He turned away from his pseudosib and steadied Madame again, touching her bruised face gently, causing necessary pain from which she did not flinch. "The bone is not broken," he said with relief, and moved quickly to find her a suit.

Afraid that Subone would recover himself and interfere again, Mischa watched him until Madame was safely suited. He had only begun to stir, to push himself up, when Mischa opened the door of the blockhouse.

The sand squealed in the tracks, but afterward was only silence. That was what had been so strange inside, this time: the absence of the scratch and howl of wind-blown sand. As the door closed behind her, Mischa blinked in the glittery light. Sand yielded beneath her feet. She looked down from the plateau of the landing field across endless iridescent black sand dunes, like a glass sea frozen in midswell. The wind had died, only briefly, Mischa thought, for the clouds still hung and shifted, low and dark, here and there breaking as they moved, revealing glints of blue-gray sky. Near the horizon, the sun glowed scarlet, rayed about with orange, vermilion, purple. Beside her, Jan whistled softly in awe. Mischa unfastened her helmet, threw it back, and breathed the fresh dusty air for the first time in months. A breeze scattered particles of sand that pattered against the blockhouse, against Mischa's suit. She glanced at Jan, also bareheaded, and he looked down at her. Suddenly she grinned, and felt laughter springing up from where it had long lain hidden. Jan smiled, the beautiful smile, untinged by irony, that Mischa had not seen in so long. The tiny lines at the corners of his eyes were deeper; only the ends of his golden hair were sunbleached white; his mustache made him look older. He was older. They both were older.

"Let's go."

Cradled in the acceleration couch, Mischa forgot her scrapes and scratches and fatigue, and tried to memorize the control room all at once. Jan was in the couch beside her, eyes closed. On a third couch, Madame lay wrapped closely in a blanket; she was groggy from concussion, but she would be all right. Subtwo, his dirty hair tied carefully back, was embraced in the navigation frame, almost every part of his body attached to a separate control system. The ship shuddered as the engines started. The acceleration began, pressing Mischa gently down.

The ship battered its way upward, into the roiling clouds. It began to vibrate on a second frequency, and the harmonic beats rose and fell. Mischa urged the ship along, feeling joyful terror when the wind pummeled and tipped them, victorious gaiety when the craft fought free. Sometimes it seemed impossible they would survive, for the force of the wind seemed beyond the ability of the ship to withstand. They crept into the sky, battered, but when they broke through the storm, the transition was instantaneous. It sounded like silence, but was merely the cessation of the wind. The engines thundered. Mischa laughed aloud, half-intoxicated. Delighted, she turned toward Jan, but his golden skin was gray-pale, and his hands were clenched white-knuckled on the arms of his couch.

"What's wrong?"

"I expected a takeoff, not ride-the-meteor in an amusement park."

She had no idea what he was talking about, though it was obvious he objected to the quality of the ride. Subtwo disengaged himself from the controls. He, too, was pale. "The winds are less steady—" It was the first time she had ever heard him make an excuse. He went to Madame's side.

"I liked it," Mischa said.

Jan laughed and lay back in the acceleration couch.

And Mischa did not know what to do. She had no idea where to go. In all the time she and Chris had talked about leaving earth, the aftermath of their escape had been a nebulous, tantalizing mystery. They had discussed how to get away, and what the Sphere would be like when they got there, but now that she thought of it, they had avoided talking about how they themselves would fit into a new society. Perhaps they had known, unconsciously, that they would not.

"What are you going to do?"

She started: Subtwo had never before showed the least talent for empathy or even intuition.

"Will you still leave me my ship?" So his concern was still his own future.

No, Mischa thought, *no, it's more than that now, it's his and Madame's.* "Yes," she said. "You can have your ship back, and then we'll be even." And then, "I'm . . . I'm sorry I didn't let you call her."

"Where may I take you?"

"You . . ." She did not know the nearest Sphere world, but she would ask for it: she had made her way in Center; she could make her way anywhere.

"To Koen," Jan said. "The coordinates—"

"I know them," Subtwo said, highly insulted.

"Is that really where you want to go, Jan? Are you sure?" She had taken so much from him, she did not want to take more, or force him into still another unpleasant situation.

"Yes," he said softly. "I'm more sure of that than I've been of anything in a long time. I want to. I have to."

"But your father—"

He nodded, his eyes still closed. "Exactly. My father." He sounded completely certain of himself, and content.

"To Koen," Mischa told Subtwo.

"We must finish an orbit." He spoke to Jan, glancing quickly at him, then back to Madame. "There is time to see earth from the observation bubble, if you wish."

Jan opened his eyes and pushed himself slowly from the couch. Mischa knew that his reluctance was not because he begrudged the time, or even that he was so completely exhausted, but that returning to the viewing bubble would bring back memories, still painful, of his friend the poet.

"You don't have to, Jan."

"Don't be silly. Just give me a hand."

He leaned on her, and they walked to the observation deck. Below them lay earth, the terminator creeping across its face, sunlight glinting from the clouds.

Jan lowered himself onto a bank of cushions, and Mischa sat beside

213

him, gazing down, picking out the gray swirls of the sandstorms, moving out of night. Most of the other clouds were gray-brown; but here Mischa found a patch of white, there of green, there of blue: the ocean. She had never seen an ocean.

She thought of all the things Val had said at the very last, all the things that needed to be done; she thought of her half-promise to Crab. She knew she was doing the right thing, for now, in leaving earth, but the future was not set.

"Jan—"

She fell silent: he was asleep on the cushions beside her. But there would be time to talk, later on.

Jan Hikaru's Journal:

Halfway to Koen. I slept through the first few dives. When I woke, we were about to dive again; Subtwo was showing Mischa how everything works. When the ship was safely under, he went back to Madame. She is recovering, and they spend almost all their time together, talking, or simply holding hands in silence. They're rather like children in some ways, inexperienced at affection, sincere, hesitant. Learning.

I never thought I'd go home eagerly, but I'm glad to be on my way, I'll be glad when we reach Koen. Ichiri can't direct my life anymore—he never could, but that I let him. Knowing that, I think I can accept him as he is. I hope someday he'll be able to do the same for me.

I'm going back to earth—not right away; I need more preparation first. At least this time I'll know what I'm preparing for. And in the meantime Mischa and I will petition the Sphere with Val's message. We in the Sphere can't ignore earth any longer. Even Mischa, who has more reason than anyone to want to forget Center, no longer seems so determined to abandon it. But she has an almost infinite range of choices, now, and can decide what she wants to do with her future and with her abilities after she has seen what all the options are. For the present, the best thing is probably for her to apply for a Special Fellowship. She's a little old for one, but the trustees value genius highly, and they'll take into account her situation. A fellowship would be ideal: it would give her liberty, resources, and independence. Murasaki's es-

tate—or even my father—could easily provide for her education, and I'll see that they do if it's necessary. But Mischa is the kind of person who prefers a prize to what she would see as a gift. From now on, I think, she'll have many prizes in her life.